PROTECTING RAVEN (SPECIAL FORCES: OPERATION ALPHA)

PREY SECURITY, BOOK 2

JANE BLYTHE

Dear Readers,

Welcome to the Special Forces: Operation Alpha Fan-Fiction world!

If you are new to this amazing world, in a nutshell the author wrote a story using one or more of my characters in it. Sometimes that character has a major role in the story, and other times they are only mentioned briefly. This is perfectly legal and allowable because they are going through Aces Press to publish the story.

This book is entirely the work of the author who wrote it. While I might have assisted with brainstorming and other ideas about which of my characters to use, I didn't have any part in the process or writing or editing the story.

I'm proud and excited that so many authors loved my characters enough that they wanted to write them into their own story. Thank you for supporting them, and me!

READ ON!
   Xoxo
   Susan Stoker

I'd like to thank everyone who played a part in bringing this story to life. Particularly my mom who is always there to share her thoughts and opinions with me. The wonderful Amy Queau of Q Designs who made the stunning cover. And my lovely editor Lisa Edwards for all her encouragement and for all the hard work she puts into polishing my work.

CHAPTER 1

October 25th

9:06 P.M.

As a child, the dark had terrified her.

Then it had become her friend.

A place to hide from the world, to find peace and solitude, a reprieve from the voices of fear, pain, and trauma that continued to haunt her half a lifetime later.

Not tonight though.

Tonight, the darkness seemed dangerous.

Raven Oswald felt like she was being watched. Coming to Colombia to chase a human-trafficking ring on her own wasn't one of her smartest moves, but she'd been trying to track down the men who stole her daughter for the last decade, and this was the closest she'd ever come.

Time was of the essence.

At any moment the tenuous link she had to the group's online presence could be terminated, leaving her in the same position she'd been in so many times before. Close but not close enough.

Not this time.

This time she needed to get close enough to stop them.

It wasn't like Raven thought she could do that singlehandedly. She was a computer expert, she didn't have the training to find the location of the next live auction and then breach it, but she *did* have the power to find that location and then pass it on to one of the teams who worked at Prey. Prey Security performed black ops missions for the government, did hostage rescue, and private security. She and her five siblings owned the company and were named after birds of prey because their parents had named all six of them after birds.

She shivered and forced herself not to look around her as the feeling of being hunted intensified. Maybe she should have waited until daylight to come out here. Her plan had been to come to Colombia on her own then call in backup when she was ready. If she came with an entire Prey team then there was no way someone wouldn't notice and report to El Entregar. Named The Deliver in Spanish, El Entregar was the biggest human-trafficking ring in the world, with seemingly endless funds and networks on every continent. One woman wasn't going to attract attention, although Raven knew she was putting herself in danger by asking questions. Still, those questions had paid off, and she had a meeting with someone tomorrow. Knowing she could be walking into a trap she'd wanted to check out the area first.

Now she was absolutely rethinking that decision.

There was still another mile to walk until she was back in the small town that was near where she believed El Entregar had their headquarters. If someone was following her, they would have plenty of opportunities to grab her. The town she was staying in was on the border of the Amazon rainforest, there was plenty of thick cover for anyone hunting her, and cell phone reception out here was spotty at best.

She was on her own.

It was a clear night, but the tall trees smothered the moonlight, and while she was walking alongside a road it was still dark and she was loathed to turn on her phone's flashlight and draw more attention to herself.

Not that it seemed to matter.

Someone was definitely out there.

While only her and one of her five siblings had not chosen a path into the military, Raven knew how to defend herself. She'd grown up on an off-the-grid farm, raised by parents who were convinced that the apocalypse was coming. By the time she was five, she had known how to shoot, use a knife and a sword, and been trained rigorously in self-defense. It wasn't that she didn't know how to defend herself, it was just that she had long ago made the decision to never use violence again.

So that left her with quite the dilemma.

If someone was coming for her, she only had three choices. One, she could run and hide. Two, she could let them take her, although since she wouldn't be able to call in Prey it would mean she'd wind up dead or wishing she was dead. Or three, she could defend herself.

The thought of it left her feeling ill.

She knew what it was like to take a life, the cost of the blood she'd shed had weighed heavily on her for the last seventeen years. Raven wasn't sure she had it in her to kill again, not even to save her own life.

Something moved behind her. It took everything she had not to react. Right now, the only thing she had going for her was that whoever was following her probably believed she had no idea they were there. She wasn't armed, not even a knife, all she had on her was her phone, a wallet tucked into the back pocket of her jeans, and the keys to the room at the small hotel where she was staying. This had just been a recon mission, nothing more, she hadn't thought she would run into trouble. It was tomorrow's meeting with her contact that she had been worried would go badly.

Her stomach churned with anxiety. Her big brother Eagle would be furious to know that she was being so cavalier with her safety, at least that was how he would see it. In her mind, it wasn't so much being reckless with her safety as it was focusing on the bigger picture. El Entregar needed to be stopped. They were the biggest human-trafficking ring in the world, and they had taken from her the most precious thing she had. Cleo had been only three years old when she'd been snatched from the park, Raven remembered the day like it was yesterday. Just like she remembered finding her daughter's picture on El Entregar's dark web auction website.

Anger burned through her now, chasing away some of the fear. How dare these men think they had the right to steal a sweet little girl, a child who was brighter than the sun, funny, smart, compassionate, and sell her to make themselves richer than they already were.

She would take them down or she would die trying.

For Raven, it was that simple.

The figure seemed to spring out of thin air.

Launching at her and yanking her up against a rock-hard body. Basically, before she could blink there was a bag over her head, and her arms were yanked behind her back, secured with plastic zip ties around her wrists.

As she was lifted off her feet, Raven sucked in a breath to scream but then stopped. What was the point? They were a mile from the village, it was quiet out here, no one would hear her screams for help.

The man didn't say anything, didn't make demands or threats, didn't tell her what he was going to do to her or where he was taking her. Was he one of El Entregar's men? Were they on to her? She'd tried to be subtle when she moved from town to town asking questions, but all it took was one question to the wrong person and the trafficking ring would know she was onto them.

Although she struggled against him, her attacker lifted her easily, threw her over his shoulder, and started walking with her. Even though Raven knew she was in danger she couldn't help but think it could wind up being a good thing if she was taken to El Entregar's headquarters. She had promised Eagle she would check in every twenty-four hours, it was the only way she had been able to convince him not to come after her. When she didn't, he would track her with the chip hidden beneath her skin between her toes and send a team in to rescue her. Which would achieve her goal, destroying the men who had destroyed her by taking her sweet baby girl.

Raven might have issues with violence, but when she was tossed into the trunk of a car, she started working on breaking the zip ties binding her wrists and effectively rendering her helpless. She had no problem with trying to escape. There was no way to know that this man was one of El Entregar so she was going to be ready to make a run for it as soon as an opportunity presented itself. Her self-defense training was impeccable, and she knew how to break the plastic zip ties, but it was awkward within the confines of the trunk.

Before she could get out of them the car stopped moving.

Damn.

She hadn't been fast enough.

The trunk opened, and she was lifted up again, tossed over the shoulder of her abductor, who started climbing stairs. Where was he taking her? They couldn't be any further away from where she'd been when she was grabbed than the town where she was staying. She was pretty sure they'd driven in the same direction too, although she had been distracted trying to get herself free.

A door opened and then closed behind them and she was tossed onto something soft.

A mattress.

A bed.

Rape.

That was the first thought that flew through her mind. She'd been there. Knew what that was like. The men she had killed when she was sixteen had raped her before she'd managed to use her knife on them. That wasn't all they'd done to her. They'd sliced at her skin, cutting her up, leaving her with dozens of thin white scars.

Raven was about to aim a kick at the man's groin who she knew was standing over her, but then the hood was yanked from her head, and instead of attacking, her mouth fell open in shock.

"I hate you," she growled.

* * *

9:31 P.M.

· · ·

"I hate you," the beautiful woman on the bed snarled at him. Her bright blue eyes were all but shooting arrows of fury at him, her lips pressed into an angry line, her black hair hung in messy waves around her face, and all he could think about was kissing her.

Yeah, Max knew he was in trouble.

"You're not going to say anything, Max Hathaway?" Raven demanded. The more she glared at him the sexier she looked.

Yep, definite trouble.

"Why are you in Colombia? And why did you kidnap me? You know *ex*-husbands are called ex for a reason. It means you're supposed to be out of my life for good," Raven snapped.

Max hid his wince of pain. Raven had no need to know that walking away from her had been the hardest thing he'd ever had to do. But what choice had he had?

None.

He'd had no choice.

Anger was a much easier emotion to deal with than pain. Easier to deal with than fear too. And finding out that Raven was down here in Colombia traipsing around on her own, putting herself in danger by asking questions about the most dangerous human-trafficking ring on the planet, had definitely raised his blood pressure a few hundred points.

"Why are *you* in Colombia?" he shot back, leaning down till he was eye to eye with her. Awareness flickered in those blue depths, although she covered it quickly. So, she was still attracted to him. Good to know.

Not that he wanted her back.

That ship had sailed, but since he'd been unable to move on even though almost a decade had gone by since they'd divorced, it was nice to know she hadn't moved on either.

It probably made him a jerk, but once in a lifetime kind of

love was special and he was relieved to know that Raven had felt the same way about him that he felt about her.

"If you're here then you know why," Raven muttered.

"So, you're an idiot then, that's not the Raven I remember."

Raven's eyes about bugged out of her head. "What did you just call me? An idiot? Because I want to destroy the people who ripped our baby away from us that makes me an idiot? And how would you know what kind of person I am now? You're the one who bailed just two months after Cleo was kidnapped."

It may as well have been yesterday that they'd lost Cleo from the raw strength of the pain that tore through him. Cleo was taken while he had been with her, one moment of distraction at the park and his precious little princess was gone. How was he supposed to face Raven after being responsible for her losing the most important thing she had? He couldn't even face himself.

"No, you're an idiot for coming to a dangerous part of the world alone. You were unarmed, Raven." The thought of her in danger scared him so much he stalked around the room and raked his fingers through his short, dark hair. "Look how easy it was for me to grab you. If I'd meant to hurt you instead of just make a point, or I was one of El Entregar, you would be in serious trouble right now."

"So, this was all just some big lesson? What exactly did you want to teach me, Max?"

Stalking across the room, Max leaned in until he was millimeters from her face. Close enough that her warm breath touched his skin, and it was all he could do not to grab her and drag her into his arms, kiss her senseless. Kiss her until she realized that it wasn't okay for her to risk her safety, not for anything. How would he cope with losing her too?

"I wanted to teach you that nothing is important enough to risk your life," he growled.

"This is," Raven insisted. "I want them destroyed for what they did to Cleo."

"And what are you willing to risk to get your revenge?"

Her blue eyes were clear when they met his, her voice calm. "Anything."

Max swore and stormed around the room again. How could he make Raven see that losing her would destroy him without letting her know that he still loved her?

He'd left because he couldn't handle his guilt. He'd been a coward, run because it was easier than having to see the pain on Raven's face every day. The hopelessness that grew as another day passed without any progress in finding Cleo. He'd filed for divorce and fled, but while his body might have left his heart hadn't. His heart still belonged to the furious woman glaring at him from the bed.

"Here, let me take these off." He grabbed a knife from his keychain and moved behind her to cut through the plastic zip ties.

As soon as her arms were free, Raven gasped as blood flow returned and she slowly rotated her shoulders so her arms were in front of her. Rubbing gently at the red marks on her wrists, he suddenly realized that this plan to make her understand she was putting herself in danger had been a mistake. There were other ways he could have made his point, but she'd terrified him wandering around in Le Entregar territory unarmed and on her own, and he'd wanted her to feel a slice of what he'd been feeling.

That had been a jerk move.

It seemed like he couldn't stop hurting her.

Walking away had been the right choice. How much worse would he have hurt her if he'd stayed?

Gently, he reached out to take her hands. She tried to tug them out of his grip, but he tightened his hold, just enough so she couldn't pull away. Max brushed a fingertip lightly over the red marks. "Look, I'm sorry I hurt you, sorry I scared you too. When I followed you out there, realized you had no idea you were being hunted, and were just wandering around unarmed in what you know is dangerous territory, I just panicked. I'm not proud of that. I could have just told you I was there, but I wanted you to realize just how dangerous what you're doing is. I know you're prepared to risk anything to take Le Entregar down, but you know what they'll do to you if they get their hands on you, Raven. And I …" he paused to swallow down the panic bubbling up inside him, "I can't lose you too," he managed to choke out.

Raven's face softened. "I know what I'm doing, okay? You always underestimated me, thought I was weak. I understood why, you know how what happened to my parents changed me, but I never liked it. I was never weak, Max."

He growled and grabbed her shoulders, dragging her off the bed. "Weak?" he snarled, furious that she ever believed he thought that about her. "You are the strongest person I know, Raven. Not many sixteen-year-olds could enter a house where two armed men had killed their parents, survive what you did, and manage to kill both of them. I *never* thought you were weak, Raven, I've never had anything but the utmost respect for you."

She nodded slowly. "Okay, look, you made your point. I need to be careful, and I'll make sure I'm armed from here on out."

He could see what it took for her to make that concession, he knew how violence affected her, but that wasn't how this was going to play out. "I'm not leaving you, Raven."

She frowned at him. "I said you made your point, there's no need for you to hang around."

Max moved closer, getting right into her personal space. "That's where you're wrong, sweetheart."

"We're divorced, Max, I'm no longer your responsibility."

"You will *always* be my responsibility, and I'm not going anywhere. I'm here to act as your own personal bodyguard."

The indignation that flared in Raven's eyes would have been amusing if the reason for them both being there wasn't so utterly personal and insanely dangerous.

"My what now?" Raven demanded.

This time he did give a one-sided smile. "Your bodyguard."

"How did you even know I was here?" she asked suspiciously.

"Eagle called me."

"My brother?" Her eyes widened then narrowed in obvious betrayal. "Why did he call *you?*"

"Because he said this is the closest you've ever been to getting to the men who took Cleo, and he knows there's no one who would take this more seriously than I would. No one who has more motivation to keep you alive and in one piece than I do," he replied honestly.

"And what motivation could you possibly have for keeping me alive?"

That she didn't know how much he had loved her—still loved her—hurt more than anything else. It made the years they had been together feel like a lie. Max reached out and placed his hand on her chest where her heart was hammering wildly. "Because of this." He moved his hand until his fingertips touched the pulse in her neck which was fluttering. "Because of this." Then he curled his hand around her nape, dipped his head, and captured her lips in a kiss that he'd been waiting far too long for.

* * *

9:53 P.M.

Her ability to think fled.

All Raven could do was feel.

Anger over Max's ridiculous way of making his point that she wasn't taking her safety carefully began to fade away.

He was kissing her.

The only man she had ever loved was kissing her.

For one beautiful moment, it didn't matter that their baby girl had been abducted or that he had abandoned her and filed for divorce a mere two months later. It only mattered that he was here, holding her, his lips on hers.

And then reality came crashing back down.

She lifted her hands and pressed gently at his shoulders. Max all but sprang away from her, shock on his face like he couldn't believe that he'd just kissed her, and then she saw what she'd been dreading.

Regret.

It was written all over his too handsome face.

Not even five seconds after he'd kissed her, Max was already wishing he hadn't done it.

It was hurt more than anger that made her want to lash out. *He* had kissed her not the other way around. And *he* had been the one to decide all on his own to end their marriage not the other way around.

"Obviously, your only reason for having any motivation

to keep me alive is so you can continue torturing me," she snapped. "You shouldn't have kissed me."

If she wasn't mistaken hurt flared in his deep brown eyes, but he nodded his agreement. "It won't happen again."

"Of course it won't because you'll be leaving now. I neither want nor need a bodyguard so I am officially relieving you of your assignment."

"Sorry, sweetheart, no can do," he said, that irritatingly sexy smirk she remembered so well curled up his lips.

"What? Why?" she demanded. The last thing she needed right now when she was closer to finding the men who had stolen her baby than she had ever been before, was for her ex-husband to throw himself back into the mix. She wanted him gone. Now. So she could get back to work. She could not afford a single distraction right now.

"Because you didn't hire me. Eagle did."

"Well, I'm a co-owner of Prey, so I have the authority to end any contracts, and I am putting an end to yours."

His smile only grew, annoying her further, mostly because she'd missed his smile. She'd missed *him*. But he had made his choice and they both had to live with it. "Prey didn't hire me, Eagle did. Him personally, my contract is with him not with Prey, which means you have no authority to fire me, which means I'm not going anywhere."

"We'll see about that." Raven huffed, stalking across the room. She grabbed her laptop and fired it up, immediately video calling Eagle.

As if he'd been expecting a call from her and was prepared, Eagle answered almost immediately. He was dressed casually in a black t-shirt and jeans, and she could see his penthouse behind him, her workaholic brother had definitely mellowed out since meeting the pretty blonde who snuggled against his side.

"Hi, Raven," Eagle said brightly. *Too* brightly. He knew she was furious with him.

"Don't *hi, Raven*, me," she snapped. "How could you go behind my back and send someone here to follow me?"

"It was easy," Eagle said calmly, "you're in a dangerous part of the world, hunting dangerous men, and you left without telling anyone where you were going. Did you really think I wouldn't do whatever I had to do to make sure you were safe?"

Since Raven knew her brother had issues when it came to the people he loved being in danger, he blamed himself for their parents' deaths, the loss of his SEAL team, and for almost losing his now-fiancée Olivia Wakefield seven months ago, she let that side of her argument go. In hindsight, she should have expected her big brother to pull something like this.

Uncaring of the fact that Max was still in the room and listening to every word she said, Raven asked, "But why *him*? Why would you send the one person you knew I wouldn't want here after me?"

"All our teams are out on missions," Eagle said.

"And you had no other contacts you could have sent if you thought I needed a bodyguard?"

"I sent the person I thought was best for the job. I'm sorry if you don't like it, but Max is there to stay. You might be focused only on bringing down Le Entregar, but I'm also focused on you. I don't want anything to happen to you, and since you don't seem to want to take your safety seriously you left me with no choice."

Yeah right.

No choice.

As if Eagle Oswald ever felt like he had no choice in the decisions he made. Her brother was well known for his ability to compartmentalize his feelings and make decisions based on evidence not emotion.

If she didn't know any better, she would think that he was deliberately trying to push her and Max together. Trying to play matchmaker. But the idea of her brother playing matchmaker was so ridiculous she immediately discounted it.

He was just being his usual controlling self.

"You're not going to revoke his contract, are you?" She sighed.

"Nope, I'm not. Sorry." Eagle grinned.

"He's not actually sorry, Raven, but I am, I told him not to do it," Olivia piped up.

"I know, Liv. Big brothers just like to be the boss sometimes, they think they always know best."

"Fiancé's too," Olivia muttered but couldn't hide the twinkle in her eyes as she looked up at the man she loved.

Raven knew that look, it was how she used to look at Max before he shattered her heart.

She didn't expect to ever look at another man that same way.

No way would she ever risk her battered heart again. Not for anyone.

"I'm still mad at you, Eagle," she warned.

"Noted. I'll work on figuring out how to make it up to you," he teased, trying to lighten the mood. He wouldn't apologize for doing what he thought was best, nor would he change his mind, but he would try to find a way to get her to forgive him, and in the end she would because she knew her brother loved her.

"Goodbye, Eagle," she said, fixing him in a glare. "Night, Liv."

"Night, Raven," Olivia said.

"Goodnight, Raven. And don't even think of trying to ditch Max," Eagle warned.

When the screen went black, she took a moment to try to get her emotions under control. It seemed she was stuck with Max, at least until she could slip away. Despite her brother's warning she absolutely decided to lose her bodyguard. Having him here was too hard, she still loved him, even the pain of his abandonment wasn't enough to change how she felt about him. She loved him, always would, and having him here played with her emotions at a time she could least afford it.

Cleo.

This was all about her sweet little princess.

She had to keep her focus on that, not on Max and kisses she knew she would replay when she climbed into bed tonight.

Deciding that for the moment her best option was to ignore Max, pretend that he wasn't there, Raven closed the laptop and stood, intending to take a shower and head to bed. Max could do what he wanted, but she wasn't going to play the dutiful little charge, she would do whatever it took to take down the men who had taken her baby from her.

"Raven, wait." Max moved to block her when she headed for the bathroom. "Is it really so bad having me here?" he asked quietly.

"Yes," she replied without hesitation. "After I was nearly killed, I doubted myself and my worthiness and attractiveness. *Major* doubts. I have scars on my body, and they took something from me that I couldn't get back, I didn't think a man would ever be interested in me. Not even you. Not even with our past. Then you were there, you tracked me down, you took away my bad memories by making love to me. When I got pregnant and you proposed, I was happy, but at the back of my mind, I always wondered if you were only with me because of Cleo. I know you loved me, but I feared you weren't *in* love with me. Then you left right after she was gone. What else could I think but that you only married me because I got pregnant? So, yes, having the person who broke my heart here while trying to find my baby is a bad thing."

"Raven," his voice was tortured as he uttered her name. "No. Just no. I was in love with you but ..."

"No, please, I can't hear anything you have to say right now," she said. There was no way her heart could take another beating. She had to be strong, her sweet little baby was counting on her to get justice. Maybe after this was done, when Le Entregar was destroyed, she could hear whatever Max wanted to tell her.

For now, he was nothing more than the ex-husband who had walked away from her when she needed him the most.

Maybe that was all he would ever be.

* * *

10:14 P.M.

Max felt gutted as he watched her walk away.

He felt compelled to grab her, hold her still and make her listen to what he had to say, but she'd asked him not to. Chances were that if he told her he still loved her today every bit as much as he had the day he'd first seen her, she wouldn't believe him anyway.

Still, it killed him to know that she had doubted him, doubted herself, doubted everything they had shared.

Leaving had seemed like the only thing he could do ten

years ago, now he was starting to believe it might be the second biggest mistake of his life.

The biggest mistake of his life would always be taking his eyes off his daughter that day.

If he hadn't, if he'd been paying attention like he should have been, then Cleo would never have been taken. If they hadn't lost their daughter then he and Raven would still be married, probably would have had other children, instead, both of them had spent the last decade suffering, in pain, with no end in sight.

The only thing that could help either of them heal was getting Cleo back, but his daughter was more than likely long since dead.

Max couldn't allow himself to think about what had happened to his little princess after she'd been taken. If he did, he'd lose what little sanity he had left. They knew human traffickers had taken her, Raven had managed to find Cleo's photo on an auction website, and he knew what happened to children who were sold. Thinking of the horrific pain his baby had gone through was too much.

Instead, he tried to remember Cleo as the vivacious, bubbly, sassy little thing she'd been. Cleo had loved pink, her entire room had been bright pink, walls, curtains, quilt on her bed. She'd loved stuffed animals and had an entire shelf full of them, she'd loved books too, she was always asking them to read to her. Cleo had loved to dance and sing and had a voice like an angel. She made friends everywhere she went and was always excited on preschool days. Her brown eyes were always sparkling with mischief, and she almost always wearing something sparkly.

She was perfection, and he had to remember her like that, it was what she deserved. To be remembered as more than just a little girl snatched off the streets and sold to monsters.

The bathroom door opened, and Raven came out, dressed in an oversized t-shirt, with her silky black hair hanging in loose waves down her back. Her skin was pale like the moon, and he couldn't not think of the night he'd first seen her. She'd been thirteen, he'd been sixteen, he'd been spending the summer with his grandparents who lived on a remote farm in the middle of nowhere. Used to his parents' arguments keeping him up to all hours of the night, he hadn't been able to sleep so he'd gone wandering through the woods. He'd been shocked to find a young girl sitting by a lake, with her thick dark hair framing her pale face she'd reminded him of night.

Midnight.

His quiet, sweet midnight.

He'd fallen in love with her right there and then, only it had taken him a long time to figure it out.

Raven wouldn't look at him as she tried to maneuver around him to get to the bed, but Max moved without thinking, blocking her path. Her gaze remained fixed on the floor, but when he reached out to cup her cheek it snapped up to meet his. There was confusion in her wide blue eyes, and he had to wonder if she was right. Was he making this worse for her? Was he distracting her at a time when she needed to be one hundred percent focused?

Should he have told Eagle no when he called and asked him to play bodyguard for Raven?

No.

His gut said no, that this was exactly where he should be right now.

His thumb brushed across her cheek. Her skin was so soft and smooth, like silk, and he'd loved to run his fingers through her hair when he was kissing her. Her mouth was heart-shaped, her lips plump, and she tasted sweeter than any sugar he'd ever had.

She was everything he'd ever wanted in a woman.

Smarter than anyone else he'd ever met, stronger than anyone he'd met too. What she'd done that night when she was sixteen, willingly walking into hell in an attempt to save her parents' lives, he couldn't imagine doing that at that age. She'd been too late, almost lost her own life in the process, but to know she hadn't hesitated to do it filled him with so much emotion he could hardly handle it.

This woman.

She was everything to him.

Everything.

Which was why he'd had to let her go.

Staying would have meant destroying her.

But now he was here and she was here, and he was finding it harder and harder to cling to his belief that he would destroy her if he didn't stay away.

Still, he didn't move.

Instead, he lifted his other hand to frame her face, allowing the feel of her to soak into him, he drank it up knowing that far too soon he would have to give her up again.

"Midnight," he whispered, leaning down to touch his forehead to hers.

Raven sucked in a breath. "Don't call me that," she said, her voice shaky.

"You're my midnight, my quiet in the storm. My peace." He should stop, release her, keep things professional between them, but he wasn't sure he could do it. Walking away from her once had all but shattered him, doing it again would destroy the few pieces that were left.

"I'm not. You left. You left *me* alone in the storm," she reminded him. Very gently she tugged free of his hold.

Max let her go only because he couldn't refute her words. He *had* left her alone in the storm, but at the time he hadn't seen any other option. He was the one who had cost them both their daughter. How could he stay with her, face her pain every day knowing he was responsible for causing it?

Call him a coward, he wouldn't disagree, but he'd made his choice and he couldn't take it back.

He was about to let it go. Head to the bathroom, take a cold shower, then sleep on the couch, but he froze when Raven stepped away from him and he saw what she was wearing. It wasn't just an oversized t-shirt she used as a nightshirt, it was one of *his* old t-shirts. When he was away, Raven had liked to wear his clothes, she said it made her feel closer to him. He'd been away a lot when they were together, he was in the military, a Pararescueman, a PJ, the air force's special forces. He'd been away more than he'd been home, which was why when he was home, he tried to spend as much time as he could with his girls.

Raven must have kept a few of his clothes when they'd divorced.

Clothes she still wore.

To sleep in.

She'd brought it here, to Colombia, where she was trying to track down the men who stole their daughter, like she'd needed his support and somehow wearing his old clothes gave it to her.

"What?" Raven asked, and he realized he was staring at her.

"The t-shirt."

She glanced down, and he saw her eyes widen as she

realized what she was wearing. "You left it behind. You can have it back if you want."

When she moved to take it off, he quickly stopped her. Partly because he was only a man and was still insanely attracted to his ex-wife, seeing her naked would likely prove too much to resist. But also because he liked knowing that she'd kept some of his clothes, that she wore then, particularly when she was vulnerable and alone in sleep.

"Don't." He reached out a hand to clasp hers, stilling them. "I don't want it back. Keep it. I like knowing you still wear my clothes."

Because he knew if he didn't leave the room soon, they'd both wind up naked and in bed, Max released his hold on Raven's hand and walked into the bathroom, closing and locking the door behind him. He sunk down against it, suddenly aware that he was in way over his head here. Not in the keeping Raven safe part, while this was the first time he'd ever played bodyguard he was no stranger to dangerous situations. His job sent him jumping into them on a near daily basis, but in the surviving Raven's company part.

How could he have ever thought he could do that?

How could he ever have thought that he could be around Raven and not want her so badly it consumed him?

How could he ever have thought he could spend the rest of his life without her?

CHAPTER 2

October 26th

4:53 A.M.

She hadn't anticipated leaving so early for her meeting, but it wasn't like she had a choice.

If she waited, then he'd want to come with her.

That was the last thing Raven wanted.

Max was already proving to be too big of a distraction. Instead of getting a good night's sleep so she was sharp and prepared for what could be the most important meeting she'd ever had—it could be the key to finding the men who had taken her baby—she had laid awake for hours, and now felt foggy and exhausted.

All she could do was pray that her exhaustion didn't wind up getting her killed.

But how could she sleep when she was ultra-aware that

she was wearing Max's old t-shirt, that he was asleep on the couch in the same room as her, that he had kissed her?

Max couldn't have shocked her more by announcing he was part grizzly bear than he had by kissing her and calling her by his old pet name for her.

If she'd known that Max would follow her down here, she never would have brought that t-shirt, but sleeping in it had become second nature, and she hadn't thought twice about shoving it into her suitcase. There had been no way for her to know that Eagle would go behind her back and hire her a bodyguard. And not just *a* bodyguard but her ex-husband.

Easing open the bathroom window, Raven shoved away all thoughts of Max. What she was about to do was dangerous, which was why maybe it was a good thing she was going to arrive even earlier than she had originally planned. She could get to the meeting spot early, hide away in the place she'd scoped out last night, and that way if this was a setup, she'd be safely tucked away where they wouldn't see her. If it wasn't a setup, then once her contact arrived and she was sure the woman had come alone, Raven would come out and hopefully get the answers she needed to take down Le Entregar.

That was what was important.

Revenge for her daughter.

Not her ex-husband who had hurt her worse than anyone else ever had.

Raven was glad she'd chosen this particular room at the small hotel because there was a large tree outside the third-story room. She'd thought that if she stirred up a hornet's nest by asking questions about Le Entregar and they came after her, this would give her another escape route.

The last thing she had expected to use it for was escaping her ex and his suffocating presence. But Max was here for a

24

different reason than she was. He was here to assuage his guilt over filing for divorce so soon after Cleo's disappearance or because he felt obligated to make sure she didn't get herself killed. He wasn't here for Cleo.

It was dark out, and she had to be careful as she swung her legs over the windowsill. It wasn't a big jump to the tree, but it had been a long time since she'd done anything like this. Not since she was a kid back on the farm she'd grown up on.

Raven concentrated then before she could back out, she leaped. She landed with a thud on the branch she'd been aiming for, and she quickly swung from branch to branch until her feet hit the ground.

Pleased with herself and her escape plan, Raven pulled out her keys and unlocked her rented SUV. It wasn't until she opened the driver's door that she froze.

"You." She scowled.

"Going somewhere without me, midnight?" Max asked. He was sitting in her car, dressed all in black, fingers drumming absently on the steering wheel.

So much for her imagined stealth. Obviously, he'd realized she planned on ditching him and pre-empted her.

"Apparently not," she snapped, annoyed that he'd managed to best her again. First last night, now this morning. Did Max always have to be so irritatingly perfect? "Can you move over?"

"Nope." He held out his hand for the keys. "I always drive, you know that."

She could stand there and argue with him about it, but Raven knew from experience it wasn't going to change anything. Max could be a control freak, always had been, and she doubted that had changed over the last ten years.

"Fine." With a huff, she handed over the keys then

rounded the car and got into the passenger seat. "Don't you need me to tell you where we're going?" she asked when he turned on the engine and started driving.

"Nope, I know where we're going."

"Then if you knew where I was going why were you waiting for me in the car? Why didn't you just follow me, or make sure you got there first? You seemed to have fun sneaking around after me last night." Okay, that came out a little snarky, but she was still a little annoyed that he'd kidnapped her last night, even if he was just making a point.

"Because I'd rather do this together."

The sincere honesty in his voice had her starting and looking over at him. His face was shadowed in the dark, but she could tell that he really meant what he'd said, which made her feel even worse. She wasn't his responsibility anymore, and yet he had taken time off his job, dropped everything, and come all the way over to Colombia to make sure she didn't get herself killed. She didn't have to like him being here, but she could at least work with him instead of against him.

"Okay, you're right." This was definitely not the time to let the past cloud the present, she had to keep her focus on Cleo where it belonged. "It's been hard finding anyone to talk to me, everyone around here is afraid of Le Entregar, but I was able to find this woman. She used to work as a maid at one of their properties, she said she broke something one day, some expensive vase, and they were angry with her, said it was really valuable. They took her daughter, said that made them even, her little girl was only eleven. She never went back, moved away, but she's been living in fear that they'll track her down. I was hoping that I might be able to get her to tell me where the property was. Max, I'm not sure she'll talk if you're there."

"I'm not letting you go in alone," he said fiercely, and she knew arguing over that was pointless. They might not be together anymore, but Max was a protector, there was no way he wouldn't do everything in his power to watch over her.

"All right, but maybe you could stay hidden. My meeting isn't until eight. I always planned to be there first so I could hide, make sure she wasn't followed, that I wasn't walking into a trap, so I was thinking that maybe we both hide. You choose a spot where you can watch over me, and that way my contact won't be spooked by having a ferocious man staring down at her while I interview her."

"Ferocious man, huh?" Max asked, sounding amused.

Raven rolled her eyes but couldn't stop a smile. "You know that look you get when you're in warrior mode, it can be kind of scary."

"Scary? Since when was my midnight ever afraid of me?"

Resisting the urge to remind him she wasn't his anything anymore, Raven instead said, "I've seen you in warrior mode before, I just wasn't scared of you when you were."

"When have you seen me in warrior mode?"

"That first night you tracked me down to my apartment after you found out what happened to me, you were in warrior mode that night."

"I seem to remember you liking my warrior mode that night."

His voice was a sexy drawl and her body clenched as she did indeed remember how much she'd enjoyed his warrior side that night. It was the first time she'd ever made love, her only other sexual encounter was being raped by the two men who killed her parents then sliced up her body. That night she had learned all about how sex should be, and even better it was with the man she had loved since she was thirteen.

"Can I take your silence as an agreement that that was one night we'll both never forget?"

Shoving down the feelings bubbling to the surface, the tingling as her body came alive after being in hibernation mode for ten long years, and the growing wetness between her legs, Raven wiped away her smile. Now was not the time for flirting. "So you'll hide so my contact doesn't see you?"

"Sure, babe, we'll play things your way for now since you know your contact better than I do, but we need a couple of ground rules."

"Ground rules?" she asked suspiciously.

"You get to ask your questions, but if I think anything feels off, we leave. If I tell you to do something you do it without arguing. Your battleground is the computer screen, but mine is out here, I promise I'll defer to your expertise if you agree to defer to mine."

The deal sounded so simple and yet agreeing to it felt harder than it should be.

He was right, they both had their areas of expertise. Maybe if they combined them, they just might be able to achieve what she'd set out to do here in Colombia.

"Raven? Deal?" Max asked, sticking out a hand.

What did she have to lose? Her sanity? Her heart? The last pieces left of her soul? If it meant finally taking down the men who had taken Cleo then she would sacrifice it all. Taking Max's hand, she shook it. "Deal."

* * *

8:08 A.M.

He didn't like this.

Max was on edge, something felt wrong but he couldn't put his finger on what.

Okay, so this whole mess was one great big dangerous disaster waiting to happen, but there was more to it than that.

Was it just because of Raven? Because he couldn't stand the thought of anything happening to her?

Or was it more?

Usually, he would trust his gut, he had to in his line of work, it was the only thing that kept him and his team alive. But right now, his gut just told him to get Raven out of Colombia and back to Manhattan where she would be safe. He couldn't trust his gut when it came to her because the idea of her being in danger sickened him.

Still, something niggled at him. Deep in that primal place you had to learn to hone if you wanted to survive in a warzone. Raven's contact was late, granted only eight minutes late, and out here people often lived a subsistence kind of life. They grew what they could, found whatever work they could, struggled to get by. It was doubtful this woman had a car, and she was going to be careful, she knew she was in Le Entregar's crosshairs.

From his perch up a tree, hidden by the thick foliage, he could see Raven, tucked away inside a large tree trunk. Branches and thick grass hid the entrance to the hole in the trunk, and unless you were specifically looking for it you wouldn't see it.

Movement caught his eye, and he whipped his attention around to find a middle-aged woman approaching cautiously. It was obvious from the way she kept looking around that she wouldn't have been surprised to see men with guns come jumping out of the trees. But was that because she was just scared of Le Entregar or was it because she knew she was leading them right to Raven?

Like she'd promised she would, Raven waited until the woman was in the designated meeting spot and then waited a full two minutes before she snuck out of her hiding place and circled around to meet with her contact. Raven had said the woman's name was Pilar Esposito and Pilar startled when she saw Raven but quickly relaxed once she realized who it was.

From his perch he could hear them talk, but he tried to keep his focus on their surroundings and looking for threats, trusting Raven would fill him in later.

He felt it a second before it happened.

A threat.

They weren't alone.

As the gunshot rang out, he was already launching himself from the tree, aiming for Raven.

By the time he located the threat and fired a shot of his own it would be too late. The shooter had the advantage, already had his targets in his sight, Max's only option was to get Raven out of the way.

Wrapping an arm around her waist he pulled her down, rolling so his body took the brunt of the fall and then rolling again so he covered her, pressing her into the ground.

A bullet whizzed by, hitting a tree behind them.

If he hadn't acted when he did it would have gone flying through Raven's heart, killing her instantly.

Keeping himself on top of her, he lifted his own weapon and scanned the area. By now the shooter had to know that it wasn't just the women out here, that meant he'd be coming in slowly and carefully. There could be others, but Max suspected that if there was more than one other man here then he would know already. They would have come storming in to confirm their kills, knowing they had the numbers advantage.

There.

Something moved at his ten o'clock.

Max didn't hesitate. He aimed and fired, a muffled thunk his confirmation that he had hit what he'd been aiming at.

Cautiously, he lifted himself off Raven when he didn't see or hear anything else. A quick scan of her body didn't show any blood but she wasn't moving. Her eyes were open, wide and scared, her dark hair made her seem even paler than usual.

"Raven, we have to go," he said, grabbing her hand and dragging her to her feet as he rose.

She swayed, and her vacant gaze moved toward Pilar Esposito. The woman's sightless eyes stared at the sky, blood soaked her shirt and puddled beneath her.

He muttered a curse. Blood. That was the last thing they needed right now. Ever since she had been sliced up by the men who had broken into her home, murdered her parents, then raped and nearly killed Raven, she had a major phobia of blood. It freaked her out, she couldn't deal with it, she'd always been particularly careful with Cleo because a simple skinned knee was enough to send Raven into a panic.

"Come on, baby," he murmured. Scanning their surroundings to ensure no one was approaching, when he didn't see anything he moved so he was blocking Raven's view of the body and took her face between his hands. "I'm sorry, midnight, sorry you had to see that, but I need you to pull it together for me so we can get out of here."

"Shot," Raven murmured.

"Yeah, babe, they shot her, but they didn't shoot you and I'm not going to let them shoot you. You hear me? I am not going to let them hurt you." Because he didn't know how else to help her snap out of her shock-induced haze, he pressed his lips to hers, kissing her hard and fast.

Raven blinked in surprise when he pulled back, but her eyes had cleared, and he knew that she was back with him.

"You good to go?" he asked.

"Yes." Her voice was still shaky, but he also saw determination spark in her. He saw the woman who had risked everything to come to Colombia to find and punish the men who had taken their daughter. Raven was strong, there were cracks in her armor, but none big enough to slow her down for long.

Grabbing her hand, he pulled her with him as he started moving. Raven stumbled at first but quickly gained her footing and kept pace with him as he led her through the trees. He had to get her back to the car, but he couldn't take a direct route because he had to find out if anyone else was out here.

He got his answer a moment later.

Bullets began to fly through the air.

Max darted sideways behind the relative safety of a tree. He shoved Raven between the trunk and his body, her front pressed against his, praying that if anyone came from behind them his body would be enough to protect her.

Three men all dressed in black were moving through the jungle toward him. It had been wishful thinking to believe the sniper was here alone. These men looked like they were well trained, but he was a PJ, the guys they sent in when someone needed rescuing, taking three men out was something he could do in his sleep.

Taking aim at the first man, he fired off a shot. The man dropped instantly. Another barrage of bullets flew at them, but he took a breath, centered himself, and fired again. The second man dropped.

Finally realizing they were up against a legitimate threat, the third man dropped low and disappeared from sight. Max fired where he suspected the man was, but he heard no thunk indicating he'd hit a target.

One of the men was still out there.

Carefully he scanned the trees, listening for the slightest sound that would indicate where the final tango was. Raven didn't move, barely breathed. He could tell she was freaked out. It was one thing to know you might be walking into an ambush, it was another to know that you had. Bullets and blood weren't Raven's thing, but she was holding it together and that was all he could ask from her.

"Max, behind you," Raven whispered in his ear.

He didn't hesitate, trusting her implicitly.

He spun and raised his weapon in one smooth movement, taking down the final tango before the man could sneak up on them and take them out. Or worse, take them with him to wherever he had come from. These men had to be Le Entregar, it was the only thing that made sense. Pilar Esposito had run from the trafficking ring, Raven was asking questions about them, they probably thought they could take out two birds with the one stone, follow Pilar to whoever she was snitching to, then take that person out too.

"That was close, midnight," he said, letting out a shaky breath as he turned back around to face her.

"Way too close," Raven agreed, still pale and shaky but still holding it together.

"You just saved my life."

"You saved mine first," she said with a half-smile. Then she grew serious and looked around them. "You think there are more out there?"

"Possibly. We'll have to move carefully. I don't want to go straight to the car in case they found it and have men there.

We'll go the long way back to it, see if we find anyone else, then head back to the hotel, and re-evaluate where we go from here."

As he took Raven's hand again and they began to move slowly through the rainforest, he knew where he wanted them to go from here. Straight to an airport and back to Manhattan, away from Le Entregar and the danger they represented.

* * *

9:27 A.M.

The drive back to the hotel was tense.

They were both on edge, both on the lookout for any more threats, of any signs that they were being followed.

Raven needed time to decompress. The sight of blood gave her flashbacks to the night her parents died. The room that night had been covered in blood, her parents', and then her own, and then finally the killers'. It was hard to see blood and not remember.

Although she'd managed to pull it together because she hadn't wanted her meltdown to get Max killed, now that they were back in the car, heading for the hotel, the shock was settling down on her again. Her hands were twisted together in her lap so tightly her knuckles were white, but she was trying to make sure Max didn't notice.

"I think we're good," he announced as he parked outside the small hotel. "No one has followed us back here."

"That's good, right?" Raven felt so out of her element. Although she had trained in self-defense and how to use a gun, knives, and swords from the time she could walk, just like the rest of her siblings, she was the only one who as an adult would hesitate to pick up a weapon even if she was in danger. Her thing was computers, from the safety of her keyboard she felt powerful, like she could do anything, but faced with a real-life enemy she crumbled.

"It's good, honey, I promise," Max assured her.

Still, despite his assurances, they were both surveying their surroundings as they climbed out of the car and headed inside. It felt wrong to leave Pilar Esposito's body out in the jungle all on her own, but it wasn't like they could bring it here with them.

"What about Pilar?" she asked quietly, aware that Max was using his body to shield her from any threats as they headed up to their room.

"Nothing we can do, Raven. I think it's best to let whoever sent those men find it there. They obviously don't know for sure who you are because they followed Pilar, not us. If we're lucky they'll assume whoever was asking questions about them was scared off and that we're long since gone."

"We know who sent those men," she reminded him. "They were Le Entregar."

"Right. No argument from me there. I'm sure they were Le Entregar, if they're operating in this area, then no one else would be stupid enough to, but you have to remember that we don't know anything for sure yet."

They both knew who this was, but she wasn't going to argue the point. Max unlocked the door to her room and they both went inside. She's tracked Le Entregar to this part of Colombia, and if she'd had more time with Pilar, she knew she would have gotten an address out of her.

But that hadn't happened.

Because a man had shot her.

As though it were happening all over again the images flashed before her eyes. The look of surprise on Pilar's face as the bullet pierced her chest, the blossom of red, the way her body fell like a ragdoll, already dead before she hit the ground.

"It's okay, midnight." Max's soothing voice penetrated the haze of shock, and she became aware of the heat of his hands rubbing her arms.

He was too close, too comforting, and she didn't know how to deal with that, which was exactly why Eagle should never have called Max and told him to come here.

"I'm okay," she said, moving away from his touch even though it was the last thing she wanted to do. *Because* it was the last thing she wanted to do. She had to be careful here. What they felt for one another was different. To her, he was the love of her life, to him, she was just the mother of his child. He was here just to protect her, she was here to get revenge for her daughter. She wished there was a way for them to have their happy ever after, but he would be leaving as soon as this was over.

"No, you're not," Max growled, stalking back and forth across the room like a caged tiger. "Of course you're not okay. Someone was shot dead in front of you just a couple of hours ago. You were almost shot. If I hadn't knocked you down, you'd be dead already. Don't you see how stupid it was to come here? Two of us are no match for Le Entregar. You need to leave, go home, collect more evidence on them, then I'll come back with all of Prey's teams and we'll take care of them."

"Don't you get it? I'm good on a computer, yes, but they have good people too, they know how to cover their tracks, how to be careful. I've been hunting them for almost ten years, and this is the only time I have gotten this close. We know they're close by even if we don't have an exact location because they took out Pilar before she could give it to us. They're having an auction soon, I need to be here so I can take advantage of every lead I get. I've never been this close to them and I'm not leaving now. No way."

His frustration was evident by the fact that he kept pacing. "And pursuing this is really worth your life?"

"Are you kidding right now? Of course it is," she exclaimed. She loved working for Prey, and she adored her family, but she would risk her life a million times over for a chance to destroy those who had taken her child.

"Try to think about this logically," Max began in what she could only describe as the kind of tone you would use to explain to a young child why something they wanted to do was dangerous.

"No," she cut him off, not in the mood for a lecture, "*you* think about this logically. I've been hunting these people for almost ten years. Every time I think I'm getting close they suddenly disappear. It took me years to connect them to the Amazon rainforest area of Colombia, now I'm narrowing that down. So far, they don't know I'm tracking the auction website but that could change at any moment. When they give the location and date and time of the auction, I'll have a couple of days tops to pull everything together and get this done. I don't know how to make it any clearer to you that this could be a once in a lifetime opportunity."

He stormed toward her, stopping just short of touching her. "And I don't know how to make it any clearer to you that this is too dangerous. Nothing is worth risking your life like this."

"Nothing?" she sputtered. How could Max of all people say that? "We're talking about our daughter, Max. I would have thought that you of all people would be on board with what I'm trying to do."

"Cleo is gone." He said it like she didn't already know that. Like she wasn't reminded of it every second of every day by the pain in her heart, and that made her angry.

"She deserves justice. I won't ever give up on Cleo like you have."

His eyes widened then darkened, and the look he gave her was dangerous. "You think I've given up on her?"

She shrugged. "Sure looks like it to me. You left only two months after she was taken, and I haven't heard from you since. I gave you updates at first on what I'd found, you never replied, so I stopped sending them. You just moved on." The last she said like it was foreign to her. Because it was. She couldn't imagine ever moving on, she would search for the men who took Cleo until she destroyed them or until she took her dying breath.

Max's breathing was choppy, and his hands clenched and unclenched, displaying his agitation. "I can't be around you right now," he snapped, storming for the door.

"I didn't ask you to be around me at all," she reminded him. "If you want to pack up your things and go home then do it."

He didn't say anything, just opened the door and slammed it behind him, leaving her standing there staring after him. She'd hurt him, and she felt bad, even though she couldn't ever understand how he could just walk away from her and move on like Cleo had never existed.

Bottom line was though that she was here for Cleo and Cleo alone and she had to keep her daughter as her focus. This wasn't about reconnecting with Max, what they'd had was over and done with even if she still harbored feelings for him.

Ignoring the pain in her chest because someone she loved was hurting, Raven locked the hotel room door, grabbed her laptop, and went back to work. If Max wanted to leave he could go home, she wouldn't miss him.

That was a lie.

She *would* miss him.

She had missed him for ten years.

CHAPTER 3

October 27th

2:36 A.M.

He couldn't sleep.

He was too angry.

Max hadn't been able to calm himself down after his argument with Raven yesterday morning. They'd barely spoken for the rest of the day. After he'd gone outside to try to blow off a little steam, he'd done a perimeter check and made sure no one had followed them to the small hotel. He'd also planned out a few escape routes if they needed one. After that there had been nothing to do but return to the room and watch Raven work.

She hadn't spoken to him.

He hadn't spoken to her.

They'd spent the rest of the day in silence except for a couple of short exchanges about lunch and dinner.

There'd been nothing for him to do. Raven had been focused on her work, which she chose not to share with him.

Nothing to do but think.

And he'd been forced to admit to himself that Raven's anger was well deserved. He had made it seem like he had just moved on. He hadn't moved on of course, he couldn't, but back in those early days when he'd been drowning in guilt, Raven hadn't been looking for justice she'd been trying to find Cleo. Every time he got one of her emails detailing a new lead she'd found, he'd had no choice but to delete it immediately, he couldn't handle hoping that they'd find Cleo only to have those hopes dashed to pieces.

Cutting off contact was the only way he had survived.

Still, he hadn't moved on, and neither had Raven. Her whole life revolved around tracking leads, and although he knew they were in danger if they stayed here, he had also accepted that she would never agree to leave. Which meant he had to decide if he could handle staying. Could he get sucked into Raven's world? A world that consisted mainly of tracking leads on Le Entregar?

Or what he really should be asking himself was, could he handle walking away from her again?

Max feared he already knew the answer to that.

No.

He couldn't handle walking away again.

What he should have done was ignore Eagle's call, pretend he was out of the country, but it was too late for that. Eagle had probably used his contacts to find out that he was on leave anyway. If Eagle had wanted him to watch over his sister, then the man would have stopped at nothing to make it happen.

He shifted again, the couch was reasonably comfortable, and he'd certainly slept in worse places, but the soft breathing coming from the bed was driving him crazy. Raven had called it a day around midnight and taken a shower then climbed into bed. He had waited till she was tucked in before taking his own shower and settling down for the night, but all he'd done was toss and turn and try not to think of Raven in nothing but one of his old t-shirts in the bed beneath the covers.

If he went to her, would she turn him away?

She was clearly still angry with him so she probably would, but what if she didn't?

Could he take one more taste of her and then leave?

Thoughts of stripping Raven naked and burying himself inside her tight, wet heat were interrupted when he heard a sound.

Immediately he focused, keeping his body still and listening intently. The hotel they were in was small—four floors, six rooms on each one. From his recon, he'd found that half the rooms were currently occupied including two others on this floor. Eagle had already vetted all of them, so he knew that none were threats.

At least they hadn't been.

But people could be bought, or they could be threatened.

A flash of light under the door had every one of his instincts screaming at him. Someone was out there, and it wasn't just one of the guests wandering around in the middle of the night. This was the only hotel in the area, Le Entregar didn't have to know who they were, all they had to do was assume that they'd be staying here and wait till dark and come looking for them, hoping to catch them unawares.

It seemed like that was exactly what they'd done, but he was always aware, his life depended on it.

Max tossed the blanket aside, quickly shoved his feet into his shoes, threw on his shirt, and then crossed the room. Grabbing a chair, he propped it under the handle and ran to the bed. Covering Raven's mouth with his hand, he shook her to wake her.

She sprung awake in a panic, thrashing against his hold. "It's me, Raven. It's just Max. Do you hear me?"

Raven went still, and beneath his hand she nodded. Tentatively he removed his hand, ready to clamp it down again if she screamed or did anything to alert the people outside their room that they were awake.

"What's wrong?" Raven whispered.

"Someone's out there," he replied, indicating the door just as someone began to wriggle the doorknob.

"Do they know it's us in here?"

"They will when they try to open the door and can't," he said, dragging her out of the bed. "Get dressed, we have to get out of here."

Raven nodded and scrambled off the bed, running to her suitcase and grabbing some clothes. "How long will that hold them off?" she asked, pointing to the chair at the door.

"Not long. As soon as you're dressed we go out the window, same way you did when you tried to ditch me yesterday morning," he said with a wink, hoping to ease the tension he could feel rolling off her.

She gave him a tight smile. "Are we taking our things?"

Whoever was out there began to shake the door more firmly, it was clear they were determined to get in here. "Are you all packed?"

"Yes, I never unpacked, in case I had to leave in a hurry."

"Then we can take anything you can carry." Max put his backpack on and zipped up Raven's case as she put on her boots.

Her gaze moved between her suitcase and her laptop. "I'll take my computer. I can buy more clothes, but my laptop has all my programs on it."

He huffed a chuckle. That was his midnight, she couldn't go anywhere without her computer. Max was about to tell her he'd grab her suitcase when the door suddenly splintered. "Go," he said, shoving her toward the bathroom. "Take your computer and go to the car. If I'm not there in ten minutes, leave."

"But ..."

"No buts," he said. While he assumed these men were Le Entregar they didn't know if their orders were to kill them or take them, and the last thing he was going to let happen was for Raven to fall into the trafficking ring's hands. He'd already failed his daughter, he wasn't going to fail the woman he loved as well.

Two men were visible through the broken door, one reached through and shoved the chair out of the way. Raven grabbed her laptop and ran into the bathroom. He could shoot the intruders, but he was sure there were more men around here somewhere and he didn't want to draw any attention. He needed to buy time for Raven to get away, if he fired his weapon then they'd know that they hadn't been caught sleeping and send in whoever else was watching this place.

Springing into action, he charged the door, catching the two men by surprise as they stormed the room. A well-placed punch to the side of the head of the first one had him dropping, already unconscious by the time he hit the floor.

The other lifted his weapon, but Max kicked out, knocking the gun from his hand. As he went to deliver a blow to the man's head, he struck out first, getting Max right in the jaw.

"Max?" Raven called, clearly worried.

"Go," he ordered. "Now."

"But …"

"Raven," he growled. He'd thought she was already long gone. "Get out of here."

The other man kicked his stomach while he was distracted, pain buzzed in his jaw and stomach, but it was nothing compared to what he'd experienced before. Allowing the next blow to take him down, letting the other man think he'd got the upper hand, he delivered a kick to the man's knee.

When he stumbled, his shattered knee unable to support him, Max pounced on him. He'd love to interrogate him, find out what Le Entregar knew about who was asking questions about them, but he didn't have time. Instead, Max snapped the man's neck, then moved onto the first intruder who was still lying unconscious by the door.

With both of them dead, he grabbed Raven's suitcase and ran into the bathroom. It was still dark out, but he didn't see or hear anyone about as he jumped to the nearby tree and quickly climbed down it.

He was about to head for the car, which he'd moved to the next street over just in case anyone had taken note of the license plate earlier when Pilar Esposito had been killed and spotted it, when he sensed someone behind him.

Max turned, aiming his weapon, but dropped it when he saw her. "What are you doing here? I told you to go."

"I couldn't leave you behind," Raven protested, stepping out from behind the vine covering the hotel's wall.

He muttered a curse but couldn't help being pleased that she cared enough to worry about what happened to him. "Come on, let's get out of here." He grabbed her hand and tugged her along with him toward the car.

"Are they …?"

"Dead? Yes. I had to kill them, I couldn't leave them alive to come after us, but Le Entregar know we're here, they'll keep trying to find us," he warned her. They were far from out of the woods, and although he had faith in his abilities, Le Entregar was powerful and had an army they could send after them.

"You saved our lives," Raven said. "Thank you."

He hadn't saved their lives to gain her gratitude, nor had he done it just because Eagle had hired him to be Raven's bodyguard. He'd saved her life because he simply could not imagine a world without Raven Oswald in it, nor did he wish to.

* * *

3:44 P.M.

Raven shifted uncomfortably in her seat. They'd been in the car for going on twelve hours now, except for a brief stop to pick up something for lunch, and a couple of bathroom breaks.

By bathroom breaks, she did not mean that they had stopped somewhere with an actual toilet. Given that they knew they were in Le Entregar territory and that no doubt meant they had eyes everywhere, Max hadn't wanted too many people to see them. That means they'd stopped at the side of the road and gone in the trees.

It had been so long since she'd roughed it like that, not since she was a kid on her parents' remote farm. Back then, it had seemed like second nature, but she'd been sixteen when her parents died and they moved to the city. She was thirty-three now, she'd spent more time in civilization than she had on the off-the-grid farm.

She shifted the computer slightly to adjust for the bumpy roads they were traveling and rubbed at her eyes. They were tired, and she really needed a break, but time was not on their side, especially if they were going to have to spend their time running from Le Entregar.

"Sometimes I can't reconcile the girl I met when she was thirteen, who had never even heard of a phone, or a TV, or a computer, or any other technology, with the computer whiz you turned into."

Raven looked over to see Max smiling at her. There was tenderness in his voice and his face, and she felt a part of herself relax. She didn't like tension, especially not with the people she loved, and things had been beyond tense between them yesterday after their argument.

She smiled back at him. "Everything was so strange when we first moved, and after everything that had happened, when I got out of the hospital I wasn't up to meeting new people. I just hid out at the house, I think the nanny got annoyed with me just sitting around moping and thrust an old laptop at me one day. From there on I was hooked." She laughed at the memory. After their parents' deaths, Eagle had taken guardianship of them since they were all minors, and he moved them to Manhattan since he was away at boot camp. He hired an elderly woman to be their live-in nanny, and while the younger kids had gone to school, she refused and had completed high school from their apartment. She'd then continued to study from home while she was in college as she took over guardianship of her siblings. Eagle was still away serving it had made sense for her to have legal custody.

"You had natural talent," Max said.

"I guess so. It all seemed to come so easily to me. It was

weird, like learning a new language, but finding out that at the back of your mind, in some hidden place, you already knew the language all along."

"It's a gift. A gift you've used to save hundreds of people."

But not the one person she wanted to save the most.

While she was glad she had played a role in saving the people Prey helped, she wanted to use her skills to save her baby girl.

"We'll get them, midnight, you're too determined to accept anything else. It was one of the first things I realized about you. Do you remember the night we met?"

"As if I could forget." Even though she had only been thirteen, Raven had known that night that she was looking at the man—well he'd been only a boy back then—that she would spend the rest of her life with.

At least that's what would have happened if fate hadn't dealt them a horrific hand.

"I don't know who was more surprised that night." Max chuckled. "Me finding a young girl sitting by a lake in the middle of nowhere, or you having some boy interrupt your midnight musings."

She laughed. "Are you kidding? It was me. I'd never met anyone outside my family before you." Every night that summer, he'd met her by the lake at midnight, they'd sat and talked about anything and everything. It was the first time she'd learned about the world outside her own little farm. He'd come back the next summer, and the one after that, and those nights had been some of the best of her life. "I always wished you had kissed me that last summer. I wanted you to so badly, but I didn't know how to get you to, and I was too shy to come right out and ask."

His hand left the steering wheel to cover one of hers. "You were only fifteen, I was eighteen, it wouldn't have been appropriate. But I always knew I would come back for you. I thought there was plenty of time," he said softly. Sadly. "I wanted to be your first. Your first everything. I wish I had kissed you that last night of the summer too. I know it wouldn't have changed what happened, but maybe it would have given you something to hold onto."

Her heart swelled at his admission. Raven turned her hand over so she was holding Max's, and she squeezed tightly. "Max, you *were* my first in every way that matters. What those men did to me doesn't count. They forced me, held me down while they cut me and raped me, and while technically that was the first time I had sex, it was nothing more than rape. *You* were the first time I made love, you made my body feel alive, you showed me what it should be. That makes you my real first."

He smiled at her now, and she felt herself relax further. Maybe having Max here wasn't the worst thing in the world. Sure, he drove her crazy, but at least he got upset because he cared. And they did share a past, he'd been her first—her only—love, and they had made the most beautiful little girl.

"Did you mean what you said before? When you said *we'll* get them?" she asked. It would be so nice to have a partner in this, someone who was as motivated to destroy Le Entregar as she was. Who better to be that partner than Cleo's father?

"Of course I meant it. I won't leave you here alone to face Le Entregar. Look, Raven, we didn't get off to the best of starts here, and that's my fault, I shouldn't have sprung it on you that I was here, and I definitely shouldn't have tied you up that night. But I'm here, and I care about what happens to you. I will do whatever it takes to keep you safe. Maybe we could form a truce."

"A truce?"

"We're stronger when we work together than when we're

constantly at odds. You're the brains, and I'm the brawn," he teased.

She laughed as she knew he had intended, and the last of the tension between them drained away. "Okay. Truce, we work this together."

"Together," Max echoed.

Raven liked the sound of that. Probably a whole lot more than she should, considering how she knew this was going to end. If they could take down Le Entregar then she would go back home to New York City and working at Prey, and Max would return to wherever his team was sent, and she would never hear from him again.

Still, for now she wasn't going to dwell on that, so Raven painted on a smile and was about to make a joke about the two of them working together when she caught sight of something in the side mirror. "Max," she said, immediately back on edge.

"I know, they've been following us for a while now."

"Why didn't you say anything?" she demanded.

"Didn't want to worry you."

"We're supposed to be a team here," she reminded him.

"You're right, I'm sorry. Next time I'll alert you immediately when we're being followed," he said and winked at her.

"You're impossible, you know that, right?" she said, but she laughed despite their dire situation. "So, is it them? Le Entregar?"

"That would be my guess."

"How did they find us?"

"No idea. Maybe they're just checking out all cars in the area."

"How are we going to get away from them?" The road they were on was narrow, and the rainforest was on either side. There was no way they could drive through the trees, and who knew when they'd come to another road.

"I don't think we're going to outrun them, midnight," Max said as he sped up.

A glance out the window showed the car was gaining on them. Just when she thought things couldn't get worse for them, someone began shooting at them.

"Those bullets are coming from in front of us," she said as she snapped around to look back out the front window where she saw another SUV speeding toward them.

They were trapped.

"Max?" She looked to him—this was his thing not hers—she had no idea how they were going to get away, and she prayed he had a plan.

"Hold on, midnight," he said as he yanked on the wheel sending them careening into the rainforest.

"What are you doing?" she squeaked.

"Trying not to get us shot," he replied dryly.

"No way we can drive through here," she said, wrapping one hand around her laptop, the other curled around her seatbelt, trying to hold herself in place as they flew over the rough terrain. The rainforest was thick, there were plants everywhere, and the trees were close together, they weren't going to get far.

A bullet cracked through the rear window and flew through the car plowing through the front windshield.

This was never going to work.

"Where are your guns?" Raven asked.

Max threw a quick glance her way. "You don't like guns."

"I haven't forgotten, but unless you have a better idea, I'm going to have to …" Raven broke off when the car suddenly lurched dangerously. "What was that?"

"They're shooting out the tires. Apparently, they've

decided we're bad news." Max was fighting with the car, but another jolt told her without him having to say anything that another of the tires had been shot out.

They were going to hit a tree.

It was inevitable.

Raven knew it, but there was no way to stop it.

All she could do was tuck her laptop under her seat. If they somehow managed to survive this then they were going to need it and try to brace for impact.

She was just straightening when it happened.

Her head and chest hit the dashboard with bone-crushing force.

The last thing she heard before the darkness forced her to surrender to it was Max yelling her name.

* * *

4:13 P.M.

His head was pounding.

It took a second for him to remember where he was and what had happened.

That second cost him his chance to grab his weapon.

Instead, Max was roughly grabbed and dragged out of the now ruined car.

Max played dead as he was tossed onto the ground, giving himself a moment to gather as much information as he could. He had to play this as smartly as he could, Raven's life depended on it. He had promised Eagle that he would watch over her, protect her, not let anyone hurt her.

He had failed.

The men were speaking Spanish, not surprising since he

assumed they were Le Entregar, and he heard at least five distinct voices, but there could be more. The men would be highly trained, and definitely bloodthirsty, but they wouldn't be as trained as he was. Just because they'd run them off the road didn't mean they knew for sure that they were the ones asking questions or that they were the ones who had evaded and killed the men yesterday.

Max couldn't hear Raven which meant she was either dead, unconscious, or too afraid of the men to speak up.

Nope.

That definitely wasn't true. If Raven was awake then she'd be questioning these men regardless of the fact that it would likely end badly for her if she did. He wouldn't go so far as to say she had a death wish, but when it came to the men who had taken their daughter he also wouldn't say that she was rational. She had known coming to Colombia was dangerous and she'd done it anyway, in her mind, destroying—or at least attempting to destroy—Le Entregar was the most important thing.

"Wake him up," one of the men ordered.

Max prepared himself for what was coming, although his eyes were closed, he felt the foot moving toward him and moved with it when it connected with his stomach, taking most of the force out of the kick. He continued moving, rolling backward, his hands reaching for the weapon tucked away at the small of his back.

They should have checked him for weapons before dragging him out of the car. Their loss was his gain.

Knowing he only had one chance at getting himself and Raven out of this alive, if he blew it they would be killed or captured, Max was already firing before he got to his feet.

He took down three of what turned out to be eight men before they had a chance to draw their weapons.

Raven's limp body lay just a couple of feet away, the man closest to her lifted his weapon to aim it at her in what would no doubt have been a threat, but Max fired as he lunged toward her, taking down the man before he could do anything.

That was four down but four still alive. They were outnumbered, and Raven seemed to be unconscious, she hadn't moved, and even though he knew she hated guns and violence she would do what she had to do to protect herself.

"You make big mistake," one of the surviving men yelled at him in broken English.

"Yeah, pretty sure it's you who've made the mistake," he yelled back, snagging the M16 that the man who'd been going to threaten Raven had dropped, he fired a volley of bullets at the car where the remaining men had taken cover.

"You make powerful enemy," one hollered.

Beneath him Raven stirred. Bullets sprayed the ground, some hit so close he could feel their heat rush past them. Instead of aiming for the men or shooting randomly at the car, he adjusted his aim for the gas tank. The men had the advantage, they had protection while he and Raven had none, and there were more of them. A couple of them could keep him pinned down while the others circled around and took them out from behind.

Grabbing Raven, he lifted her over his shoulder, already getting to his feet as he fired at the gas tank. Because he was already running when it exploded, they avoided being hit by burning metal, but the force of the explosion still knocked him down.

Max made sure he took the brunt of the fall, tucking Raven into the safety of his arms and hiding them both behind a tree.

"Max?" Her eyes were glassy as they looked up at him, and he was worried about a concussion.

"We're okay, midnight," he soothed, wanting to keep her calm. "I need you to stay here for me, okay?"

"Where are you going?" Raven blinked, and her eyes cleared a little, at least she was lucid and asking questions.

"I need to make sure they're all dead." He reluctantly let her go, the idea of leaving her here alone didn't sit well with him, but he didn't have a choice. The car was ruined, they needed to put as much distance as they could between it and them. He had to make sure that none of the men followed. "Here, take this," he said, passing her his weapon, keeping the M16 for himself.

Raven nodded but was clearly reluctant to take the weapon. She held it loosely in her hand as though afraid it would bite her, and he knew she wasn't happy with the idea of having to shoot anyone.

But she didn't complain, and he turned and cautiously made his way back toward the burning vehicle. He'd have to be quick, it wouldn't be long before the smoke alerted someone, and Le Entregar would send more men after them.

The first three bodies he found were all dead, but the last of the men who had attacked them made a feeble attempt to reach for his weapon when he spotted Max.

Max placed his foot on the man's arm, applying just enough pressure to cause pain. "Who do you work for?"

Blood dribbled from the man's mouth, a piece of metal from the vehicle was embedded in his stomach, he wasn't walking away alive and he knew it.

His fury spiked when the man pressed his lips into a thin line, and he pressed harder on the man's arm, hard enough that he heard the crack as the bone broke. The man howled in pain and Max leaned down close. "Who do you work for?"

"L-Le E-Entregar," he stuttered.

"Why did you shoot at our car?"

Again the man pressed his lips together and stared up at him in defiance. Since he didn't have time for this, he kept applying pressure to the man's arm, then nudged the protruding piece of metal, causing the man to scream in agony.

"I'm going to ask you again. Why did you shoot at our car?"

"S-someone been a-asking q-questions about u-us. A w-woman. W-we ch-check all c-cars." Tears were streaming down his face, and he coughed up blood, he was fading fast.

"Do you know who she is?"

"A-American."

"Do you know her name?"

"No." The man's eyes fluttered closed, and he had all he needed. Because the man had been helpful Max ended his life quickly with a bullet between the eyes instead of leaving him to succumb to his injuries.

He was halfway back to where he'd left Raven when he saw her. She was up on her feet and moving slowly toward him. Even from here, he could see the pain in each movement, and he hurried toward her.

"Max, you're okay." She sunk down against the nearest tree when she saw him, relief evident in her face. "I was worried one of them shot you."

"No such luck, midnight, you're not getting rid of me that easily," he joked, wanting to see a smile chase away her worries, if even for a moment.

She smiled as he'd hoped, but the worry was still there. "Are they all dead?"

"Yes."

"Le Entregar?"

"Yes."

"Do they know who we are?"

"They know a woman has been asking questions, but they don't know your name. Yet, anyway, but they're going to assume that we are who they're looking for. How badly are you hurt?" They needed to get as far away from here as quickly as they could, but Raven was in obvious pain. He assumed she had a concussion so he'd have to monitor her carefully, but he needed to know if she was injured anywhere else.

"I'm okay," she replied but shifted her gaze so she wasn't looking directly at him.

"Liar," he murmured as he stepped closer and reached out to palm her cheek. There was a large lump on her forehead, blood dribbled from the wound, and she had an arm braced across her stomach, just under her ribcage. "Your chest."

Raven nodded reluctantly. "I was putting my laptop under the seat when we hit, my head and chest took the brunt of the impact."

"Broken?" That was the last thing they needed, broken ribs could puncture her lungs or heart, even cracked ribs would slow them down substantially.

"I don't think so, just bruised."

"Let me see." Her eyes widened then narrowed. "I am *not* going to let you see my chest."

Max grinned. "Babe, I've seen you naked lots of times. We were married, remember? And if I want to see you naked again all I have to do is close my eyes and picture those perfect breasts of yours."

"Max," she exclaimed, but she laughed. "You're incorrigible."

"With you, always. I do need to see your chest though, see how badly you're hurt."

Raven sighed but grabbed the hem of her long sleeve t-shirt and lifted it up. As soon as it moved above her bra, he could see that her chest was already red and starting to turn black. She would be a mess by tomorrow. He lifted his hand and brushed his fingertips along the marks, hating that she was hurting.

"Sorry you got hurt," he whispered.

"You saved my life," Raven corrected, lifting a hand and covering his. "I'd be dead or a prisoner of Le Entregar right now if it wasn't for you. Thank you, Max."

"We're partners, remember? Can't have my partner getting herself killed." He smiled, then rested his forehead against hers. "I'll find a way to get us out of here."

"I believe you, Max. I'm not used to this side of you, you were always so sweet with Cleo and me, but I like seeing you like this. It's kind of sexy," she finished softly.

Her admission surprised a chuckle out of him. "Only kind of sexy?"

She smirked. "Yeah, only kind of."

"Come here, midnight." He tugged her gently into his arms, snuggling her against his chest and tucking her head beneath his chin. He could have lost her today, either to bullets, the accident, or Le Entregar, none of those were acceptable outcomes. He needed to find a way to keep her safe while also helping her destroy the trafficking ring, but right now he just needed a moment to hold her.

CHAPTER 4

October 28th

1:19 A.M.

Raven wasn't sure she could walk anymore.

They'd been walking through the thick, dense rainforest for hours now. The sun had long since set, making walking that much harder. The dark felt oppressive, smothering, and she longed to get back to some sort of civilization. They couldn't walk down the road, they'd be too easily spotted, and she had lost track of which direction they were heading in, but Max was moving with purpose so she had to assume he had some idea of where they were going.

Her chest sent a stab of pain through her with every single step she took, she was exhausted, shaky, thirsty, and all she wanted to do was lie down and sleep. Her head was pounding with a constant headache, and the world was fuzzy and almost like it was spinning around her.

She stumbled, but before she could completely lose her balance an arm wrapped around her, and she was tucked in against Max's side.

"I'll find a place for us to bunker down, get some sleep," he said, taking most of her weight.

Raven snuggled against him, soaking up his strength. "No, we haven't gone far enough," she reminded him. They had to put as much distance between them and the car as they could because more men would be coming after them.

"I hate that you're right. You need rest to start healing, but we haven't gone far enough yet. If they've already found the car, then they've already sent people out after us. The best we can hope for is that they'd assume we'd stick close to a road. How about I carry you for a while?"

"Max, no," she protested when he went to pick her up. "I'm too heavy, and you're hurt too, you can't carry me."

"Are you calling yourself fat?" he asked, a reprimand in his tone.

She laughed. "No, I'm too willowy to be fat." Raven had always thought she was a little too thin, she didn't have the kind of figure men seemed to like, and she wasn't tall enough to look elegant. At least in her mind, she's always thought her body looked more like a kid's than a woman's, but she just couldn't seem to add enough pounds, even while pregnant, to get the figure she desired.

"You're perfect is what you are," Max said, making her blush. He had always seemed to like her body even when she'd been unhappy with it and unable to see what he saw in her.

"Only you think that," she said with another smaller laugh.

"Only *you* think that," he shot back. "You don't seem to notice that men stare at you. You're gorgeous, Raven, and I wish you saw that."

Raven yawned, her head lolling against his shoulder. "I don't care if men look at me or not," she said, suddenly very tired. "Only ever cared how *you* looked at me."

"You have nothing to worry about on that front, midnight," he murmured as he gathered her into his arms. "Rest for a bit, honey."

It wasn't a conscious decision, her body had just reached its limit and checked out against her permission.

When she woke up, she was alone.

She was sitting on the ground, resting against a tree trunk. Branches covered her so at least she knew that Max hadn't just dropped her and been attacked. He'd left her here, carefully covering her so she wouldn't be spotted before leaving.

But where had he gone?

Raven went to move the branches and found that there was a gun sitting in her lap. He'd left her armed. Was that because he thought he wouldn't be coming back?

Max wouldn't leave her alone out here, she knew that, but he also couldn't carry her indefinitely. Maybe he'd found a village and wanted to scope it out. Or perhaps they'd been found and he'd tucked her away so he could eliminate the threat. Or maybe he'd known the only way they were getting out of here was for him to leave her behind, get help, and then come back for her.

"No, Max wouldn't leave you," she whispered to herself as she stood on shaky legs. However long she'd been out was enough to regain a little of her strength, her head still pounded, her bruised ribs still ached, but at least she felt clearer and not like the world was spinning beneath her.

It was still dark so she couldn't have been asleep more than a couple of hours tops, probably not even that long. Raven wasn't sure what she should do. If Max hadn't intended to be gone long, then she shouldn't wander far otherwise when he came back for her, she wouldn't be there. But if he needed help, she didn't just want to be sitting here in safety, leaving him to fight off Le Entregar by himself. Especially when she was the reason Max was even in Colombia.

Moving slowly, cautiously, she crept forward, unsure what direction she should go in. It was probably best to try going a short distance in one direction, then backtrack and try a different direction. That way she should spot Max if he was nearby.

Putting that plan into action, Raven hadn't gone more than a dozen yards or so when a shadow fell over her. Stifling a scream, she spun around, weapon rising automatically to aim at whoever was coming.

"Whoa, don't shoot, midnight, it's only me."

Letting out a sigh of relief, Raven sagged against the closest tree. "Where did you go?"

"Found us a small shack to hole up in, get some rest. I wanted to check it out, make sure it was safe. You were still out, and I thought I could be back before you woke up. You didn't think I'd left you, did you?"

She had. Just a teeny little bit. It wasn't like she wanted to think he'd abandon her, but he had walked away after Cleo was taken, so maybe she had a small bit of doubt when it came to him sticking around. "I was worried you were in trouble."

"You worried about me getting hurt, sweetheart?"

Raven simply huffed. She knew he was teasing her, but

she didn't want to be the first to admit that her feelings for him still existed. He was the one who had left her, he had to be the one to make a move if he wanted anything to change between them. "Wasn't worried for a second, I know you can take care of yourself," she said with a smile, ignoring the tension that simmered between them.

Max smiled back and reached for her hand. "Let's go get some sleep. I don't have anything for us to eat, but there's a well beside the shack so we can at least drink something. We'll sleep for a few hours and then start walking again. I'm hoping we'll be in the next town by sunset tonight."

Sleep and water sounded pretty good right now, her stomach was still a little queasy so she wasn't really hungry anyway, but she was thirsty. "Sounds good," she agreed, fighting another yawn.

Hand in hand, he led her a short way off where a tiny shack stood between the tall trees. It was mostly dilapidated, but it had four walls and a roof and would give them some shelter from the weather, and also some protection from the men hunting them.

"Water first," Max said.

They stopped beside the well and Max drew up a bucket filled with cool water. It felt so good sliding down her parched throat that she moaned in delight. When she finished drinking her fill, she licked a drop from her bottom lip, and Max groaned.

"Babe, don't do that," he said tightly.

She was going to ask him what he meant, but she caught sight of the growing tent in his pants and giggled. "We're dirty, exhausted, hungry, and injured. Are you really thinking of sex at a time like this?"

"Honey, when you're around it's *all* I think of."

Raven was still laughing as he ushered her inside. It was filthy, there was no furniture, and because there were no windows it was even darker than it was outside. Still, it was better than sleeping outside amongst the trees and the creatures that lived there. She was *not* a fan of creepy crawlies, and there should be less in here.

Max guided her over to the corner furthest from the door. "You sleep next to the wall, that way I can take out anyone who comes in here.

With Max between her and the door, Raven knew she would feel safe enough to sleep, but when they both lay down and he curled an arm around her shoulders, urging her to use his chest as a pillow, Raven found that sleep wouldn't come. Exhaustion had Max passing out immediately, and she lay there for a long time listening to his deep, even breathing. It was a comforting sound, and he was pleasantly warm, but she couldn't stop thinking about the danger she'd gotten him into.

This was a personal vendetta to her, it was her own personal crusade, but now because of it Max might die.

The thought made her feel ill.

Stomach churning again, Raven inched out of Max's hold. She'd go outside, drink a little more water, then maybe she could clear her mind enough that sleep would finally come. They both needed all the rest they could get, they had hours of walking ahead of them, and she didn't want to be a burden and make Max have to carry her again.

The night was quiet, peaceful, like they'd reached the hour where all living creatures joined one another in slumber. Her aching feet protested taking another step, but she headed for the well. Pulling up another bucket of water, she drank greedily like she'd never consumed the earlier one.

Raven had just released the bucket, heard it splash into

the water below when a hand covered her mouth, and she was yanked up against a hard chest.

* * *

2:57 A.M.

Max woke as soon as Raven slipped out of his arms, but he didn't go after her.

He knew she needed more rest, she hadn't been out for more than an hour earlier and had to be exhausted and in pain, but he also thought that maybe she needed a moment alone to process what had happened.

Things between them were ... well, he wasn't quite sure where this was heading, but at least they could be in the same room again without resorting to trying to kill each other. The truce seemed to be working well, she had accepted that he wasn't leaving, and he had accepted her need to do this. Coming to that understanding had made things almost feel like old times between them.

Everything between him and Raven had always felt so simple. They'd gotten along from the moment they first met, companionship and friendship had quickly grown into something more, and he'd always known that she was his.

But then Cleo had been kidnapped, and everything had changed.

Was it possible to go back?

Were second chances a real thing or something for fairytales and romances?

Did he even want Raven back in his life?

Handling the guilt he still dealt with daily for failing her and their daughter would be harder to deal with if he had to see Raven every day, but was it worse than letting her go again?

Now that he was back with her, it was getting harder and harder to remember why he'd walked away in the first place. Maybe he was getting ahead of himself, his feelings for her might be getting stirred back up, but that didn't mean that Raven felt the same way. Getting along with him, and forgiving him and taking him back were two completely different things.

She'd been gone too long.

Unease prickled at every one of his senses.

Something wasn't right.

Quietly, he grabbed his weapon and crossed the small shack so he could peek through the door. Although Raven had closed it behind her the wood had split in places, and he could peer through the gap.

His blood froze when he saw Raven. A man had a hold of her and was dragging her away from the shack toward the trees. Raven was fighting against him, but the man was bigger than her and easily able to maneuver her small frame where he wanted to take her.

Instead of disappearing into the rainforest, the man shoved Raven up against one of the trees and moved so he was in front of her. One of the man's hands curled around Raven's slender neck, holding her in place while his other hand roughly grabbed one of her breasts.

Max saw red.

Shoving the gun into his waistband, he pulled out his knife, the only other thing that had survived the explosion since he had it on him when he'd been pulled from the car. If there was one man here there had to be others in the area, and since Le Entregar obviously operated here then they controlled the whole area, this man had to be one of them.

It seemed this man wanted a little alone time with Raven before he turned her in. That mistake would cost him the hand that was currently trying to find its way inside her pants, and his life.

The man was too focused on assaulting Raven, who was still fighting vainly against him, and didn't notice Max approaching. He was almost to them when Raven managed to free one of her legs from her attacker's hold and kneed him right in the groin.

The Colombian grunted in pain and backhanded her hard enough that her head hit the tree with a thunk he could hear from here.

Anger took over and Max flew at the man.

Wrapping an arm around the Colombian's neck, he hauled him off Raven and grabbed the hand that had been touching her. Max shoved it against the tree and held the blade of his KA-BAR against his wrist, pressing hard enough to draw blood.

"You like touching women without their permission?" he snarled quietly in the man's ear. "That make you feel like a big man?"

His arm on the man's windpipe was pressed too tightly to allow him to answer, but the Le Entregar squirmed in his hold, trying unsuccessfully to get free. The man's free hand alternated between clawing at the arm against his neck and trying to move the hand holding the knife at his wrist.

"How many of you are out there?" Max lightened his grip on the other man's neck just enough to allow him to speak, but the man remained mutinously silent. They didn't have the time, nor did he have the patience to drag this out. He and Raven needed to get moving again. In one swift move, his sharp blade sliced through the man's wrist and then moved to sever his carotid artery. Dropping the body, he grabbed Raven's hand and pulled her close. A trickle of blood dribbled from the corner of her mouth and the cut on her forehead from the accident yesterday had started bleeding again. "You okay?"

"You cut off his hand," she murmured, her voice shaking with shock.

"He touched you." While he was sorry he'd done it in front of Raven and upset her, he couldn't summon up an ounce of remorse. Touching a woman against her will was not something he tolerated. Someone touching *his* woman against her will filled him with fury that was too hot to bury.

"You saved me. Again. Thank you." Although she was still shaking, she summoned a smile. "That makes four times now, in only two days. That has to be some sort of record."

Despite the grimness of their situation, Max couldn't help but laugh. Raven was a survivor, even terrified and hurting she was looking for a way to keep going. She'd been through a lot over the years, battled through pain and trauma, and yet no matter how many times she was knocked down, she bounced right back up again.

Fighting down his fear, he might have eliminated this threat before either of them were hurt or captured, but more men would keep coming. Max lifted a hand and caught the small rivulet of blood trickling down her forehead with his thumb. Raven's questions had stirred up a hornet's nest, and there was no way Le Entregar would let it go. They couldn't if they wanted to remain in business.

"Maybe no more needing to be saved though," he said, brushing a finger across the dark circles under her eyes, his heart wasn't sure it could take much more of Raven in danger.

"Max, I ..."

"Shh," he said, touching a finger to her lips. "I'm not

asking you to give this up and go home, I just hate seeing you in danger. Four times in forty-eight hours I could have lost you."

In the dark, her eyes met his, the blue shone brightly in the moonlight, and her brow furrowed. "You already lost me." She winced at her words and quickly added, "I mean, you already walked away. You didn't want me."

"That's where you're wrong, honey. I *always* want you." Before he could talk himself out of it, Max leaned down and captured her lips in a soft, sweet kiss. The kiss reminded him of the first one they'd shared when he'd managed to track her down. She'd been nineteen, he'd waited until she was a legal adult before coming back for her. But when he'd gone back to where she'd lived he'd found her and her family gone. It had taken him a year, tracking her down only when he was on leave, to finally find her. By then he knew what had happened to her and he hadn't wanted to come on too strong.

But that night when he had knocked on her apartment door, she'd looked up at him much like she had tonight, with hope in her eyes like he was her knight in shining armor. He'd kissed her then because he couldn't not, and he kissed her now because he couldn't not.

This woman was so twisted inside him that he couldn't be rid of her even if he wanted to, and he didn't want to. For ten long years he'd thought about her daily, he wore his wedding ring with his dog tags, carried a photo of her and Cleo in his wallet, she was a part of him, she lived inside his heart. Maybe it was time to listen to his heart instead of his head.

Raven uttered a soft sigh and leaned into him. "You kissed me," she whispered.

"Yeah, I did."

"I don't understand why."

71

He loved her honesty and her willingness to be open and upfront, Raven didn't play games and he appreciated that. "I know, midnight. I messed up—big time. We need to talk but not here, not now. There'll be more like him out there," he said, nodding at the body that lay at their feet, tucking Raven closer when she winced at the sight. "We need to move out, get someplace safe, then we can talk."

Taking her hand, he kept her close as he headed away from where they'd crashed the car, deeper into the rainforest, more determined than ever to keep Raven alive. They had a lot to talk about and sort out, and he wanted to know if she could find it in her heart to forgive him and give him a second chance.

* * *

4:43 A.M.

She would have blisters on her blisters by the time they finally got out of this jungle.

Well, assuming they *did* in fact get out.

With each minute that passed, Raven was starting to doubt that they would.

"Need to take a rest?" Max asked. He stopped walking and immediately tugged her into an embrace. It was what he did every time they paused for a short break, and it was starting to feel natural. How easy it would be to allow herself to open her heart up to Max again, to lean into him, soak up a little of his strength.

For so long she'd had to be the strong one. Facing the men with the knives alone so her siblings would be safe, keeping them all together when they left the safety of their farm to move to the city and Eagle went back to the military. Taking responsibility for her younger brothers and sisters, even whilst raising her daughter. Then singlehandedly trying to find and take down Le Entregar. She'd gotten used to being on her own, but now Max was here and it felt so good, she didn't want to let him go.

It was taking conscious effort on her part to keep her heart from getting carried away.

Max had left once, he could do it again.

"Honey?"

"Oh, sorry," she said, "I don't need to take a break."

"Liar," he murmured, nuzzling her temple and touching his lips to her skin in the lightest of kisses.

"Okay, I do *need* to take a break, but I don't *want* to," she corrected. They didn't have time to rest. Besides, time meant her mind would wander back to what had almost happened outside the shack. The man's hands on her, what he'd been going to do, the blood as Max killed him. The sight of it had thrown her mind right back to the blood-streaked cabin she'd almost died in as a teenager. But this time the only dead body was her attacker's, that was what she had to focus on. "Let's keep going a little longer."

Although she thought he would argue, Max sighed. "Okay, just a little longer though, then we're going to have to stop and find a place to rest, you can't keep going forever."

"You can't either," she reminded him, pulling back so she could look up at him. There were dark smudges under his eyes, lines of exhaustion around his mouth, he was every bit as wiped out as she was. They needed to get to a town, find a hotel to hole up in, someplace they could both feel safe enough to get the sleep they needed.

"I'll sleep when I know you're safe," Max said. Then he took her hand, and they started trudging forward.

This time they hadn't been going far when she spotted something up ahead. She knew that Max saw it too because he quickly yanked her behind a tree, pressing her up against the trunk, much as he had the day she'd met Pilar when he'd protected her from the flying bullets. This time there were no bullets, but they might have just found the answer to their prayers.

"Look, a car," she whispered, excited at the prospect of being able to get off her aching feet and not have to walk to a town.

"Yeah, babe, I see it," Max said, sounding amused by her enthusiasm but as relieved as she felt.

"Can we take it?" There was no way to know if it had been abandoned here, or if it belonged to someone who lived in the area, or if it was a Le Entregar car and they were still nearby. If it belonged to an innocent, she would feel bad stealing it, but if it belonged to the men hunting them then she wouldn't at all.

"Yes. First, I need to scout around, there could be some of them nearby."

"You think it's their car? Le Entregar?"

"Yes. The car is too new and clean. It doesn't belong to anyone who lives in the area."

That made her feel much better. Although she didn't like him leaving her, she took the gun he shoved into her hand and didn't protest when he turned his back and slunk away into the trees. He seemed to disappear, and even though she knew where he had to be going, she couldn't spot him at all. Max was good at the warrior stuff. When they'd been together, he'd never let her see that side of him. He'd been protective of her and Cleo and a bit of an alpha, but he had never allowed her to see how deadly he could be.

She didn't hear any gunshots, not that it meant that Max

hadn't killed anyone. Since she knew he didn't want to draw attention to them, he would slit someone's throat like he had the man back at the shack.

Raven felt her throat tighten as she remembered the spurt of blood when Max's blade sliced cleanly through the man's carotid artery.

It wasn't the first time she'd seen that.

The night of her parents' murder, she'd had a knife on her when she snuck into their home to try to take out the men who were there before they could find her siblings who were hiding in the barn. They'd got her first, held her down while they cut her and raped her, but then they made a mistake.

They thought they'd destroyed her.

Thought she was too broken, inside and out to be a threat.

That was when she'd struck.

She'd gotten the closest one in the leg, piercing his femoral artery. At his friend's scream, the other man had lunged. Raven had flung out her knife a second time, this time aiming for the carotid artery.

She hit what she aimed for.

The blood had spurted out almost in slow motion, raining down on her already blood-streaked body.

The feel of it was etched into her mind. Usually, it came for her while she was vulnerable in sleep, but today it hadn't been a dream, it had been real.

"Raven."

The sudden presence, hands on her arms, would have made her scream but his scent filled her, his warmth seeped into her, his strength surrounded her.

Max.

Her Max.

He had the power to break her heart all over again, but he

would never physically hurt her. In fact, he would travel to the ends of the earth, risking everything including his life, to keep her safe.

"It's only me, midnight."

"I know." She blinked and the images from the past cleared away leaving her firmly in the present, just as dangerous, but at least she wasn't alone. "Did you have to kill any of them?"

"A couple."

She just nodded. That wasn't something she needed to be dwelling on right now. "I should drive."

"Uh uh, sweetheart, you have a concussion, don't want you passing out or seeing double and driving us into a tree or something."

Raven poked her tongue out at him when she heard him snicker as he took her hand and led her to the vehicle. "Are you making a quip about my driving skills?"

Smothering a laugh, he shook his head. "Of course not. Totally concussion-related only. You are *definitely* a good driver."

"Max," she growled, shoving him with her free hand. "The time I hit the mailbox it was because a squirrel ran in front of the car and I tried to avoid it."

"And the time you hit the fire hydrant? Or got the car stuck in a ditch? Or somehow got the car tangled in the swing set when we were on vacation that time?"

"Max," she said, shoving him again, only this time she was giggling. "All of those were accidents."

"Well today we can't afford one of your *accidents*," he said with a chuckle.

"Did you just do air quotes when you said that?" she said, pretending to sound aghast but couldn't keep back a giggle. It almost felt like old times with Max. Then she sobered, now wasn't the time for joking, they were on the run for their lives. "My head hurts but it's not spinning, I can drive, Max, and that means you can shoot at anyone who tries to follow us." Although the idea of violence sickened her like it always did, she knew that in a fight for survival, they had to do whatever it took to stay alive.

"Yeah, okay," Max agreed, and she knew he hated to do it, but she also knew she was right. Max wanted to protect her, and while she might hesitate to take another life because she knew how that destroyed a part of your soul, she could also hold her own. She wouldn't allow another person she loved to be snatched away from her, and despite their history and the broken heart he'd given her, she still loved Max.

Always would.

* * *

6:28 P.M.

Something was dinging repeatedly.

Still half asleep and exhausted, it took Max a moment to realize what it was.

Raven's phone.

Thankfully, no one had come after them as they'd driven out of the jungle. They'd driven for a few miles before he'd insisted they were safe and made Raven pull over so they could swap places. She'd dozed a little and he'd woken her when they'd reached a town with a hotel. They'd ditched the car, walked the rest of the way here, and as soon as they'd gotten to their room they'd both showered, he'd tended to the blisters on Raven's feet, then they'd both collapsed into bed. They'd been too tired to be hungry, but his stomach was rumbling now that he was waking up.

They'd been asleep for going on seven hours, and he felt completely rested, he'd slept a lot less when he was on a mission, but Raven really needed more sleep. Still, he knew she'd be angry if he didn't wake her to tell her she'd received a message. They were lucky they'd had their phones on them when the car crashed. Both had been useless in the rainforest, there was no reception out there, but when they'd gotten here they'd bought chargers and plugged their phones in while they slept.

Climbing off the couch, Max stretched his back, then crossed to the bed. While he would have loved to share it with Raven, sleep with her in his arms like he'd wanted to for the decade they'd been apart, he knew they weren't there yet. Things were improving between them, but they still had a way to go.

"Raven," he said softly, giving her a gentle shake.

"Mmm?" she mumbled, rolling over but not opening her eyes.

"Your phone went off."

"My what?" She blinked sleepily up at him and stretched, the blankets shifted, exposing the smooth skin of her stomach and the band of her panties, and his length immediately responded.

"Your phone, honey, you know that thing you use to communicate with people," he teased.

Raven sat up and poked her tongue out at him. The sight of it made him grow harder, and he shifted so Raven couldn't see, he didn't want to make her uncomfortable when he was actually making progress with her. She leaned over and snagged the phone from the nightstand, unplugging it and letting the cord drop to the carpet. She touched the screen, and when it came to life her entire demeanor changed in an instant.

"What is it?" he asked, immediately on guard.

Her eyes were wide when they looked up at him, and he saw that spark of determination in them. The same spark of determination that he knew had gotten her through everything life had thrown at her. "It's an alert for Le Entregar. I have it set that all my programs alert me immediately of any hits. I was worried that me asking questions would make them edgy and they'd cancel the auction, but they haven't. It's going ahead."

Despite Raven's obvious enthusiasm, Max found himself having a more mixed reaction. He was glad that the opportunity to take down Le Entregar was still on the table, but he was also terrified that now Raven was in more danger. She wasn't letting this go, not for anything, and certainly not for him, but he was afraid he might not be able to keep her safe from such a dangerous opponent.

"We need to get an invite to that auction," Raven said, bouncing out of bed. They didn't have any clothes but the ones they'd been wearing when they fled the hotel yesterday, and she was already putting them back on and running her fingers through her hair. "I have to call my brother and Tex."

"Tex?"

"You remember, my mentor, John Keegan, but he goes by Tex, he's a retired SEAL, a friend of my brother, he can do anything on a computer. I mean it, anything."

"You can do anything on a computer."

"I'm good, but Tex is the best. I'm definitely going to need his help to pull this off."

Dressed, she dropped down onto the sofa with her phone in her hand. Because he was going to make sure Raven's safety was the top priority, and he knew she would disregard that completely, he sat beside her.

A moment later, Eagle appeared on the screen. A second after that a man he hadn't met before that he assumed was Raven's friend Tex appeared as well.

"What happened to you?" Eagle asked as soon as he saw his sister, his eyes narrowing as he no doubt took in the lump on her forehead.

"We ran into a little trouble," Raven said dismissively.

"Looks like more than a little," Tex said in a southern drawl. The man had dark hair and deep brown eyes and looked to be a few years older than Raven.

Apparently having already moved on from that topic, Raven said excitedly, "I got another hit. The auction is going ahead, it's on the thirty-first, that doesn't leave us with much time to come up with a plan."

"A plan for what exactly?" Eagle asked suspiciously. Max knew that Raven's big brother was extremely protective of his siblings, and it had to be killing him to know that Raven was here in Colombia actively painting a bright red bullseye on her back.

"A plan to get an invite to that auction," Raven replied.

He'd known she would say that, but he still got a stab of fear to the gut. The thought of Raven going to an auction where a bunch of rich men were buying people was enough to make him feel ill, but he also knew she was doing this with or without their support so he wanted to give it to her. Max reached out and took the hand that didn't hold the phone, she looked at him in surprise but didn't pull away.

"An invite to the auction?" Eagle growled, sparing their joined hands only a quick glance. He knew his former brother-in-law wasn't pleased with how he'd left after Cleo was taken, but Eagle had been the one to reach out to him, so he had to assume that meant the man wasn't opposed to the idea of him and Raven getting back together.

"Don't say it's crazy," Raven said.

"It *is* crazy," Eagle grumbled.

"Tex, tell him this is the only way." Raven turned imploring eyes on her friend.

"Oh no, don't look at me to convince your brother that this is a good idea," Tex said, holding his hands out. "This is your plan, you need to sell it to us."

"I've been looking for an opportunity to get this close to Le Entregar. I'm doing this even if you guys don't want to help," Raven told them.

"I don't like being blackmailed," Eagle snapped.

"I'm not blackmailing, I'm being honest. I've been tracking Le Entregar for almost ten years, never have I been able to narrow down a location, and never have I been able to get accurate intel on an auction. If I don't take advantage of this opportunity, then I don't know when I'll get another chance. If I can get an invite to the auction, get into their inner sanctum, then I can get the names of the top guys. I know there are six of them, one from each continent except Antarctica, but I don't know who they are. Then I thought that we could send in one of Prey's teams to take them down. You'd get the major players, the main location, and a lot of their customers. Their operation would be left in shambles, the men who took my daughter will be punished, and this would be a major feather in Prey's cap."

"I care more about you than the company," Eagle said.

"The plan has merit," Tex said slowly.

"You jumping ship, Tex?" Eagle growled.

"I told her to sell me on the idea, and she did. Taking out Le Entregar would put a major dent in the world human-trafficking trade," Tex countered. "What do you need from me, Raven?"

"I need you to access my programs, make any changes you need to, and make sure we don't lose this track I've got on them. I've thought I was closing in on them before only to lose the contact, and it can take me months before I get another hit on them. They're smart and they have good tech people working for them. Good, but not as good as you, Tex," Raven said sweetly, shooting her friend a winning smile.

"Flattery will get you everywhere," Tex said with a wink.

"How do you think you're going to get yourself an invitation?" Eagle asked.

"I was hoping we might have been able to create an identity, someone who would have a background that was compatible with Le Entregar's buyers. Rich, ego, disdain for women, maybe add in some assault charges that money made go away. That was my plan, but I wasn't expecting the auction to be so soon, no way we can pull that together in enough time to make contact with Le Entregar in three days." She sounded dejected, but he knew that Raven wouldn't give up.

"We can keep working on the details," Tex encouraged. "For now, we just gather every bit of information we can on them so we can figure out the best way to get in. Send me access codes to your programs, and I'll get right to work."

"Thanks, Tex, your support means a lot to me," Raven said.

"You always have my support," Tex assured her.

"I'll have Alpha team on standby," Eagle said. "I don't want to fly them into Colombia in case Le Entregar gets wind of it and thinks Prey is making a move. We don't want them to cancel the auction because they got antsy. Alpha team will be prepped and ready to fly out at a moment's notice though."

Tears shimmered in Raven's eyes. "Thanks, Eagle."

"Nobody messes with the Oswald family and gets away with it," Eagle said fiercely.

Family was everything, and Max would always regret walking away from his. Now he just prayed there was a way he could reclaim what he'd lost, and that started with destroying the men who had stolen his daughter.

CHAPTER 5

October 29th

12:53 A.M.

"Come on, honey, you can hardly keep your eyes open any longer."

Large hands lifted the brand-new laptop from her lap, closing it and setting it on the dresser, then they cupped her elbows and eased her from the sofa.

"Just a little longer," Raven said, fighting a yawn.

"No, it's after midnight, and you've hardly slept for days. You've been shot at, knocked unconscious, and walked through the jungle for hours. You need rest, Raven. If you want to take down Le Entregar, you have to be at the top of your game," Max reminded her.

She hated that he was right. She wanted to keep working at this until it was done, but she was playing a dangerous game. If she wanted to come out on top, she had to be clear-headed.

"Okay," she agreed, rubbing at her bleary eyes. She'd taken painkillers earlier, and it had helped with the headache. They'd eaten too and that had helped with the lingering nausea. While she and Tex had worked, Max had gone out to get them clean clothes and surprised her with the laptop, she could work off her phone, but this was so much easier.

"Come on, honey." Max's hands stayed on her as he guided her to the bed.

He folded back the covers and then took the hem of the oversized sweatshirt she was wearing and pulled it over her head. She was wearing a bra beneath it, and as his fingertips brushed across her nipples as he removed the shirt, her breasts suddenly felt heavy. She wanted him to touch them, play with them like he used to. While she didn't think her breasts were much to write home about, Max had always loved them, spending hours playing with them, touching them, turning her on until all she could do was beg him to make love to her.

Raven shivered at the memories and Max looked down at her. "Cold?" he asked.

"No," she said, her voice a breathy whisper. She wanted him almost more than she could bear. There hadn't been anyone for her in ten years because her body craved only this man. She'd dated a little, mostly to pacify her siblings who worried about her, but she'd never let it get far enough to involve sex because she couldn't imagine offering her body or her heart to another man.

It already had an owner.

She'd thought he would have commented about the reason behind her shiver, with her answer that she wasn't cold, and his close proximity was pretty obvious what had been the cause. But Max simply hooked his thumbs into the waistband of her sweatpants and eased them down her legs. He moved with them, his thumbs trailed a line of fire down her skin until he crouched before her, lifting each of her feet, caressing each sole as he removed her pants.

It felt like a seduction, but again he never touched her panties, which if he did, he would surely have found wet. Instead, he just stood and carried the clothes to the dresser, then shrugged out of his t-shirt.

"Here," he said, holding it out to her.

"I can find something of mine to sleep in," she told him, not taking the t-shirt.

"I'm sure you can, but you were sleeping in one of my old t-shirts before and it got blown up with the rest of our clothes. I bought this one specifically to give to you to replace the one you lost, I just wore it first so it would smell like me." He shrugged as he continued to hold out the shirt to her.

Well, if that didn't melt her heart, she didn't know what would. "You really bought it for me?"

"I like seeing you in my clothes." Max's gaze was hot, scorching, like fire. No, definitely hotter than fire, it was like lava, although fire kind of sounded sexier. Still, when she took the t-shirt and put it on, he made no move to touch her. Once she had the t-shirt on he gestured for her to get into bed, and once she was lying down he tucked her in. "Goodnight, Raven."

"Night, Max." She wanted to ask him to kiss her, make love to her, something, anything, but she didn't know how to ask. She didn't know where she stood with him or what he wanted.

When he stooped, her heart sped up, sure he was going to kiss her, and he did.

On the forehead.

It wasn't nearly enough, and yet she didn't say anything as he switched off the lamp on the nightstand, then the rest of the lights. She watched as he removed his jeans then stretched out on the couch.

This was crazy.

She wanted him. They were two adults, if he wanted her too then they could have sex. There didn't have to be strings, it didn't have to be anything more than sex.

"Max?"

"Yeah, midnight?"

Raven drew in a breath. Even with Max she'd never been particularly forward when it came to sex. But she was older now and hopefully wiser, so she said boldly, "I want you."

"You have me, I'm here, I'm not leaving you."

She huffed a chuckle and rolled her eyes even though he couldn't see her. "I mean here. In bed."

"Raven ..."

"If you don't want to that's okay, just say so, don't give me some stupid excuse."

"Midnight, I thought we went over this already, I *always* want you."

"Then come here."

He didn't move, and she thought he was going to reject her, but then all of a sudden he was there, flinging the blankets aside. "I don't deserve you, baby."

"No past tonight, no history. Just you and me," she said, reaching for his hard length that was already standing to attention.

Max brushed her hands aside and took her mouth in a powerful, hungry, desperate kiss. He plundered her mouth, and she opened to him, giving him all of her.

Tearing his lips from her, he rained kisses down her neck.

He buried his nose between her breasts and inhaled, and she thought he was going to shove the t-shirt aside, rip away her bra, and take them into his mouth, but he didn't.

Instead, he settled between her legs. His large hands curled around her bottom, and he lifted her off the mattress, this time burying his nose in her pulsing center and breathing deeply.

"You smell so good," he murmured.

"Max," she begged, shifting restlessly. Her body had been humming with need from the moment she realized that Max was the one who had kidnapped her from the rainforest. Despite the way things had ended between them, the hurt and anger that still simmered there, she wanted him more than she wanted her next breath.

"Okay, babe," he chuckled. "Here you go."

He ripped her panties away, literally ripped them, which was way sexier than she thought it would have been, and tossed the material to the floor, and then his mouth was on her. It was hot and wet and perfect. His tongue slid along her core before his lips circled around her needy little bundle of nerves and sucked hard.

Her hips lifted off the bed as electricity sparked through her. "I missed your mouth."

"I missed those sexy little whimpers you make when my tongue is driving you wild."

Max swirled a finger through her wetness and then slipped it inside her, stroking deep. They'd been married for close to four years. He knew every inch of her body, knew what she liked, knew how to drive her wild, knew how to make her come so hard she forgot anything but the pleasure he was giving her.

His fingers pumped in and out of her, his mouth claimed her bud, alternating between flicking it with the tip of his tongue and sucking on it. His hand moved faster, his fingers curled to find that special place inside her.

Moans fell from her lips, her head shifting on the pillow as her body was assaulted with sensations it had all but forgotten.

She was close but the pleasure she needed still shimmered just out of reach.

"Max, I ... I need ... more ... more ... please," she begged mindlessly. She couldn't quite get there, but she wanted it so bad.

"Relax, sweetheart, stop trying to force it, just feel it."

Raven was panting, squirming, pleading, begging, but she stopped trying to force the orgasm to come and just focused on Max's mouth and his fingers. He added a third, stretching her and making her insides quiver, then he sucked her hard and swirled his tongue on her bud, and her world disintegrated into a burning mess of fiery embers of pleasure.

It tore through her, almost too much, more than she remembered it being, but it was everything she needed.

He was everything that she needed.

Did she have it in her to give him a second chance?

"Don't break my heart again," she whispered. Raven knew that was something she would never come back from.

* * *

6:28 P.M.

She had said the words more to herself than to him, but Max stopped what he was doing and lifted his head.

He felt everything she wasn't saying. This time there

would be no going back. If he hurt her again, any chance he had with her would be gone forever. He had betrayed her love and trust once, there couldn't be another time.

"Pretty sure if there's any heart breaking this time around it will be my heart that gets shattered," he admitted. As much as he knew they needed to talk, Max was so desperate to be buried inside Raven's tight, wet heat that it was all he could think about. "If you don't want to, we don't have to," he said. If Raven wasn't ready for sex he'd wait, it would just about kill him, but he wasn't doing anything she wasn't comfortable with.

Raven reached down and grabbed his shoulders, tugging his body up so he was stretched over her. "Don't you even think about backing out now."

Max chuckled. "Not backing out, sweetheart, just don't want to push you into doing anything you don't want to do."

"*I'm* the one who asked for this in case you've forgotten."

"Not forgotten." Not touching her when he'd been undressing her had taken every ounce of his self-restraint, but he was the one who ended things, who had hurt her, so she had to be the one to let him know what she was and was not ready to allow him to do. "Just don't want to do anything you don't want."

"I want you, Max. No, I *need* you."

There was no mistaking the fire burning in her eyes or the way her body moved restlessly, seeking something more. His body echoed that restlessness, so many years wasted wandering in a wasteland of emptiness, loneliness.

He was ready for more.

Ready to live again.

Ready to come home.

Shoving his boxers aside, he let his length spring free,

noting the way Raven's tongue darted out to wet her bottom lip.

"I forgot how big you are," she said as she reached out and curled her fingers around him. His length quivered at her touch, and he took her hand, pulling it away from him.

"Not going to last long if you keep that up."

She arched a brow. "Is that a problem?"

"Don't want to come until I'm inside you." It had been too long; he hadn't been with anyone since Raven. Although he'd tried, he just couldn't summon any enthusiasm for touching another woman. His body belonged to Raven just like his heart did.

"Then hurry up and get inside me." Raven's fingers dug into his backside and her hips thrust up as she tried to take him inside her.

Because it was clear both of them needed this, he positioned himself at her entrance and buried himself inside her in one smooth thrust. Raven moaned in delight, her head falling back against the pillow, eyes fluttering closed.

He was already close to bursting, and his hands gripped Raven's hips as he began to move, but he didn't want it to be like this. This wasn't just sex, this was the woman he adored, who owned him, who he loved more than life itself. This was making love, he wanted it to mean something, he craved a connection with her.

"Hey," he said, reaching out with one hand to tuck a lock of hair behind her ear.

"Yeah?" Raven opened eyes that were glazed with desire.

"I want to see you come, midnight."

"I already came, it's your turn now."

"Uh uh, nope, no way. My girl always comes first." Okay, so maybe as a teenager he'd been a little less restrained, hadn't yet known how to give pleasure to a woman, and hadn't really cared if she came or not, but now he knew better. His release was always so much stronger and more powerful when he was coated in his woman's pleasure. There had been a couple of women before Raven, back when he'd thought that the connection between them wasn't real when he was too young to know that following your heart was more important than following the crowd.

"Not sure I can come again."

"Touch yourself," he said, adjusting his angle to increase friction on her sensitive bud.

"Max …"

"Gotten shy, sweetheart?" Given that her first sexual experience was with the men who raped her, Raven had been extremely shy when they first got together. It had taken time and patience to get her to open up to him, but he'd been rewarded by seeing her learn to embrace her sexuality.

"It's been a long time," Raven said, but her hand moved between them and brushed against him as she touched herself.

"Too long," he agreed as he took one of her perfect little breasts in his hand. Raven had always complained that they were too small, but they were perfection as far as he was concerned. Thin white lines marred her soft skin, but he barely gave them more than a second's acknowledgment before he worked his fingers in the sensitive flesh, massaging it and watching the pleasure flush across Raven's face.

Her fingers moved faster, becoming almost frantic, and her eyes fell closed again.

"Eyes open, Raven," he said, stopping his thrusts.

She murmured a protest, but her eyes opened again, and she locked her gaze on his.

He held it as he started moving again, faster, harder, the same neediness that was in Raven spread to him and he was suddenly increasingly desperate for release. To watch Raven fly apart again.

Max pushed her t-shirt up then pushed aside the lacy cups of her bra to bare her breasts, then bent his head, took one of her nipples into his mouth, and sucked hard, making the nipple peek into a hard little bud, then he swirled his tongue around it, scraping it with his teeth.

Raven gasped, and he felt her body begin to tremble. As her orgasm hit her, Max claimed her mouth, wanting to take her pleasure inside him. He needed it to heal from the pain he'd caused her.

Her internal muscles began to clench around him, and still kissing Raven, he felt his own pleasure hit. It flooded over him, almost too strong, too powerful, he held onto the woman he loved as his entire world seemed to be thrown about. Max was vaguely aware of Raven's continued orgasm as her body continued to squeeze him, prolonging his own release.

When it finally faded enough that he could think again, Max lifted his head to find Raven watching him with a sleepy and sated expression. "We forgot a condom."

He hadn't even realized it until she said it. "I'm so sorry, Raven. That was irresponsible of me."

She shrugged like she didn't really care. "I didn't remember either, and I was the one who wanted sex."

"I wanted it too, I just didn't want to pressure you. I'm clean, haven't been with anyone since you."

"Max, you don't have to say that. We're divorced, you don't have to pretend you didn't move on," she said softly.

They *were* divorced, and if Raven had moved on he couldn't blame her, he was the one who left after all, but the idea of another man touching his woman—yeah, he was caveman enough to think of her as his, but he thought of himself as hers too—made him sick. "Not pretending anything, I haven't touched another woman since you."

Surprise was evident in her face, but she smiled and reached up to caress his face with gentle fingers. "I haven't been with anyone either. I'm not on birth control because there was no reason to be, but I don't think the timing is right."

"If it is, would you want another baby?" he asked, already knowing how he would feel about it.

"Yes," she replied without hesitation. "I'd love to have more kids. How would you feel?" she asked uncertainly.

"Thrilled," he answered honestly. It would be a lot easier to win Raven's heart and trust back if she was carrying his baby, something that would bind them together forever. But they already had that, didn't they? Cleo might be gone, but she would never be forgotten. For the rest of their lives she would always be something they would share.

His answer obviously pleased her, and she smiled and relaxed back into the mattress. "I like feeling you inside me, I'm not sure I want to let you go."

"We both need sleep, but no reason we can't do that again later," he said as he reluctantly pulled out of her.

"Yeah, later," Raven said on a yawn.

Max stood and went to the small, attached bathroom, wetting a face washer and bringing it back to clean Raven up. She smiled up at him again, and her fingers lifted to twirl through his hair as he sat on the side of the bed and wiped between her legs. When he was done, he disposed of the cloth in the bathroom and didn't hesitate to slide into the bed beside Raven. He tucked them in then curled his body around hers, spooning her.

With her tucked all warm and safe against him, Max closed his eyes and fell into the best sleep he'd had since Cleo was taken. His daughter might be gone, but Raven wasn't, and when this was over he wasn't letting her go again.

* * *

12:52 P.M.

"Here, you need to eat something."

Raven was sitting on the floor, her back against the couch, and she looked up as Max set a sandwich on the coffee table next to her laptop then sat on the couch behind her so his legs were on either side of her. His legs didn't cage her in but were close enough that she could feel them lightly brushing against her arms.

He'd been doing this all day. Touching her, gentle caresses here and there, allowing his fingers to brush against hers when he passed her something, letting their shoulders bumped when they walked past each other in the small hotel room. Max also stared at her when he thought she was too engrossed in what she was doing and wouldn't notice, but she did notice. She could feel his eyes on her because it felt like his gaze was wafting over her skin in a sensuous dance much like his fingers and his tongue had done when they'd woken up this morning.

She knew what he was doing. At least she knew what it felt like he was doing. He was wooing her, courting her, letting his body and his eyes do what his words couldn't.

But the thing was she needed the words.

Raven needed to know if this was just a fling for him. If he wanted to get off while the two of them were forced to be here together then she didn't want to build up expectations in her head that this was going somewhere. And even though she still loved him, she could never take him back without an explanation as to why he had left, otherwise she would always be waiting for him to leave again, and that was no way to live. Maybe his reasons for leaving weren't ones she could forgive, and she wouldn't want to be with him anyway.

"Midnight, eat," Max said, nudging her shoulder with his knee. "You haven't eaten since breakfast."

Not food anyway.

The thought made her blush as she remembered their post-breakfast lovemaking, and to try to cover it so Tex didn't notice, she quickly picked up the sandwich and took a bite. "Thanks, chicken and avocado, my favorite."

"Thought one of your favorites was the only way to pry you away from your laptop for a bit," Max said. He shifted behind her, and his calf's brief contact touching her side had her whole body reacting. She was like a starving woman being shown food for the first time in months—years—it didn't matter how many times they made love it wasn't enough.

She had to stop thinking of it as making love.

It was sex.

Just sex.

Only it didn't feel like just sex.

Max holding her in his arms all night and buying and wearing a t-shirt only to give it to her to replace the one she'd lost in the explosion, being so attentive to her needs today, bringing her snacks and coffee while she and Tex worked, all of it suggested he cared, but she'd always known he cared about her. The question was, did he love her?

"You want to take a break, Raven?" Tex asked.

She focused her gaze back on the laptop. "Nope, I'm good, but if you need a break we can stop for a while." Although she said the words and meant them, Tex was doing her a favor and they'd been working for five hours straight, she hoped he didn't. Time was not on their side, they only had two days to figure out a way to get to that auction and pull the plan together.

"I'm good to keep going," Tex replied.

"You guys come up with a plan yet?" Max asked.

"Well, I was thinking about something," she said as she nibbled at her sandwich. Ideally, they would have been able to create a background of a man similar to those who already attended the auctions and then send someone in undercover. Time constraints meant that was completely out, no way they could make contact with Le Entregar, build trust, and get an invite in only forty-eight hours. That was a long game, and right now they needed a short one, which meant there was only one solution she could see.

"What's that?" Tex asked, and she felt Max's hand lightly stroke between her shoulder blades, offering his silent support. She needed that support more than he could understand.

"I've been keeping detailed notes on every buyer I could link to Le Entregar," she said.

"Of course you have," Tex teased her. Although he was every bit as detail-oriented as she was, she had been known to be a little obsessive when it came to working this particular case. She had more files on Le Entregar than she did on every other case she'd ever worked at Prey combined.

Raven poked her tongue out at him good-naturedly before continuing. "What if we can use an existing invite instead of trying to figure out a way to fast track ourselves an invite to that auction, something we know we can't do given the time we have to work with?"

"Existing invite?" Max asked, straightening behind her.

"You want to go after one of the men you have notes on?" Tex asked.

"That's exactly what I want to do," Raven confirmed.

"So you want to what? Put pressure on one of the guys you know will be going to the auction and get him to wrangle you an invite?" Max asked.

"Not exactly. I don't think that will work. Le Entregar haven't been around for more than a decade because they're stupid. No way are they going to issue a last-minute invite to someone they don't know just because one of their clients asks them to."

"I don't understand then," Max said. "What exactly do you want to do?"

"You want to use his invite to get into the auction," Tex said.

"Like take it from him and use it to get in the door?" Max asked.

"Well, yes, but it's more detailed than that. Le Entregar survives by being smart and cautious, they're going to be checking to make sure that everyone is who they say they are, so that means we're going to have to be smart and careful too. But once we know who's going to go undercover ..."

"*I'm* going to go undercover," Max interrupted. There was a ferocity in his tone that hadn't been there when he first came to her in Colombia. Then he'd thought she was foolishly risking her life for vengeance for Cleo, but now he seemed to understand that while that was her driving force in this mission, she also wanted to stop others from suffering like they had. The only way to do that was to cut off the head of the snake.

"Okay, if it's Max, then we choose one of the men on my list who looks similar enough to him that with a bit of work he can pass for him. Max studies everything about the man there is to know, and it should be enough to get us in," Raven explained.

"Us?" Max asked, and she could tell from the sudden tension rolling off him that he didn't like that idea.

"We're going to need both of us in there if we're going to bring them down. It's not unheard of for some of the men to bring one or more of their slaves with them so it shouldn't be a problem for me to pretend to be your slave and get in there with you."

"I think it's safer that I go in alone," Max said.

"I agree," Tex added.

"Traitor," she muttered, throwing her friend a glare.

"It might be safer, but you're going to need me in there if we're going to bring them down. They won't think anything of me, I'm no threat, I'm a woman, a slave, these kinds of men don't think very highly of women. We can use that to our advantage. All I need is one chance to get to one of their computers, and I can infect it with malware that will give us access to everything."

"Everything?" Max asked.

"Everything," Tex echoed.

"Tex helped me with it. Once it's uploaded to their computer it will give him access to everything. That means names and details on the men who run Le Entregar, information on all of their clients, and details on the women and children who have been bought and sold. You know what that means, right?"

"That we'll be able to dismantle them," Max replied.

"Yes, and we'll be able to find our daughter," she added.

"You mean find out what happened to her?" Max asked.

"And find out where she is."

"Wait a minute." Max stood and moved so that he was

standing in front of her. "You think that Cleo is still alive? That's what all of this is about? You're not here for revenge, at least not completely, and while I know that you want to take them down to save others that's not what you're here for either."

"Of course that's not the only reason I'm here," she said. She'd thought that was obvious but it seemed she was mistaken. "I'm here to find my baby and finally bring her home."

* * *

1:19 P.M.

How could he not have seen this?

It seemed so obvious now.

"Raven, honey, Cleo is dead," Max said gently. While he hated voicing the words, he couldn't deny that they had to be true. Cleo had been only three years old when she was taken, whoever had bought her was after a small girl. That was ten years ago. Ironically, their daughter's birthday was the same day as the auction, and she'd be turning thirteen, no longer appealing to whoever had bought her as a toddler.

Cleo was dead, but he'd had no idea that Raven hadn't come to terms with that. She was still holding out hope that they'd one day bring their little girl home. But then again, of course he wouldn't know that, he'd run away just a couple of months after Cleo was abducted because he couldn't handle his guilt when he had to see Raven's face every day.

Max couldn't help feel this was partly his fault. He should have been there to keep Raven grounded, help her come to terms with what had happened.

Instead, he'd bailed.

And Raven had apparently spent the last decade trying to find Cleo.

Raven's blue eyes darkened, and she glared at him. "I'll call you back, Tex," she said, then closed the laptop screen before her friend could reply. "What did you just say to me?"

"I know you don't want to accept it, but Cleo is dead." While he tried to keep his voice gentle from the fire spitting from Raven's gaze, he was clearly taking the wrong track.

"We don't know Cleo is dead," she said, getting to her feet and all up in his face. She was five-four to his six-two, he towered above her, but at the moment her attitude and unbridled fury made her seem ten feet tall.

"She's been gone for nearly ten years," he reminded her, like either of them could have forgotten.

"That doesn't mean she's dead," Raven shot back. "You might have given up on her, but that doesn't mean I have to. I won't *ever* give up on my daughter."

"So, you're going to go on suicide missions until you wind up dead like her? Is that what you want?"

"How dare you," she screamed. "I've never once gone on a suicide mission. I've chased down every lead I've gotten, and compiled every piece of information I could find, and this is the only time I've ever been in a remotely dangerous situation. You wouldn't know because you bailed on Cleo and me, but I don't have a death wish. At all. I want to stay alive, I want to find and destroy the people who kidnapped and sold my baby like she was nothing but a piece of meat. I've played this smart, not reckless at all, this is the closest I've ever come to actually taking down Le Entregar. When I came here, I weighed the pros and cons and decided the best move was to come on my own. I didn't ask you to come, that was Eagle, and I don't need you to be here. I can take care of myself. So leave, Max. I'll ask Eagle to send someone from Alpha team to come and go undercover with me. I don't want you here, and you don't deserve to be here. You turned your back on Cleo, not me, and you have to live with that."

Her words hit their mark.

The pain of knowing that he had given up on his daughter—who he absolutely believed was in fact dead—while Raven had fought daily for Cleo made him feel like the worst father in the world.

"I'm not leaving."

"I don't want you here," she growled. "You aren't here for the same purpose that I am."

"I'm here to keep you alive," he said firmly. While he didn't think that Cleo was alive, there was no way he would allow Raven to risk her life in a crazy pursuit of the daughter who was no doubt long since dead.

"It's not your job," she ground out.

"I'm not leaving, end of discussion."

"It's not the ..."

"I'm not arguing with you on this, Raven."

"Of course not," she said with an overly dramatic eye roll. "The great Max "Zen" Hathaway doesn't argue with anyone, he's too good to have a discussion with us mere mortals."

"You know why I don't like arguing." Bickering was all his parents had done his entire childhood. He'd been the only kid in his class in elementary school who prayed his parents *did* get divorced. There had been no reprieve from their fighting, they fought about anything and everything, down to the smallest most irrelevant of details. As a child, he had vowed that if he ever got married he wouldn't spend his days arguing over things that didn't really matter, and that's what he'd done. Now, though, he stepped closer into Raven's personal space. "Is that what you want, Raven? An argument?"

"What I want is for you to care enough about your daughter to believe in her. You walked away like she meant nothing to you."

"She meant *everything* to me," he countered.

"You wouldn't know it. You just left, like she didn't even matter. You left like *I* didn't even matter. She was our daughter, and she was out there somewhere. How could you just move on with your life like nothing had happened?"

"Because I knew she was dead. How long do you think the monster that bought our little girl kept her alive? You really think he didn't kill her almost immediately?" At the most, he would have been surprised if Cleo had lived more than a year or two, but his gut said she was dead within the month. How did he convince Raven of that though?

"I think there's every chance that she could still be out there, and I won't ever give up on her. Not ever. She's all I have, and I will fight for her until I get her back or until my dying breath."

"That's all very noble, Raven, but you're fighting a battle that is already lost. So yeah, I do think you're here on some suicide mission. You can't live without her, I get that, I feel the same way, but we have to, don't you get that?"

"You seem to be able to live without her pretty easily," she spat.

"Every day since she's been gone has been like living in Hell on earth."

Tears brimmed in her eyes now. "If that's true, how could you leave? You knew I was alone. Eagle was in the SEALs, Falcon was being courted by Delta, Sparrow had joined the Air Force, Hawk and Dove were seventeen and fifteen, still my responsibility. I had no one when you left."

His guilt surged. He'd been so very selfish. Letting his own guilt rule his mind, not giving any thought to what Raven might be going through. "I'm sorry."

"I don't want your apologies. I want to know how you could walk away without even fighting for Cleo. How are you going to feel when I find her? When I get her back and she asks us if we were looking for her, you have to look her in the eye and tell her that you're her daddy but you gave up on her and wrote her off as dead. How are you going to feel then?"

"Cleo *is* dead," he bellowed.

Raven flinched at his harsh words. Her mouth opened and then closed. Then her entire face shuttered and he could feel all the progress he'd made with her over the last few days fade away. She was shutting down, shutting him out, and since he could never agree with her that Cleo was alive, he couldn't see any way to bridge the sudden gaping gap between them.

"I don't care if you hate me for the rest of my life, I will keep you alive. I failed Cleo, but I won't fail you too, Raven. I won't lose you like I lost her. I won't lose another person that I love." With that, he turned and stormed from the room, desperately needing fresh air.

Once he was outside, he planted his hands on his knees and leaned over, dragging in lungfuls of air in a seemingly vain attempt to calm his racing heart. If Raven truly believed Cleo was still alive, and it was painfully obvious that she did, then she would risk anything in her attempts to find who had bought Cleo and bring her home.

He was going to lose her.

Already he could feel his grip on her slipping.

She was going to get herself killed, and he had no idea how he would stop it from happening.

Worse, was the niggling doubt.

Was she right?

Could Cleo be alive, out there somewhere, praying that someone save her?

Had he failed his daughter a second time?

If he had, how was he going to live with himself?

* * *

1:48 P.M.

What had Max just said?

Raven stared after him as he stormed out of the room. She didn't know what to make of everything he'd just said. Nor did she know how she felt about it.

Anger.

There was definitely a whole lot of anger. He'd given up on their daughter and was insisting that Cleo was dead. That was something she couldn't accept. Of course she wasn't stupid, she knew there was a chance that Cleo had been killed, but until she was holding her daughter's body in her arms, she would never be able to believe it.

Along with the anger she also felt … sad.

Max had looked so tortured when he'd yelled that he wasn't going to fail her like he had failed Cleo. He blamed himself for Cleo being taken, she'd known that. He was the one with their daughter when she was taken, and Raven had always known he thought it was his fault, but she hadn't realized it was this bad.

Had she been selfish?

After Cleo disappeared, her entire focus was on finding her daughter and trying to cope with her own pain, but now she couldn't help but feel like she had missed some major signs when it came to Max.

He wasn't coping with Cleo's disappearance at all. He was completely avoiding it, trying to ignore anything that might remind him of Cleo. He was basically doing the exact opposite of how she had coped. While she'd gone all in, dedicating every second to finding Cleo, Max had completely removed himself from the equation.

Her heart broke for him. What must it have been like to try to banish all thoughts of their sweet little girl from his mind and his life?

Max had said that he loved her.

Was it true?

Could he really still love her?

This was ridiculous. Why was she sitting in here on her own trying to figure out what was going on with Max instead of following him and asking him?

Raven slipped her feet into her sneakers, grabbed the hotel room keys, and headed out into the hall. It didn't take her long to find Max, he was standing outside on the street, leaning against the side of the building, his hands over his face. She knew he was suffering because no way would her Max cover his eyes when he was worried about Le Entregar finding them. He would always be on alert when it came to her safety, but right now, all he could think about was his pain.

"Max?" she said when she walked over to join him, gently resting a hand on his shoulder.

His body shuddered beneath her touch, and when he slowly lowered his hands, she could see that his cheeks were wet.

He'd been crying.

Her heart broke wide open, and the anger she'd been holding onto for a decade suddenly melted away.

"I'm so sorry, Raven. It's my fault, it's all my fault."

"You're right, it is." Pain flared in his eyes, and she knew her words had cut him open inside. "Oh, Max," she said sadly, letting her hand trail down his arm until she reached his, then she entwined their fingers. "It's your fault for leaving me, for not trusting me with your feelings, not thinking of me as a partner, for not loving me enough to stay. But it is *not* your fault that Cleo was taken. I never thought that, not once. You were a fabulous father, and while I hate that you've given up on Cleo, I know that she was your world. It was the park, it was busy, I know you were watching her, it could easily have been me there with her that day. I don't blame you, Max, please try to believe that."

For a long moment he said nothing, she would have thought that he hadn't even heard a word she said or that he didn't care, but he'd tightened his grip on her hand until it was almost crushing. "You're wrong."

"No, Max," Raven insisted. "It wasn't your fault, you couldn't ..."

He silenced her by touching a finger to her lips. "It *was* my fault that Cleo was taken, but that wasn't what I meant. Cleo wasn't my world, *you* and Cleo were. Are. I didn't leave because I didn't love you enough, I left because I loved you so much, I wanted to spare you the trauma of having to see me every day, knowing what I cost you."

Raven ached for him, for herself too, and their daughter, their lost love. "I never blamed you, Max. I thought you left because Cleo was gone and you were only with me because of our daughter."

A growl rumbled through his chest, and he grabbed her biceps, dragged her close, and crushed his mouth to hers, kissing her greedily. "How could you not know how much I love you?" he murmured against her lips.

"You know why," she replied softly. "I'm scarred and damaged, and I had doubts about myself. Then when you left, I wondered if you'd ever really loved me. I knew you cared but ..."

Max growled again, a tortured sound. "But you didn't know that I loved you. Raven. You're everything to me. I love you more than you can ever know, and because of me you lost your daughter. *That's* why I left. Guilt. Not because you didn't mean everything to me."

"You mean it?" she asked, feeling vulnerable, raw, from their talk. She wanted so badly to believe that Max still loved her, but she was afraid of being hurt again.

"I've never meant anything more in my life," Max assured her.

"When we go back home, are you leaving again?" She wanted her family back. Even if they didn't find Cleo on this mission, she still wanted to have Max back in her life, but she was trying to be cautious. Max might still love her, but he'd left for a reason, and she didn't know if he had any plans to change that.

He hesitated for a moment then reached out to smooth a lock of hair behind her ear. "Have I completely ruined what we had?"

Had he?

He'd broken her heart when he left, and she hated that he didn't think there was a chance that Cleo was still alive out there somewhere, but bottom line was she loved Max, and if there was even a slim chance they could rebuild what they'd had then she didn't want to give it up.

"No," she said softly.

Max's body sagged, and he dragged her into his arms,

holding her tight against his chest. "I'll make it up to you, spend the rest of my life apologizing for walking away when you needed me."

"That's not what I want, Max. You've apologized, I've accepted, I want to look to the future, but …" Raven hesitated, he had made his position on Cleo's fate clear, was he going to understand her need to keep looking for their little girl?

"I know, Raven. It's okay, I might believe that Cleo is already gone, but I will do everything I can to help you find out what happened to her."

His arms lifted her, and she wrapped her legs around his waist, her arms around his shoulders, and pressed her forehead to his. All of a sudden her world, which had been dark and empty, filled with possibilities. With Max back at her side, she might be able to find peace, happiness, a future, and maybe, just maybe, together they could find their daughter.

Max carried her back up to their room, then set her down, reverently removing her clothes. Last night had been hot, fast, desperate sex. The air between them hadn't been cleared then, it had been an explosion of passion, pent-up desire, but this was different. This was sweet lovemaking.

As soon as he had them both naked, Max's lips found hers, and he laid her down on the bed, his large body covering hers. His kisses were gentle, his hands roaming her body attentive and focused on the sole goal of bringing her pleasure. Her own hands found his hard length, and she stroked it as his hand teased her between her legs.

By the time he eased inside her, she was already close to coming. Max flipped them so she was on top, and Raven did her best to make this last as long as it could. She moved slowly, lifting her hips until only his tip remained inside her, then lowering them until he was buried deep. One of Max's hands fondled her breasts, while his other touched her where their bodies were joined. His thumb working her little bundle of nerves, and the feel of him inside her as he started meeting her thrust for thrust, set off internal fireworks. It sparkled and glittered, showering her in a fiery display of ecstasy that sizzled and scorched her. She felt Max come inside her and somehow that increased her satisfaction.

Sated, she sunk down so she was plastered across Max's chest. He was still inside her, and he lifted one hand and began to stroke her hair, locking his other arm around her to keep her close.

"I love you, sweetheart, always and forever and completely. Please never doubt that again."

Even if his words hadn't been enough—which they were —the pleading desperation in them smothered the last embers of her doubt. Max loved her, she loved him, surely there was a way for them to work things out and be happy together again.

CHAPTER 6

October 30th

8:17 A.M.

"We have to go." Although Max said the words, he made no attempt to release his hold on Raven and continued to drop kisses all over her face.

"I'm not stopping you," Raven said, smiling up at him.

How had he lasted almost a decade without seeing that smile?

One thing Max knew for sure was that he was never going to let her go. Guilt would always be a part of his life, but he had to learn how to not let it control him. One of his hands drifted from her hip to her stomach, they hadn't used a condom any of the times they'd made love, and he couldn't not wonder whether they'd made a baby. While no other children they might have could take the place of Cleo, maybe it would be a fresh start for them. And if Raven wasn't pregnant then it didn't matter, they'd have kids when and if they were ready for them.

"I can't seem to stop kissing you," he said.

"Then don't."

"Ugh, you're killing me, midnight. We have to go. Alpha team is waiting to pick us up at the airport so we can go get ourselves an invite to this auction." After he and Raven had finally talked yesterday, the two of them and her friend Tex had managed to come up with a plan on how to get the invite. To do that, they were going to have to fly into Venezuela. From the list of men Raven had notes on, a man named Joseph Calder was the closest physical match and was also a well-known former mercenary with a penchant for disguises. He was also close enough that they could get there and take the man into custody so Max could impersonate him at the auction.

Raven sighed. "Then I guess we better get going."

"Hey." He snagged her wrist when she stepped out of his embrace and tugged her back again. "Once we get back home, I'm taking you away for a couple of weeks. No interruptions, no bad guys chasing us, nothing but you and me, and all the time we need to reconnect."

"Sounds perfect," Raven said, resting her head on his chest and wrapping her arms around his waist, squeezing him tightly.

"All right, time to get back to reality." Grabbing the duffle with their clothes, Raven got her laptop, and they headed outside. He'd hired them a new car last night, so all they had to do was check out, pay, and then they were on the road. It was an hour's drive to the airport, and once they got on that plane everything was going to start moving really quickly. The auction was tomorrow. They needed to work everything out with Alpha team who would be coming in to rescue the victims at the auction and take everyone else into custody.

Max just prayed everything went smoothly. The last thing he wanted was to lose Raven when he'd just been blessed with a second chance. He'd love to talk Raven into letting him go in alone, but he knew it was already a lost cause.

"What are you thinking about so hard over there?" Raven asked, reaching across to rest a hand on his thigh.

He immediately took one hand off the wheel to cover it. "Just thinking how scared I am that you want to attend the auction."

"I'm going, Max."

"Not trying to talk you out of it, honey, just being honest. The thought of you being in danger almost paralyzes me."

"How do you think I felt every time you left on a mission?" Raven asked gently. "Danger is a part of life, and I have always been proud of you and what you do, but it doesn't mean I don't worry about you. But just because I would worry, I would never ask you not to do it because being a PJ is what you do, it's who you are. This is who *I* am, I need to do this, even though it's dangerous."

There was nothing he could say to argue with that. She had always respected and supported his job, even though it meant he was away from her usually more than he was home. She'd basically been a single mother for most of Cleo's life, and she had never once complained or made him feel bad that he was often away.

"You're something else, you know that? You're right, I don't like you being in danger, but I need to respect that this is something you need to do. And if I have to have a partner in there, there isn't anyone I'd rather have by my side."

She huffed a laugh. "Yeah, you totally wouldn't rather have one of your PJ buddies, Alpha team, any of the other teams at Prey, one of my brothers, my sister Sparrow, or basically anyone with actual training."

"I'd trade them all for you in a heartbeat."

"Then you're crazy," she said with a laugh.

The sound of her laughter was like music to his soul. They lapsed into silence, but it was a comfortable one, and a peace settled over him, dulling the terror at knowing Raven would soon be walking into the lion's den. The miles ticked by, and the closer to the airport they got the more his temporary peace vanished.

Something felt off.

He'd expected that Le Entregar would have tried finding them in the village. He'd disabled the GPS in the car they'd stolen, but there weren't that many towns around, he would have thought the trafficking ring would have sent men to check them all. But no one had come hunting for them, and now they were mostly to the airport, and there had been nothing.

Le Entregar wouldn't give up, they couldn't. Not if they wanted to remain in business. They had to eliminate the threats, and they didn't know how much Raven knew or even her name, which meant they had to go after her while she was still in Colombia.

"We're here," he said as he turned into the airport.

"What's wrong?" Raven asked, looking nervously around.

"Nothing."

"Don't lie to me. Something has you on edge. What is it?"

"Just wondering why everything is so quiet."

"You were expecting them to try another hit on us?"

"Yeah, I was."

"Well, thankfully they didn't. There's Prey's plane," she said, gesturing to the small plane parked in the airfield. This was a small private airport, there was no terminal, just a half dozen hangars and the airstrip. Right now there was only one plane visible, and Max started driving toward it.

They were passing the first hangar when the bullets started flying.

Three SUVs pulled out of it, aiming for them, assault rifles were hanging out the backs of each of the vehicles, it was only a matter of time until they were hit.

Alpha team immediately sprang into action and bullets were flying from the plane as well. He and Raven were trapped between them, Prey shooting on one side at Le Entregar, and Le Entregar on the other shooting at them and Prey.

"Get down," he said, struggling to control the vehicle.

"Guess you got what you expected after all," Raven said as she unbuckled her seatbelt and ducked down.

Instead of wasting time trying to track them down in a hotel, Le Entregar must have decided to stake out all the airfields in the area. The more he tried to drive, the more he risked crashing and killing them both. He needed to get as close as he could to the Prey plane, then get one of the guys to come and bring him a weapon. Once he was armed, he could cover Raven so she could get to the plane.

Yanking the vehicle so his side was facing the shooters, Max quickly unbuckled. "Get out," he ordered Raven.

She knew better than to argue in a situation like this. She was the expert when it came to computers, but they were on his turf now. Raven opened the passenger door and slid out, Max climbed over the center console and got out too.

Without him even having to call them and ask, he could see that Luca "Bear" Jackson and Asher "Mouse" Whitman, Alpha team's leader and second in command, were running flat out toward them. Snipers Dominick "Domino" Tanner and Christian "Surf" Bailey, and medic Antonio "Arrow"

Eden, were picking off Le Entregar one by one, and he assumed Caleb "Brick" Quinn was in the pilot's seat ready to fly them out of here as soon as they were all on board.

"Need this?" Bear asked, grinning as he held out a weapon.

"Perfect, thanks," he said, more relaxed now that he was armed.

"And this?" Bear held up comms.

"Thanks." With a team at his back, Max finally felt like they had the upper hand.

"Mouse, get Raven to the plane," Bear ordered as he and Max started firing back at the Le Entregar men still standing.

"Be careful," Raven said. "Don't get shot, I'll be mad if you do."

"Ditto, midnight," he said, fighting a grin as he took aim at a man and dropped him.

Although he wanted to be the one running with Raven to the plane, he was going to stay right here making sure his girl got to safety. Nothing was more important to him than Raven's safety.

His heart stopped beating when she screamed, and he whipped around to see she was on her knees beside Mouse. It took his brain a second to register what his eyes were seeing. Raven hadn't been shot, Mouse had, she had her hands clamped around his leg.

"Raven, go," Mouse's voice echoed in his ear.

"No, not without you," Raven's came next, quieter since she wasn't wearing a comms unit.

"Raven," Mouse gritted.

"Don't argue with me," his stubborn woman said, and then he saw her move behind Mouse, grab him under the arms and begin to drag him toward the plane.

Fighting his urge to go running after her, Max did the

only thing he could, continue to take out as many of the men shooting at them as possible.

"We got them," Arrow said, and Max let out a breath he hadn't known he was holding.

"You guys need to get here now," Brick said, "we need to get out of here."

"We'll provide cover fire," Surf added.

Turning around, he and Bear took off for the plane as quickly as they could. Somehow, they managed to make it, probably because they'd already taken out most of the Le Entregar trying to kill them.

As soon as they were inside the plane, Domino slammed the door, and then Brick started them moving. A minute later they were lifting off into the air.

Only then did Max's gaze search the cabin for Raven. When he found her, he hauled her into his arms and crushed his mouth to hers.

*** * ***

9:50 A.M.

Raven couldn't stop shaking.

Mouse's blood was still on her hands, she didn't want to look at it, but she couldn't seem to stop.

Brick was flying them toward Venezuela. Arrow was working on Mouse who they had put on a gurney with Max helping him. Bear was snapping out orders and looking stressed, she knew he and Mouse had been friends since they were kids, and she didn't know where Surf and Domino were because she kept getting distracted by the blood.

"What were you thinking?" Max growled, making her jump when he suddenly appeared before her.

"Thinking?" she echoed. The world was still a little hazy, and if she was going to have to figure out what he was talking about, he would have to be more specific.

"You should have run to the plane, not stayed and dragged Mouse with you," Max said. His expression was fierce, and anger dripped from each word.

For the life of her, she couldn't figure out why he was upset about that. "What was I supposed to do?"

"Run for the plane like Mouse told you to," Max snapped.

"But he was shot, he was bleeding." Her gaze returned to her blood-stained hands. She hadn't made a conscious decision out there, bullets had been flying. Mouse got hit because he was covering her, she couldn't leave him out there alone, so she grabbed him and pulled him toward the plane.

"Not your job to get him to safety."

Now Raven frowned. The fog around her clearing. "Actually, it is. He works for me, that makes him my responsibility."

"No one is arguing that, but ..."

"I know, I know, you guys are the fighting experts and I'm the computer expert. But I was there, and you weren't, and no way was I leaving Mouse out there. He has a daughter, Lolly is only four," she finished softly. She knew all the families of every one of Prey's employees, and she definitely had a soft spot for Mouse's little girl Lauren, nicknamed Lolly. He was a single father, and while his mother helped out with his daughter, the child had already lost one parent, and she wasn't going to stand by and let the sweet little girl lose the only one she had left. Hurrying over to Mouse, she knelt beside him. "Is he going to be okay?" she asked Arrow.

"Gonna be fine," Mouse grunted.

When she looked to the medic for confirmation, Arrow nodded. "Bullet missed the artery, we've stopped the bleeding, he's going to need surgery though. Eagle is sending another plane to Venezuela, we'll stay with you and Max, and Mouse will fly back Stateside for surgery."

Relief wiped away more of the fuzziness in her head, and she knew she had to pull it together. She went to stand but a hand reached out to grip hers.

"Thanks, you risked your life for me," Mouse said, "I won't forget that."

"You're welcome." She squeezed his hand back but then made the mistake of looking down and seeing the dried blood coating her hands.

"Come here," Max said, gentler now. He gripped her under her elbows, tugging her to her feet and guiding her to a chair. "I'll get something to clean you up," he whispered, then leaned down and touched a kiss to her forehead.

Clean.

As if anything could clean her.

Sure, Max could wash away the blood, but it would still be there in her mind. Seared into her memory just like the day she'd been covered in her parents' blood, her own blood, and the blood of the men she'd killed.

But not today.

Not today, she reminded herself.

Today, the only people to lose their lives were the ones who had been trying to kill them. No innocents. No one she cared about.

"It's okay, honey," Max soothed as he sat in the seat opposite her and picked up one of her hands. His touch was gentle as he carefully wiped away all traces of Mouse's blood. When he was done, he picked up her other hand and cleaned it just as carefully. Then he set the washcloth down and held both of her hands in his, his thumbs brushing lightly across the inside of her wrists. "You doing okay?"

Raven nodded. She wasn't really doing okay, but it wasn't like she had a choice. When they got to Venezuela, she had to be ready to do her part to get them access to Joseph Calder's house.

"I need you to hold it together for me, honey," Max said, scooping her up and then sitting in her seat, setting her on his lap.

"I'm trying," she whispered, pressing her face into his neck, wishing she could block out the rest of the world.

"I know you are. I know how much the sight of blood upsets you. Even though I was terrified when I saw you out there dragging Mouse toward the plane, I was proud of you too. You're so strong, Raven. Strength isn't not being afraid, it's not even conquering your fears, it's facing the things that scare you and doing them anyway. That's what you do. It's who you are. You can do this, sweetheart. You can set aside how much blood scares you because you know we're doing this for a good cause."

"The best cause," she whispered back. Max was right, she just had to focus on why they were doing this. Mouse was going to be okay, it wouldn't take them long to get to Venezuela, and when they got there she had the most important role to play.

It was up to her to get them access to Joseph Calder's house.

If she couldn't pull it together, they wouldn't get into his house. If they couldn't get into his house, they couldn't put him in custody. If they couldn't get him in custody, then Max wouldn't be able to take Joseph's place at the auction. And if they didn't get into that auction, her chance to find Cleo could be gone.

"I can do this," she said firmly, lifting her head.

"Never doubted you for a second," Max said, pressing a quick kiss to her lips.

Arrow dropped into the seat beside them and touched his fingertips to her wrist.

"What are you doing?" she asked Alpha team's medic.

"Taking your pulse," Arrow replied.

Raven rolled her eyes. "Yeah, I got that, I meant why?"

"You were having a panic attack when you got back on the plane," Arrow said calmly.

"It was just the sight of the blood, I'm okay now." She was embarrassed to now be the center of attention and to have had a meltdown in front of men who worked for her, but the panic in her chest had receded and she was feeling better with each passing second.

"Your pulse is still elevated," Arrow said.

"I'm fine," she gritted out.

"Do you want me to give you a mild sedative?" Arrow asked.

"No, of course not."

"Actually, maybe it will help with our plan," Max said.

"How?"

"You're supposed to be running away from someone, you've got the lump on your head still from the accident, and bruises, we were going to make you dirty and give you ripped clothes to wear so it looks like you're escaping someone who's been holding you prisoner," Max said.

"Yeah, I know all that." Since Joseph Calder bought women, they thought the idea of seeing her vulnerable, injured, seemingly running from her captor would be a turn-on and get her access to his secluded jungle estate. Since they were running this op without time to do proper recon, they needed a quick and easy in, and this was it.

123

"We were going to put a handcuff on you, but I think he'd notice that your wrist isn't all red and bruised so he'd know you haven't been cuffed for long. But if Arrow gives you a mild sedative, then he'll think you've been drugged, and that's how your captor has kept you under control," Max explained.

"I could just pretend to be drugged," Raven protested. It should be easy enough, there was no need for her to be drugged for real.

"This guy buys women. According to the notes you have on him he has several already, he's not going to be easily fooled. Arrow isn't going to give you anything that would knock you out, just make you a little woozy. We're only going to have one chance at this," Max reminded her. "We need access to his estate as quickly as possible because we still have to get things prepared for the auction tomorrow. Up to you though, midnight, if you're uncomfortable with the idea we don't have to do it, chances are you could fake being drugged enough to convince him."

Raven was sure she could, but there was just a teeny tiny little bit of niggling doubt. Max and Alpha team minus Mouse would be watching over her, they wouldn't let anything happen to her. She trusted them, and if taking the sedative would make their story more believable, she'd do it. Anything to get this chance to find Cleo.

Lacing her fingers with Max's, she nodded. "Let's do it. Nothing can mess this up."

"Nothing will mess this up, honey," Max promised. "We're going to get our baby back."

Her gaze flew to his. "Do you mean that? You think we're going to find Cleo?"

"I don't know, midnight, but what I do know is there are

answers we both need in that place, and we're going to get them. Together."

She liked the sound of that. "Together," she echoed.

* * *

1:26 P.M.

"Last chance to back out," Max told Raven.

"I don't want to back out," she said. Although he knew she was one hundred percent committed to this plan, and that in her mind she had said the words firmly, Arrow had given her a sedative, and her words instead came out weak and a little slurred.

The idea of sending Raven into danger drugged didn't sit well with him even if it was his idea. It made her vulnerable, but it also increased their chances of this working and her getting into Joseph Calder's estate. According to Raven's research, the man didn't have a lot of security. Joseph was a former Marine turned mercenary who made his fortune and now lived in this remote Venezuelan estate with the women he purchased with his enormous amounts of wealth. As soon as Raven ran onto the property all attention would be on her, making it that much easier for them to breach the property without letting anyone escape. There could be no one to leak to Le Entregar that it wasn't Joseph Calder who turned up for the auction.

"We'll be watching and listening to everything," Tex's voice through the comms reminded them all.

Raven was wearing a wire and a camera so even though they weren't with her they would be aware of everything that was happening and could get to her if they needed to.

"We gotta get moving," Bear reminded them. Alpha's team leader was six foot five with thick dark hair and a beard, he looked every bit as lethal and dangerous as the grizzly bears he was named after.

"It's going to be okay, Max. I trust you guys," Raven said, squeezing his hand.

There she was trying to reassure him when she was the one who was about to go running unarmed into the house of an amoral monster. "All right, let's do this before I change my mind," he agreed. Before he released her, Max pulled Raven into a tight embrace and kissed her long and hard. "You got this, midnight."

"I'll see you soon," she said.

"Yeah, you will."

With a last quick kiss, Max released his hold on her and she took off running. Alpha team had patrolled the jungle surrounding the estate and taken note of where all the cameras were. Raven had to be running when she came into view, had to look exhausted like she'd been running for miles. As it was, they had positioned themselves just over a mile from Joseph's house, with the drugs in her system, the bruises from the accident, her hair messed, clothes dirty and ripped, and her feet bare, she'd certainly look like she was a woman running for her life by the time she reached the house.

Through the camera, they watched the jungle move past, Raven's ragged breathing was the only sound as all of them watched and waited. He hated this plan, hated that anything could go wrong, hated that even if everything went the way they hoped Raven would still be hurt, her feet cut up from running through the jungle. She'd assured him she'd love to run around barefoot as a kid on her parents' farm, but that was years ago, and this was the jungle not a farm. The idea that she might wind up seriously hurt or with a deadly infection made his stomach churn.

"She's going to be fine," Tex assured him. "Raven is a lot tougher than she looks."

"I know," he murmured. She was, he knew that, but he loved her and he didn't like this.

Raven was a reasonable runner and could probably run a mile in ten minutes, no more than fifteen, but without shoes and the drugs in her system it took her more than twenty before the trees began to thin out and the property's fence came into view. Using drones, they'd done a sweep of the entire property, and the fence had a hole in one place. Since it would look suspicious if Raven went running straight for it, they had her come in close and then run along the fence until she got to it.

His jaw clenched when Raven cried out as the wire must have cut her as she squeezed through the hole, and then she was off and running again.

"Easy, she's okay," Tex soothed.

"Barely," he muttered.

"Hello? Help me, please," Raven cried out as she ran, immediately attracting the attention of the nearby guards.

Max sucked in a breath, held it, this was it. There was always the chance that she would be shot on sight. There was nothing he could do to stop it from happening. He was over a mile away, a bullet could end her life in a second.

"I see at least half a dozen guards watching her progress and moving in," Tex informed them. As well as watching a feed of what Raven was seeing, he was also monitoring two drones.

No gunshots echoed through their comms units, and Raven continued to gasp for breath as she staggered across the manicured gardens.

"Someone please help me, I need help. Please," she said on a sob, and even though he knew she was acting, he couldn't help but react to the sound.

"Ma'am?" a voice spoke, but they couldn't see anyone, so whoever it was wasn't approaching from in front of Raven.

"Hello?" Raven said, looking around and a man dressed in a simple white shirt and pair of chinos appeared. "Oh, thank goodness, when I saw the fence I prayed someone was living here."

"What are you doing here?" the man asked, stepping closer to Raven who was still moving.

"I don't know where I am," Raven wept. "He took me, he had me in his car but when he stopped, I just got out and ran. Please help me, call the police."

"Is that him?" Surf asked, brushing a lock of his blond hair from his forehead and leaning closer to get a look at the footage on the tablet.

"Looks like it," Domino said.

"Confirmed. That's Joseph Calder," Tex told them.

"All right, let's move," Bear announced.

They all collected their weapons and put their backpacks on. Just because they weren't expecting this mission to be difficult, it didn't mean things couldn't go bad. Only two dozen guards patrolled the estate, no doubt Joseph thought he was trained well enough to protect himself should it come down to it.

Since they were all highly trained, they took barely five minutes to reach the fence. Just as they were there, the comms suddenly went quiet. "What happened?" Max asked.

"We lost her," Tex replied.

"Lost her?" he echoed.

"Either he made her as a plant or he's just extra cautious,

but it looks like he's using some sort of jammer to block any signals," Tex explained.

"Drones?" Bear asked.

"Lost them too. Working on getting them back online," Tex replied.

"So we're going in blind now?" he asked.

"Looks like it. His men are going to be on high alert," Tex said.

"We stick together, take out the guards, but we want Joseph Calder alive," Bear said.

Although he hadn't worked with these men before, he was used to working as a team and slipped seamlessly into Mouse's spot. They entered the property through the same hole in the fence that Raven had used and met the first guard almost immediately.

Max dropped him and kept moving without a second thought.

A large white mansion was up ahead, the grounds were manicured gardens, palm trees, flower beds, ponds, but nothing to provide much cover. At least the fence was simple, no guard towers, just miles of wire fence topped with barbed wire. It was clear that Joseph Calder felt safe enough out here, probably because he was so remote it was unlikely anyone would ever find him. Raven had found him only because she'd managed to get a virus onto his computer when he'd contacted Le Entregar and used it to track his location.

They took out another two guards as they made their way toward the house, but as they moved closer, a spray of bullets hit the ground just before them.

"They're shooting from the roof," Bear said.

"Coming at us from the house too," Domino added.

"Behind us too," Arrow said from their six.

"They're trying to circle around us," Surf said, a grin on his face. "Guess they think if they get us surrounded they can take us."

Little did Calder's men know what a mistake they were making. Instead of getting the upper hand, all they were doing was making it easier to take them out. Now they didn't have to worry about tracking down all the guards, the men were coming to them.

Snipers Domino and Surf took out the men on the roof, Bear, Brick, Arrow, and Max took out the men slowly closing in on them. Minutes later everyone but them lay dead or dying.

"Calder should have invested in better security," Bear muttered.

Max agreed, but the man's cheapness had worked in their favor. No one was shooting at them, and the six of them hurried across the remaining yard.

"Tex, we need those cameras operational," Max said. Raven was nowhere in sight, they needed to find her ASAP.

When he entered the house and saw what was inside, he couldn't stop a horrified gasp from escaping his lips. He knew that Joseph Calder bought women. Knew that the man had an obsession with flowers. What he didn't know was that inside his home he kept the women in what could only be described as large human-sized engraved crystal vases. The women looked at them with large, terrified eyes, their skin had been tattooed to look like petals, and crowns of flowers sat on their heads.

Human flowers.

The sick, demented monster had made himself his very own garden out of stolen women. And Raven was with him.

* * *

1:59 P.M.

"Ma'am?"

"Hello?" Raven called out, catching sight of a man dressed in a simple white shirt and a pair of chinos. "Oh, thank goodness, when I saw the fence I prayed someone was living here."

"What are you doing here?" the man asked as she continued to stagger toward him.

Was it him?

Was it Joseph Calder?

In her mind, the biggest problem they might have faced was that Joseph had already left for the auction. From what Tex had found, access to the property where the auction was to be held wouldn't be allowed until late tomorrow afternoon, but that didn't mean that Joseph hadn't decided to fly into Colombia early.

"I don't know where I am," Raven cried, willing tears to fall from her eyes. "He took me, he had me in his car, but when he stopped, I just got out and ran. Please help me, call the police." Raven stopped running when the man crossed the distance between them.

It was him.

Since she was out of breath, woozy from the sedative Arrow had given her, and in pain from her feet and her chest, there was no pretending involved when she swayed unsteadily on her feet.

This was it. Do or die time. Either Joseph believed she was some helpless woman running for her life and didn't see her as a threat, or he figured out he was being played and shot her here and now.

"Who took you?" Joseph asked, and as she blinked and got

a good look at his face, she saw he really did have an uncanny similarity to Max. Only her Max was good and kind, he risked his life to save others, and he had come to Colombia for her because despite their rocky history, he still loved her and wanted to protect her. Joseph was a monster who bought women like they were property. Still, she hoped the physical similarities were enough to bring down the world's largest human-trafficking ring.

"I-I don't kn-know who he w-was. I was o-on v-vacation, and he j-just grabbed m-me," she stammered, allowing her body to shake along with her words. She knew she looked a mess, with the bruises and her wooziness she could pass as a kidnap victim who had managed to escape, it all boiled down to how suspicious Joseph Calder was. "Can you h-help me? Can w-we call the p-police. Please?"

He smiled at her. It wasn't a pretty sight. "Of course, why don't you come inside, sit down, and I'll get you a drink?" Joseph said.

It was her job to keep him and his men distracted while Max and Alpha team got into place, so she gave a shaky nod of her head. He held out a hand to her, the last thing she wanted to do was touch this sick monster, but she didn't have a choice. She wasn't supposed to know who he was as far as she should be concerned, he was just a random man who lived out in the jungle who was going to be her savior.

Raven couldn't help a shudder passing through her when his hand closed around hers, but she was sure he just attributed it to her current mental state.

The house was large with a huge balcony. Joseph bypassed the closest door and instead led her around the side and through a smaller door into a kitchen. The kitchen was also white, with white tiles on the floor, white painted walls, and white countertops and cupboards. There was even a large wooden table and twelve chairs that had been painted white. It felt like being inside a very warm and tropical igloo and was almost too bright for her eyes.

"Why don't you sit," Joseph suggested, guiding her toward the table.

She dropped down into one of the chairs and watched as Joseph grabbed a glass and a pitcher of chilled water from the fridge. Raven tried to get a read on him, he didn't appear to be upset or on edge, so she suspected for the moment at least that he was buying what she was selling.

That was all going to change the second he heard the bullets start flying.

As far as she could see, he didn't appear to be armed but that didn't mean he couldn't kill her with his bare hands. Joseph had been in the US military, he'd been a Marine, and once he'd gotten out, he'd decided to become a hired killer. He'd made his millions as a mercenary, in part working for Le Entregar. She knew that if he wanted her dead there was nothing she could do to stop it from happening.

"Here you go," he said, bringing her a glass of water.

"Th-thank you." Raven took a sip of water, just a sip in case he'd slipped something into it. She didn't want to make herself any more vulnerable than she already was. "Are you g-going to c-call the p-police n-now?"

He gave her a onceover, it was slow and deliberate and made her feel like he was undressing her with his eyes, picturing her naked, and she assumed he was trying to decide if she could be added to his collection.

"Sure, darlin'," he drawled.

Raven began to squirm in her seat. Any moment now, Max and the others were going to breach the estate. As soon as he heard the gunfire, Joseph was going to know she was a plant. It would be the only thing that made sense. She'd hoped he would have gone for a phone leaving her to find a place to hide. Then all she had to do was wait for the others to come and get her.

She looked around the room then tried to sound innocent when she asked, "Wh-where's the ph-phone?"

"Thought I'd let you relax a little first," he said with a wink that made her shiver, sexual innuendo was heavy in his tone.

"But …" she broke off when it happened.

Gunfire.

Max and the others were here.

Joseph's calm demeanor changed instantaneously. With a growl he grabbed her, throwing her up against the nearest wall. "What did you do?"

Continuing to play the innocent victim card, Raven widened her eyes. "I-I d-don't know wh-what you m-mean," she stuttered.

"Cut the act," he snarled. "Who are you? Cop? Military? Your accent says you're from the States. You working some kind of sting?"

Raven pressed her lips together and remained silent. All she had to do was hold on just a moment longer. Using the knowledge that Max was listening to and seeing everything she was to keep herself grounded, she met Joseph's angry gaze.

"You think they can get to you before I kill you?" he sneered.

Deciding he'd already made up his mind and she may as well drop the act, Raven shook her head. "I know you can, but it's worth it. I want your invite to the Le Entregar auction."

That caught him by surprise if the narrowing of his eyes

was any indication. "You think you can take on Le Entregar and come out alive?"

"Yes, I do."

"Stupid woman." He threw back his head and laughed like a firefight wasn't happening right outside. "You won't even take me on and come out alive. Too bad we don't have more time, I would have liked to have a taste of you."

She aimed her knee at his groin, but the man was well trained enough to anticipate the self-defense move and easily pin her in place, using his much larger body to his advantage. One of his hands clamped around her neck, squeezing tightly, cutting off her air supply. His other hand grabbed one of her breasts, roughly kneading it, and she knew he would leave bruises.

Not that that was her biggest problem right now.

Raven struggled, trying to dislodge him, but to no avail.

The hand on her breast moved and began to attempt to fumble its way inside the waistband of the torn skirt she was wearing.

He couldn't get past the buttons so instead he reached down, grabbed the hem, and bunched it around her hips.

She wished she'd worn pants.

They'd decided to make her look as vulnerable as possible so Joseph wouldn't see her as a threat.

That had worked.

But now he was going to take advantage of her vulnerability.

Raven clawed at the hand strangling her.

She heard the shooting stop.

Prayed Max was coming.

Joseph's hand trailed up her thigh, then moved between her legs.

One second a finger was snaking its way inside her

panties, and the world was going gray around the edges, the next, Joseph was gone.

Without him holding her up, Raven's legs buckled, and she sank to the ground.

She heard the blows, was aware of being surrounded by people.

She wondered if it was Joseph's guards. Had they killed Max and the others?

Then hands were clutching at her, shoving her skirt back down, framing her face, stroking her cheeks which she just now realized were wet with tears.

"Raven, honey, are you okay?"

Max.

Her Max was here.

Relief made the world go a little bit fuzzier.

Because she didn't want him to worry, Raven nodded. She *was* okay, just shaken up by what had almost happened. But they'd done it. They'd successfully taken out Joseph's guards, they had him in custody which meant they could use his invitation to get into the auction, and her chance to take down Le Entregar and get her daughter back was finally within her grasp.

And it was all thanks to her ex-husband.

"Thank you," she whispered through her sore throat as she reached out to Max.

His lips found hers, and she wrapped herself around him, drawing strength and comfort from the only man she would ever love.

* * *

3:03 P.M.

136

"How are you feeling?" Max asked Raven as he walked into the living room. He knew how lucky they'd been to get to her in time. Just a couple of minutes longer and not only would Joseph Calder have killed her, but he would also have violated her. It would have been a horrific way to die, and he wasn't sure he'd ever get the images out of his mind of entering the kitchen to find Raven's skirt bunched around her hips and a hand around her throat, squeezing the life out of her.

"Better," she said and offered him a tired smile. Arrow had checked her out and given her some oxygen and painkillers, and she seemed to be holding it together, but she'd been through a lot in a short space of time, and she still had a lot more to go through, he was worried about her.

"You sure?" There were dark circles under her eyes, the bruise on her forehead was turning an awful shade of greeny-yellow, and red marks were forming on her neck from Joseph Calder's hands. He knew they would be dark black and blue bruises within a few hours.

"I'm tired, I'm hurting, but so far everything is going the way we'd hoped. We got our access to that auction, and that's all that's important."

"It's not *all* that's important," he corrected as he pulled up a chair and sat beside her. "You are important too. How you're handling this is important. Bringing down Le Entregar is important, but it's not the only thing that is. I know how much you want to do this, and because it means a lot to you, it means a lot to me too, but I don't want to lose you in the process."

"You won't lose me." Raven held out her hand and he took it and squeezed. Although he liked her confidence, there was no way to know for sure what was going to happen. She'd weighed the pros and cons and made her decision, but he hadn't had a chance to do that because Raven had already decided, she was going ahead with her plan with support or without it. That meant he had no choice but to offer his support.

"You can't know that," he said softly. His thumb brushed lightly across her knuckles. Her hands were so much smaller than his, she was so much smaller than him, just like she'd been much smaller than Joseph Calder. His instincts told him to protect her, tuck her away someplace where nothing could ever hurt her, and treat her like she was fragile. But she wasn't fragile. She was tough, stronger than he was. While he'd run from the pain of losing their child, she had faced it head-on and made it her mission to right that wrong.

Now she was prepared and willing to walk into a dangerous place. A place filled with men who thought nothing of buying and selling their fellow human beings. She was putting herself into a situation where she would have no rights. She would be playing the role of a slave, sitting here now having temporary tattoos put on her skin so she looked like one of Joseph Calder's flower women, she would be beyond vulnerable.

"I can because I trust you, you won't let anything hurt me," Raven said confidently.

But that was the thing.

When they went through with this, *he* would be the one hurting her.

"You understand how this is going to be, right?" Max asked.

"I understand that when we arrive, you'll be my master and I'll be your slave," she said, watching him while the tattoo artist worked on her, covering her skin with dozens of flowers.

"But do you really get what that means?"

"I understand how sexual slavery works."

"Do you? Because I'm not sure you do," he said harshly. The idea of what he would have to do to Raven once they arrived at the auction made him feel physically ill. "You're going to be my *slave*, Raven. That is what everyone there will believe. There will be cameras everywhere, probably microphones too, including in our bedroom. That means we're always going to have to be on, playing our roles. I won't be able to hold you in my arms, or kiss you, or make sure you're okay. If we want them to believe that I'm Joseph Calder and you're one of his slaves, then I'm going to have to act like Joseph. That means I'm going to have to mistreat you, honey."

Her brow crinkled like that particular piece of information hadn't occurred to her yet. "Mistreat me?"

"What did you think I'd be doing?"

"I don't know, I didn't really think about it. I guess I thought I'd just follow you around, stare at the floor and not make eye contact, act submissive."

"Is that what you think Joseph would do with his slaves? Just have them follow him around and look at the floor?"

She cast a glance over her shoulder in the direction of the kitchen, and he knew she was thinking about how the man had overpowered her and almost killed her while he was right outside. Joseph Calder was currently being interrogated by Bear and his team. Eagle had sent in a cleanup team and alerted the authorities on what had happened out there. The women who had been held captive had been transported to a hospital where they would be debriefed, receive medical care, and be reunited with their families.

"No," Raven said quietly. "Joseph Calder would enjoy hurting and humiliating his slaves."

"Right," he said grimly. "That means I might have to hit you, I might have to make you do things that you're not going to like. I might have to make you do things that will upset you, embarrass you, probably traumatize you. But if I don't do them, we risk Le Entregar figuring out we're not who we say we are, which will get us killed."

"What things will you do to me?" she asked, her voice wobbling.

"I might have to strip you naked and have sex with you, even knowing they'll almost definitely be watching us. I'll have to berate you in front of everyone, order you around, pretend I don't care about you. But one thing I will not do is allow anyone else to lay a hand on you." That was a hard line he had drawn in the sand, and he would not cross it for anything, not even if it ended up blowing the mission. It was one thing for him to have to pretend that Raven was his slave, hurting her in the process, it was another for a stranger to put their hands on her.

"Whatever you have to do I can take it," Raven assured him, and she squeezed his hand tightly as though to remind him of her strength.

"It's not too late to back out." Max would so much rather go in and do this alone, she could teach him what to do with the virus, and without her there, he wouldn't have to worry about anything but gathering as much information as he could.

"I think it is." She nodded at the woman doing the temporary tattoos. "And even if it wasn't I want to do this. I trust you, and I'll know that whatever you're doing to me to keep our cover will hurt you a whole lot more than it'll hurt me."

She was right on that. Putting his hands on a woman, talking down to her, berating and humiliating her were all things he abhorred. But he didn't have a choice, if they weren't convincing as Joseph Calder and his slave then they'd lose their lives. It was as simple as that. So, he would do what he had to do, he would just hate himself afterward for doing it.

"I'll hate every second of it, baby," he said, reaching out to smooth a lock of hair off her cheek and tucking it behind her ear.

"I will too, but just keep reminding yourself we're doing this for a good cause. I'm not naïve enough to think that taking down Le Entregar will end human-trafficking, but it will at least put a major dent in the operation until someone can rise up and take their place. And we'll remove a lot of the key players and buyers with the information we'll get once I upload the malware onto their computers. Plus, we'll get to save all the women and girls who are there, and hopefully track down a lot more with what we learn, that's going to feel good. Our temporary pain and discomfort are worth it, especially if we get answers about Cleo."

"You're a smart woman, you know that?" he asked, touching a kiss to the tip of her nose.

"I know." Raven grinned at him, and it felt like things between them were back to the way they always had been. Their love had grown from friendship. As a teenager, he'd shared things with Raven he hadn't with anyone else, and he knew she had done the same. They had always respected each other, and they had created the most beautiful little girl together. Raven was his forever, he wasn't letting her go ever again.

"I love you, midnight."

"I love you, Max."

"We'll get through this."

"Together."

"Yeah, babe, together. Because we're stronger together."
He wished he had always remembered that, but he vowed he
would never forget it again.

* * *

7:17 P.M.

"Whoa. Those tattoos are something else."

Raven stopped in the doorway, feeling self-conscious at
Max's exclamation. She hated being here in Joseph Calder's
house even though they had to be because someone from Le
Entregar was flying in to pick them up from here tomorrow
morning. The women who had been kept captive here were
free, Joseph's guards were dead, Max was now impersonating
Joseph which meant he was spending the night in the man's
room, she was now the only "slave" in the house, and Alpha
team were now patrolling as Joseph's "guards". It was creepy
being here and she'd reached the end of her rope with
nothing to do over the last several hours except sit there
while the temporary tattoos were sprayed on all over her
body and dwell on everything.

And she meant *everything*.

All that had happened the last few days and what would
happen tomorrow.

She felt spent, empty, exhausted, and yet things were only
just beginning. What had happened so far was just the
prelude for what was to come next.

"Hey, you all right?" Max crossed the room to her and
brushed the back of his knuckles across her cheek before
curling his hand around her nape and tugging her forward so
she rested against his chest.

Raven couldn't stop a smile at the way Max's other arm circled her waist and held her anchored tightly against him. He was strong and solid, and offered her that strength until she had restocked her own supply. It was nice. It wasn't that she couldn't get through this on her own, she could, in the past she had, but it was nice not to have to.

"Honey, you're scaring me. Did something happen? Are you feeling worse? Do you want me to call Arrow, have him come take a look at you?"

She loved that he didn't ask if she was backing out, it bolstered her confidence, and she gave a content sigh and snuggled closer. "I'm okay, I think everything just hit me all at once."

"It's okay to be scared, Raven. What we're doing is extremely dangerous, but we have your guys watching our back, and you have me by your side, I won't let anything happen to you."

"Just remember, I don't want anything to happen to you either." Maybe that was her biggest fear right now. Raven had made her peace with the idea that Le Entregär might end up killing her when she decided to take them down, but even the possibility that Max might wind up dead froze her heart.

"Sweetheart, I have every reason in the world to make sure I don't get myself killed." He gently pulled her back so he could frame her face with his large hands. His dark eyes were tender, and she could see the love shining in them so brightly that she had to wonder how she could ever have doubted his love for her. Max leaned down and kissed her forehead. "I'm sorry that I left you when you needed me, sorry that you doubted yourself because of it, and I'm sorry that I gave up on Cleo instead of standing by your side and fighting for her."

Raven lifted her hands to cover his. "I forgive you, Max.

We all handle grief in different ways, and you were dealing with guilt that I wasn't."

"I won't ever give up on you—or Cleo—again. Ever. I vow that to you right here and now. Whatever happens tomorrow at the auction, whatever happens with us in the future, I won't ever give up on you, or our daughter, or us."

"I believe you," she whispered, moved by the intensity in his words. Max was a warrior, and she knew that giving up on their family would always be his biggest regret, but they had the whole rest of their lives before them, and she was more than ready to leave old hurts in the past where they belonged.

His fingertips brushed lightly across her face. "These aren't going to wash off if we take a bath are they?"

"No, well at least not after one bath. The tattoo artist said they'd last about a week, more than enough time for us to get to the auction, take down Le Entregar, and get out. Why? You want to take a bath."

Max's gaze heated. "Oh yeah."

She giggled as he took her hand and led her into the large master bathroom. There was a jacuzzi tub, and Max headed straight for it. Turning the water on hot, he put the plug in and let the tub fill. Then he turned to her and looked at with what could only be described as insatiable hunger in his eyes.

"These tattoos are …"

"Creepy," she supplied. "They're creepy. I feel like some sort of weird attraction. You know like in one of those old freak shows. Step right up, ladies and gentlemen, and see the human vase, she's covered in flowers and looks like a meadow." Raven shuddered, she was glad she hadn't seen the women who had been kept here in giant life-size vases. Apparently, they had extensive damage to their legs from being kept submerged from the waist down in water, and she could only imagine that the psychological damage was so much worse. Max hadn't wanted her to see them and insisted that Arrow check her out in another room after Joseph had almost killed her. She'd argued at the time, but now she was glad she hadn't seen those women. She wasn't sure she could carry their fear and humiliation with her tomorrow.

"Yeah, the flowers are a little creepy, but you are beautiful, and the tattoos will be gone in a few days." He snagged the hem of the knee-length sundress she was wearing and pulled it up and over her head, letting it drop to the floor at their feet. "You're not wearing underwear," he groaned.

Raven grinned. "The tattoos are pretty much everywhere. I only put the sundress on because we're not alone here. If it was just the two of us, I wouldn't have bothered."

"Midnight," he ground out.

Her grin just grew, she'd missed teasing Max, bantering with him, hadn't even realized how much until he was back in her life.

"Did I mention how much I missed this body? How responsive it is? How much I love that I'm the only man who's ever touched you." His hand slipped between her legs, touching her where she was already wet for him. "I'm sorry you're not my only."

"It's okay," she said with a shiver as he made her body come alive with a few simple touches. "If I was your only one you wouldn't have learned how to be so good at making me feel good." She sucked in a breath when one of his fingers thrust inside her, making her internal muscles clench in delightful anticipation.

"I think I would have learned just fine how to make you moan and scream my name," he said. "Bath's full."

She moaned a protest as he withdrew his finger, and from the twinkle in Max's eyes, she knew he liked that he'd turned her on and left her desperate for more. He turned off the tap, stripped off his clothes, then scooped her up and stepped into the bath, settling her between his spread legs.

The water was deep, coming right up to cover her bare breasts, and perfectly hot, helping to ease her stress.

What helped ease her stress even more was when Max picked up a loofah, poured a generous amount of body wash onto it, and ran it over every inch of her needy, trembling body. He took his time gently scrubbing her, paying special attention to her breasts before dipping across her stomach. Max cleaned each leg, hovering for longer than necessary on her inner thighs, making sure to brush insanely softly across her center, enough to keep her turned on but not enough pressure to get her even close to coming.

When he was done, instead of finally giving her what she knew they both wanted, he picked up a bottle of shampoo and set about washing her hair. His magic fingers worked her scalp, and down her neck to her shoulders before scooping up water to rinse the suds away.

"Max," she pleaded. Her whole body was super sensitive. How wet she was between her legs had nothing to do with the bathwater and everything to do with his slow seduction.

"Yeah, babe?" he asked as his fingers stroked the length of her spine.

"Hurry, please?"

"You begging, babe?" His fingers trailed over her hips and settled between her legs, playing the same light dance they'd done all over her body.

"Yes," she said, shifting so that she caused friction against his hard length that pressed between them.

"Not nice, babe." He chuckled, his breath warm against her neck as he kissed and then lightly sucked on her collarbone.

"No, what's not nice is teasing me like this," she said, shifting again.

"Then beg me," he murmured.

"Please, Max."

"Please what?" He positioned one finger at her entrance but didn't slip it inside her.

"Please touch me, I need you inside me, I need to feel you now, when it's just the two of us, no human-traffickers, no auction, nothing but us. So please hurry up and let me come," she begged.

"Okay, honey."

His finger slipped inside her then, stroking deep and then curling to catch that special spot inside her. His thumb found her needy little bud and he worked both until she was panting, and squirming, and out of her mind with desperation.

When he added a second finger inside her she broke.

"Max," she screamed as pleasure burst through her, spiraling around and around, touching every inch of her body, filling it until it was almost too much.

"You're gorgeous when you're coming on my fingers, screaming my name," Max whispered when she could finally think of something other than the overwhelming ecstasy he made her feel.

"Don't be smug," she rebuked mildly.

"Can't help it, babe. Now get on your knees, hands on the rim of the bath." He guided her up onto her knees and put her hands where he wanted them, then he entered her from behind in one smooth thrust.

Raven moaned in delight as he held onto her hips and moved in a steady rhythm, making her already overly sensitive body come alive all over again.

"Touch yourself, babe, make yourself come, I can't hold on much longer," Max ordered.

She slipped one hand between her legs, found that little bundle of nerves, and began to work it with her fingers. Max thrust, she worked her bud, and a moment later she was screaming his name again as pleasure rushed at her like a tsunami. It poured down upon her, relentless in the seemingly never-ending series of waves that crashed over her.

By the time it ebbed, Raven wasn't sure she could move, wasn't sure she could think, wasn't even sure she could breathe.

But it turned out she didn't have to do anything other than rest in Max's arms as he gathered her up, stepping out of the bath and wrapping her in a soft, white fluffy towel. They didn't speak as he dried her off, and then himself, then picked her up again and carried her into the bedroom.

She didn't have time to think about whose bed they were getting into because her head was on the pillow, Max was spooning her from behind, and her eyes were fluttering closed, cherishing this moment of peace before the world turned to Hell around them.

For now, it was just the two of them, and Raven snuggled deeper into Max's embrace and allowed her mind to float away into sleep, safe in the knowledge she was cocooned in the arms of the man she loved.

CHAPTER 7

October 31st

9:52 A.M.

Gone was the tranquility he'd felt last night in the bath with Raven and lying in bed holding her in his arms.

Every second of the next twenty-four hours, he had to be completely focused on what they were doing. He couldn't walk in there armed, well not properly armed anyway. He had snuck a few knives into his luggage and one tiny gun. He couldn't treat Raven as anything more than a piece of property. And he had to be aware of everything going on around them and gather as much intel as possible to send to Alpha team.

"You ready to go?" he asked Raven, mainly because he couldn't stand the stifling silence a second longer. They were waiting on the porch for the car Le Entregar would be sending to collect them. They'd be taken to a small private airfield and flown to the location. Since there was no way Alpha team could follow them, Tex was tracking the tiny chip Raven had inserted between her toes. Although it was a risk not removing it, if it was located, he could always claim he'd put it in her because he hadn't wanted her to be able to escape. That should be easily bought, and although the tracking device would likely be removed and destroyed, it would distract them from finding the secondary device she had hidden at her hairline behind her ear.

"Yes," she answered shortly. He was dressed in one of Joseph Calder's crisp white suits. It was not something he'd ever wear, and he hated it, but he had to play the part. Raven, too, was playing her part. There was a ring of flowers sitting on top of her lightly curled hair. She was wearing a white G-string and a sheer strapless dress that flowed around her slim frame. He hated that everyone she would come into contact with would be able to see her breasts and most of her body, but again there was nothing he could do about it.

"Raven …"

"I said yes, Max. You should try to get out of the habit of speaking to me. I'm just an accessory, a slave, your own personal toy, you wouldn't be worrying about me and constantly looking at me if you were Joseph. They're going to be here any minute, I think it's time we fully embrace our roles.

"I hate our roles," he said, standing and dragging Raven into his arms to hold her one last time.

"I do too, but anytime you have the need to make sure I'm okay just remember that I am, that this was *my* plan, and that nothing is more important than finding information on Cleo. That should be enough to keep you in your role."

"You're smart as well as beautiful." He covered the back of

her head with his palm and pressed her face against his chest, holding her tight and trying to memorize every single thing about what it felt like to hold her. Just in case. Just in case the worst happened and he lost her.

"And you're one smooth talker," she said with a small laugh, but her arms came around him and held him just as tightly as he was holding her, and Max knew she was thinking the same thing he was.

There was a chance this was the last time they would hold each other.

"One last kiss," he said, taking her chin between his thumb and forefinger and tipped her face up. His eyes closed as his lips touched hers, drinking in her taste, letting it sustain him. "I love you, midnight."

"I love you too, Max. Always have, always will."

Max let his hands trail down her body slowly before taking a step back. "This is it."

"I know. Don't hold back, Max, do whatever you have to do to me to make this believable. We might never get another chance at Le Entregar, this has to work. For Cleo."

"For Cleo," he echoed.

"They're here," Bear said, stepping out of the house to stand beside him.

"Wait for them in the driveway," he said and took a seat on the porch swing. "Raven, get on your knees beside me, hands on your knees, eyes down. You got this, babe."

Between the two of them, her role was a million times harder than his. Raven was a strong woman, and there was a difference between doing something that you didn't want to do and having all choice taken away. For the next twenty-four hours, she would have to do whatever he ordered no matter how much she didn't want to. Max knew she would do it only for their daughter, and he couldn't be prouder of her determination. Finding out what happened to Cleo would happen only because of her dedication.

A black limousine came down the driveway and pulled to a stop outside the house. Bear stood between them and the vehicle like he was Max's personal bodyguard. A man dressed in a black suit opened the back door and stepped out, eyeing Bear before looking over at him.

"Mr. Calder?"

Max stood slowly, stretching, taking his time. He'd spoken with the women Joseph had bought to get a feel for who the man was and how he had treated them and his staff, and the one thing they all had said was that he thought of himself as the king. And the king didn't spend time worrying about others or their schedules.

"I'm Joseph Calder," he said as he moved to the top of the steps so he could look down at the man.

The man's gaze jumped from him to Bear and back again. "You're aware that you can't bring a bodyguard with you?"

"I know, doesn't mean he's going to allow just anyone to come near me. I pay him handsomely to put himself between me and any potential threats. I believe you have something for me?"

With a nod, the man—who hadn't bothered to offer them his name—pulled out a piece of gold-leaf paper, the other half to the invitation that they'd gotten from Joseph Calder. Bear intercepted the man before he could walk over to Max, and he had to fight back a smile at the scowl on their visitor's face.

Bear brought him the paper, and he pulled out Joseph's half and put them together. "It's a match," he said with a grin.

The man gave a terse nod. "We have a schedule to keep to, Mr. Calder, so if you're ready we really need to depart."

Leaving Bear to grab his luggage, Max walked back to

Raven—who to her credit hadn't moved a muscle from where he'd told her to sit—and tangled a hand in her dark hair, yanking her to her feet.

She let out a surprised yelp, and he delivered a swift blow to her backside.

"Did I give you permission to make a sound?" he growled, making sure to put in every drop of power and control and domination he could into his tone.

Raven dropped her gaze to the ground and didn't utter a word.

"Better," he said, then kept his hand in her hair, making Raven walk on her tiptoes and prayed she forgave him for this when it was all over. Just because she said she understood, and they'd talked about it, it didn't mean she could cope with the man she loved treating her like this. "I've got one more piece of luggage."

"Sir, you're aware that there will be women there to attend to your needs," the man told him.

"I'm aware," he snapped, looking down his nose at the man. "But I don't like to share. I prefer to bring my own." Max shoved Raven inside the car, hiding a wince as she fell awkwardly onto her side.

"Very well, sir," the man agreed. They'd known he would because the intel Bear and his team had extracted from Joseph included the fact that he had brought one of his own slaves with him to the last two auctions he had attended.

The man joined them in the back of the limousine, and as soon as the door was closed the driver took off. Once they were on the move, the man pulled out a phone and began to tap away on it, so Max ignored him and stared out the window. The drive to the airfield was a short one, only twenty minutes, and they were quickly ushered toward a small plane.

Two men with guns stood on either side of the steps that led up to the door, but no one stopped to check them for tracking devices. Instead, they were led inside the darkened cabin, the blinds were all drawn, covering the windows, no doubt to make sure they couldn't identify where they were going.

He tossed Raven into the seat beside his, giving her the window one so that he was at least between her and the others on board, then demanded something to drink as he buckled his own seatbelt.

Someone delivered him a beer, which he would sip at slowly because he did not want to impede his senses even a little. The engine roared to life, and a minute later they were taking off.

There was no backing out now.

2:33 P.M.

"Since this isn't your first time attending an auction, I'm sure you already know all of this, but just as a reminder there can be no weapons taken onto the property. There are armed guards there to protect all of us as I'm sure you know we all have a lot to lose should the authorities try to interrupt. There is no cell phone reception, there is however wi-fi. Should you need to make an urgent call you will need to do so under supervision. The auction starts at nine, dinner will be served at seven, any woman you successfully bid on will be kept in our custody overnight and handed over to you in the morning when you leave. This afternoon you are free to wander the grounds and indulge in any activities on offer.

There's a pool, a golf course, and of course there is both an indoor and outdoor bar. Or of course you are free to spend the afternoon in your room with your ... luggage."

Although Raven kept her gaze locked on the floor, doing her best to maintain her cover as a broken and obedient slave, she took in everything the man was telling them. It was clear that their escort was used to seeing naked women as he'd barely spared her a glance back at Joseph Calder's house, and she knew that basically everything was on display under this sheer dress.

The plane journey had taken a couple of hours, and although they had not been able to see where they were going, she knew they were back in Colombia, close to where they'd been before. No one had checked her or Max for a tracker which meant that Bear and his team would currently be on one of Prey's planes following them.

The knowledge did little to comfort her.

For now, she and Max were on their own.

While she still knew that this was their best chance to take down Le Entregar and find Cleo, it didn't mean she wasn't terrified out of her mind.

Things had gotten real very quickly when Max had grabbed her by the hair and yanked her to her feet. The stinging pain in her scalp had surprised her, and she'd made the mistake of making a sound, meaning that Max had had to strike her. He'd been careful not to hurt as he'd delivered the blow to her backside, but she had vowed never to put him in that position again. She knew better than to have made a sound, a slave would already have had it beaten and tortured out of them that they were not to speak without permission, and Max was an honorable man, having to hurt her would hurt him in ways he would never recover from, even knowing that they were simply playing a game.

She had to do better. Not only did finding Cleo and taking down Le Entregar depend on it, but so did her and Max's lives.

The car stopped at a large metal gate, deep within the Colombian rainforests, and their escort got out of the vehicle and stopped to speak with someone. Although she could feel Max wanting to reach out to her, take this moment alone to offer her contact and reassurance, they both knew that there was likely a camera in here somewhere, watching their every move.

On the plane, Max had mostly ignored her and for that she was grateful. She knew that couldn't last, but she had used the last couple of hours to make sure she truly understood what she was going to have to do to maintain cover. Whatever Max asked of her she had to do, no matter how much she didn't want to. He'd told her that several times already, but she wasn't sure it had sunk in until she'd felt his rough hand in her hair and him hitting her backside.

The man returned and they started driving again. As much as she wanted to look up and out the windows, see where they were and how many guards there were, how easy or difficult it was going to be for Alpha team to breach, Raven kept staring at the floor.

They drove for maybe two minutes before finally pulling to a stop again. This time she knew they were at the house, she could hear the activity around them, the excited voices of the men who were here to purchase a sex slave, sounding more like children on Christmas morning than the vile monsters they were.

"You are in room 312, it's on the third floor, down the end of the corridor on the right. If you need assistance in finding it, please don't hesitate to ask one of the staff. Your luggage will be delivered straight to your room. Would you like me to have her delivered there as well? And if so, are there any instructions she should be given in how you expect her to be waiting for you when you arrive?" their escort asked.

Raven bristled at being discussed as though she were of no more importance than the suitcase of clothing, but quickly counted to ten in her head to distract herself and calm down. She knew slaves had no rights. To these men, they *were* of no more importance than a suitcase full of clothing. This was nothing compared to how Max and everyone here would treat her over the next twenty-four hours, so she better get used to sucking it up and dealing.

"No, I like to have her with me, never know when the urge will strike," Max said as she'd known he would. There was no way he was going to let her out of his sight.

"Very well, sir, then please enjoy your stay, and I will see you tomorrow around noon when it is time to take you back to your residence."

With that, the car doors opened again, and their escort seemingly disappeared. Raven dragged in a breath and made sure she didn't flinch when Max grabbed her arm in a rough hold and pulled her from the car. While keeping her head down, Raven risked a couple of glances around and was very quickly appalled with what she saw.

At least a dozen men were lounging around on the large veranda, most were drinking as they laughed and talked. Armed guards were standing at the door, and she was sure there were some positioned on the roof as well. There were also several naked and near-naked women standing about. One was on her knees in front of a man, performing oral sex while he chatted with someone, his hand tangled in her hair as he thrust violently into her mouth.

Raven shuddered at the sight, and Max immediately took

a step closer. She knew he wanted to wrap her up in his arms and take her away from here, but he couldn't, it was too late for that now.

"Good afternoon, sir. May I get you a drink? Something to eat?" a man dressed in a black suit and bowtie asked as he approached.

"Not right now, I think I'm going to head to my room, take a shower first. I hate traveling on planes, always feel dry and dirty, even if it's only a short flight," Max said.

"Very well, sir. When you're ready, please don't hesitate to ask for anything you require."

Max guided her up the steps and across the veranda, then into the enormous mansion. There had to be a couple of hundred rooms in this place, and it wasn't at all decorated as she would have suspected. Instead of muted tones, or large pieces of antique furniture, the interior was bright and colorful, and looked more like a beachfront hotel than a place where evil transactions were made.

She spotted more guards as they made their way to their room, and Raven started to realize they might have underestimated Le Entregar. They'd known there would be guards, but she hadn't expected to find this many inside, she'd assumed they would mostly be stationed around the perimeter with perhaps a few indoors.

Alpha team were good, she trusted them with her life, would trust them with Cleo's life, but they were down Mouse, and they weren't prepared for this much resistance. She was wearing the same camera and microphone, carefully hidden in her earrings that she had been yesterday as she went into Joseph Calder's place, but that would only help them once they were already here.

They needed to use the enhanced satellite phone to inform them, let them know they would need to come in with more men. The plan had been to wait until the early hours of the morning when the auction was over. Most of the visitors would be sleeping off their alcohol-induced highs, then she would infect the computers with the malware. Once that was done Alpha team would breach, taking out the guards then rounding up the auction attendees and taking them into custody, along with the Le Entregar leaders.

But this number of guards changed everything.

She knew what it meant.

It meant that in the event that the place was attacked any and all guests, slaves, and staff would be killed. Dead meant you couldn't talk.

As soon as Alpha team's arrival was known, she and Max and all the women here waiting to be sold would be gunned down. And Max wasn't armed with anything that he could use to stop it from happening.

* * *

3:06 P.M.

This wasn't good.

Max realized as he dragged Raven alongside him through the maze of hallways toward their room that they had made a tactical mistake.

They had underestimated their enemy.

They'd known that Le Entregar was good, and he knew Alpha team had a plan to take out the guards they expected to find along the perimeter, but they hadn't expected the house itself to be so well guarded.

He was no fool, he knew that the guards inside were Le

Entregar's backup plan. If the place should be attacked, then the guards inside would kill everyone but the top players in the trafficking ring, then get those men out of here while the guards on the ground did their best to hold off those attacking.

The only weapons he had on him were a couple of knives and one tiny gun, nothing that would match up with the guards' weapons.

Max was very afraid that by agreeing to this plan he had just signed his and Raven's death warrants.

While he knew she had been willing to risk her life for this chance to take down Le Entregar, he wasn't sure that he was willing to risk her life.

Too late for that though.

They were here now, and they had to follow through no matter how much he didn't like it.

Finding his room, he took the key their escort had given him, unlocked the door, shoved Raven inside, and locked the door behind him. Because he knew there were cameras in here, probably microphones too, he wrapped a hand around Raven's neck and slammed her up against the wall.

Her eyes widened in surprise, but she didn't make a sound and quickly dropped her gaze from him to the floor.

Pressing his body against hers, pinning her in place, he crushed his mouth to hers in a kiss and then moved it away a mere millimeter.

"Don't say anything," he murmured, "don't know if they have microphones in here but if they do, we don't want them to hear you talking." That would look more suspicious, and if he kept his voice low so it didn't carry, then they would just assume he was giving instructions to his slave on what he wanted her to do to him.

Raven didn't say anything, but he felt one of her fingers

brush lightly across his hip and knew she was telling him she heard him.

"We need to get a message to Bear that he needs to bring in another team," he said when he moved his mouth to nibble on her earlobe.

Her finger pressed more tightly against him, and he knew she wanted to say something to him.

Grabbing her wrists, he pulled her arms above her head and pinned her wrists against the wall. "Gonna have to be a bit dramatic here, midnight, but I want to give them a quick show before I take you into the bathroom, don't think there will be cameras in there."

She didn't say anything, and she didn't lift her gaze, playing the dutiful slave to perfection, and he hated that he had to do this.

Despised it.

But it was that or get her killed.

"Sorry, babe," he whispered in her ear. Then he used his free hand to grab hold of her dress and rip it from her body. He felt her flinch but didn't react to it and released her hands and said in a louder voice this time, "On your knees, flower."

Raven immediately complied with his order, dropping to her knees at his feet.

He couldn't for the life of him call her a derogatory name, not even as part of this game, so instead he stuck with calling her flower. That was how Joseph Calder thought of his slaves anyway, as his living, breathing, human flowers. "Come, flower," he ordered as he started walking toward the bathroom where he was fairly certain there would be no cameras.

Unable to look at the sight of Raven crawling on her hands and knees after him like she was some sort of pet, he strode into the attached bathroom and switched on the lights. There was a large glass-enclosed walk-in shower, the perfect place to be able to discuss their next steps without being overheard.

"Stand," he commanded as he closed the bathroom door. Then because he couldn't be one hundred percent certain that there wasn't a camera in here, he reached out and snagged a hold on the G-string Raven was wearing and ripped it, leaving her standing naked before him.

Max turned on the shower and stripped out of his own clothes while he waited for the water to heat, then he took the flower crown off Raven's head and set it down on the counter. When steam filled the room, he took her hand and pulled her into the shower after him.

Immediately, he made sure she was tucked between him and the wall so any potential cameras couldn't see her. Once he had her blocked, he touched a light kiss to her lips, knowing the steam would blur any images being broadcast, giving him the chance to offer at least a little solace.

"I'm sorry, honey," he murmured. "Did I hurt you earlier, when I hit you and when I grabbed your hair?"

"No, Max, I'm fine. I knew what I was getting into. The guards inside, they're here to kill us all if anyone breaches the fence," she whispered urgently.

"Yeah, babe, I figured that out too," he assured her, proud of her for realizing what that meant. Raven was the head of Prey Security's tech team, her forte was computers not tactical operations, and yet she had correctly interpreted what the excessive number of guards inside meant.

"We have to let Bear know," she said softly.

"Yeah, we do."

"Carefully though. The satellite phone looks like a cell phone, but I don't know how closely they're monitoring things here. If you use the phone in our room and they pick up on it, they'll know we're up to something."

"We need to use it in a common area when other people are also using phones, that way they won't be able to tell which one of us it is," he said.

"Dinner."

"You're right. Most of the guests will have their phones then, checking through the catalog for the auction and making sure everything is set for them to make payments." According to the man who had escorted them here, the catalog of women in the auction wouldn't be available until during dessert. After the meal, they would all head straight to the auction room where they would be seated and then the auction would begin. He had no intention of doing anything other than a cursory flip through the catalog in case he was being monitored.

"What are we going to do between now and dinner?" Raven asked.

Hating what he had to say, he knew there was no way around it. "I don't want to take you back down there. Too many people, and I don't want to have to keep telling people I don't share." According to what Joseph had told them, it was common for any slaves brought to the auction to be shared with the other guests, and that wasn't happening. It was a hard no for him to allow anyone else to touch Raven. She'd already lived through being violated and while it was one thing for him to have to touch her in front of these monsters, that was something she had agreed to, it was quite another thing for her to be touched by strangers.

"So, we stay in here," she said, and he knew from the tone of her voice that she already knew what he was going to say.

Just in case, he had to make it clear because if she said she couldn't do it, he'd leave her in here and go and walk around downstairs, gathering as much information as he could. He didn't want to leave her out of his sight, but he'd do it if she couldn't go through with this. "We can't just sit around in here, honey, at least not all afternoon."

Her throat moved as she swallowed. "I know."

"We're going to need to show them what they're expecting to see."

"Sex," she whispered. "We're going to have to have sex knowing that they're watching."

"Maybe watching," he corrected. "There are cameras in here no doubt, but that doesn't mean that anyone is sitting there watching them continuously." He figured there had to be close to one hundred bedrooms spread over the house's three floors, then there would be cameras in all the common areas and across the grounds. He doubted anyone was watching every second of footage, just keeping a watch over everything to make sure nothing untoward was happening. "We'll keep a blanket over us, they won't see much, and we won't actually have sex, we'll just fake it, make it look real enough so when the images from our room show up on the screen it's assumed we're having sex."

"I can do it, Max, stop worrying about me."

"Not gonna happen, sweetheart."

He just wanted this over and done with. The next few hours were only going to get worse. Sending the text at dinner would be risky, he was going to have to do something with Raven to keep their cover, and then he'd have to watch a parade of stolen women without killing anyone or alerting them to the fact that he didn't think buying people was okay.

Yep, he was pretty sure pretending to have sex with Raven was the easiest thing he would have to do today.

* * *

8:20 P.M.

Her stomach was churning, and Raven was glad she hadn't really eaten anything. She was pretty sure that with as nervous as she was, if she had anything substantial in her belly, she would have thrown up already.

She and Max had spent the afternoon in their room. After their pretend sexual romp under the covers, Max had ordered them room service. Well, he'd ordered himself something to eat but he hadn't gotten anything for her since he didn't think that was something Joseph would have done. Instead, he'd pretended that she'd done something to anger him and made her stand in the corner as a punishment. Raven hadn't minded, she would much rather have been hiding out in their room than watching the guests downstairs abuse the women forced to work here against their will.

They couldn't hide in their room forever though.

Now they were down with the others in the huge dining room. She estimated there had to be well over fifty buyers here, and there were a few other slaves like her who their masters had brought along. Some of them were sitting like she was, on their knees, head bowed, sitting beside their owner's chairs. Others were being forced to pleasure the men, either those who had brought them here or others.

Of course, as a slave she hadn't participated in the meal, but she had been given a bowl of some sort of stew which she'd had to eat with her fingers because she hadn't been given utensils. It had been humiliating, and her heart ached for the women who were made to live their lives like that because they'd been snatched and sold.

Fire also burned inside her, a thick, heavy hatred for Le Entregar and everything they stood for.

"Come here, flower," Max ordered, his voice cold and commanding, nothing like the man she knew. He was good at playing this role, she'd been listening to him throughout dinner, and he'd been talking up a storm, bragging about his —Joseph's—legendary record as a mercenary and the many slaves he'd owned. He'd also managed to learn the names of a couple of the Le Entregar leaders. If she hadn't known how much he detested this, and that he was nothing like he was pretending, she would have believed he fit in with these men.

She stood and waited to be told what to do next. As awful as this whole thing was, she was so grateful Max was doing everything he could to shield her as best as possible while still maintaining their cover.

"Sit," he said, patting his lap, and she allowed him to pull her down so she was straddling his lap, her chest to his. The dress she was wearing now wasn't as sheer as the other one, but it was still possible for people to see her breasts through it, and she knew Max had her facing him to keep as many eyes off her as possible.

"You like flowers, Calder?" one of the men at the table snickered.

"You got a problem with that?" Max growled. "Granted, this one is getting a little, shall we say, wilted, but that's why I'm here, I need a new flower for my house." His hand went between her legs, and to anyone else it would look like he was fondling her, but in reality, his hand rested against her inner thigh, and when his fingers stroked against her skin, not her center, it was in a gentle caress, him offering her the only comfort he could.

"No problem," another man spoke up, "we all have our preferences."

"Here you go, sir, dessert," a waiter spoke as he set down a plate with chocolate mousse and chocolate-covered strawberries. "And as you know, the catalog is now accessible on your phones."

Immediately, most of the men snatched up their cells, eager to see what was on offer tonight, and Raven realized Max had timed this perfectly. While the others were checking out the catalog of women who could be bid on after dinner, he would send a coded message to Bear. If the message being sent was noticed, it would be all but impossible for Le Entregar to figure out which of the dozens of men on their phones had sent it. And with her on Max's lap, and his hands apparently touching her, he wouldn't look like a likely candidate.

Lulled into a sense of security on Max's lap, with his warm hand stroking her, calming her, making her forget for a moment where they were, Raven was caught by surprise when Max suddenly shoved back from the table and grabbed her arms, shaking her violently.

"Did you just come?" he bellowed, causing all eyes in the room to turn in their direction. There were a few chuckles, a few snickers, and even a few cheers.

His actions were so unexpected, Raven just stood there, her cheeks flaming, staring at him in shock. What was he doing? He knew she hadn't come, he hadn't even been touching her, and given where they were and the anxiety churning in her gut even if he had been she doubted she could have.

"You don't get to come," he snarled. "This one has a bad habit of trying to sneak in orgasms, she tries to hide it like I don't know what it feels like when a woman comes all over my hand," he announced to the room, making a wave of laughter roll through it. "Get down on your knees," he ordered her, shoving her down and maneuvering her so she was under the table.

Raven had no idea if he really wanted her to suck him off here, surrounded by people, but when he carefully covered her with the white linen tablecloth, making sure it covered his lap as well, she knew that even though he unzipped his pants he didn't intend for her to do anything.

The moans he started giving though certainly gave the impression that her mouth was currently on him.

His hand tangled in her hair, but it was gentle, and his thumb stroked the back of her neck, reassuring her that this was nothing more than an act to make sure no one caught on to who they really were.

Despite his reassurances, a tear tumbled down her cheeks, her head knew this was all pretend, but sometimes her feelings still acted as though it were real.

Max grunted like he'd just come then zipped himself back up but left her where she was. He was talking away with the other men at the table like he wasn't pretending to be getting off, and it wasn't until she heard someone announce that it was time for the auction to begin that he pushed back his chair and pulled her out.

He tucked her close to his side as everyone headed from the dining hall to the auction room. His head dipped and his barely audible voice whispered in her ear, "You're okay, sweetheart. Someone came in and was looking around, I think they noticed the text go off. I wanted to make sure they had no reason to even be looking at us. I'm sorry, honey."

She gave a tiny nod to indicate she'd heard but otherwise kept her blank mask in place. She was glad she hadn't done something stupid back there where he'd caught her by surprise, something that would have given them away.

They went to their seats and Max immediately put her on

his lap. She suspected it was more for his own benefit than for hers, but she wasn't going to protest the comfort his touch brought her.

Even though she wanted to pretend that none of this was happening, her gaze couldn't help but move to the stage where a line of women were standing, all of them dressed in beautiful white gowns. Some of them weren't even women, the ones down the far end looked more like girls. They couldn't be older than early teens.

Her gaze swept over all of them, praying that she and Max and her team could pull this off so all of these women could go home. She couldn't imagine what they had gone through, how terrifying it would be to be snatched off the streets, imprisoned and told you were going to be sold. At least when she was recovering from what had happened to her, she'd had her siblings by her side, but these women had nothing and no one, with no end in sight to their suffering.

Raven froze when her gaze fell on the final girl. Pale skin, wide brown eyes framed by long lashes, and long brown locks that tumbled down her back in gentle waves.

There was something familiar about the girl, who looked like she was about thirteen.

The girl lifted her head, looked over in her direction, and Raven froze as their eyes met.

It wasn't possible.

Yet it was.

She knew it.

Felt it.

Cleo.

That girl was her daughter, she knew it in her heart, down to her very soul.

Her daughter was standing on the stage waiting to be sold.

Raven didn't think, in this moment nothing mattered but the fact that the child she had lost almost ten years ago was just yards away.

* * *

9:10 P.M.

Max tightened his hold on her just in time to stop it from happening.

Raven had lost track of what they were doing and where they were, her mind focused only on the stage and the women there.

No, not on the women, on one in particular, little more than a child.

He felt it too.

The connection, the girl on the end looked so familiar, and while he knew without her having to say anything, knew by the tightness in her body, the way she was breathing much too fast, the way her gaze was locked on the kid, that Raven believed it was Cleo.

Was it?

He was much more pragmatic about it than Raven was. He believed their daughter was deceased, that there was no way she could have survived almost ten years when she'd been taken as a toddler. A pervert who wanted a toddler didn't want a teen. And she was too old to be sold to a family, those kinds of people wanted to buy an infant not a three-year-old.

Cleo was dead.

Gone.

And yet …

The girl looked exactly like he would have imagined his daughter would look if she had lived and was almost a teenager.

No, she *was* a teenager now.

October thirty-first was Cleo's birthday. Halloween. It had always been one of Raven and Cleo's favorite holidays, they'd go all out, dressing up, decorating the house, baking treats, and of course the candy. That last Halloween, Cleo's third birthday, they'd thrown a party for all of Cleo's friends, then they'd gone trick-or-treating for hours. He'd been exhausted but his girls had been hopped up on sugar, excited, and full of boundless energy.

That day he'd thought they had the whole rest of their lives to enjoy Halloween birthdays together, not knowing that would be the last one.

Cleo was taken just under two months later, between Christmas and New Year.

Now there was a girl who looked just like their daughter standing on the stage in front of a bunch of sick perverts with more money than humanity waiting to be sold. Anger burned inside him, if Cleo was still alive then she had spent the last decade suffering horrendously. Even if they saved her, they wouldn't get back the sweet, bubbly, sassy child they'd lost.

That girl was gone forever.

Raven was straining against his hold, desperate to get to the girl, but he tightened his grip until he was worried he was going to leave bruises. Raven had checked out, focused only on the girl, but they were still at the auction, men were ogling the women on the stage. If she went running up there it would ruin everything and they'd all pay with their lives. The girl included.

Max gripped her tight enough he knew he was causing

her pain, but when she flinched, he knew he had momentarily drawn her attention away from the stage, and he took advantage of her distraction.

"Hold it together, babe," he murmured low so only she would hear.

He could feel her internal struggle, but she relaxed against him, and he knew she was making an effort to control herself.

The auction began, Max held onto Raven in case she lost it and ran to the girl on the stage. Each woman was paraded across the stage, the men threw out bids, Max joined in, Joseph's bank account had already been linked to Le Entregar from his previous attendance at auctions so there was the money in there Joseph had intended to spend to buy a new slave.

One by one the women were sold off until all that remained was the final girl. Her eyes were large and terrified in her pale face, she was slim, just like Raven, and he couldn't deny the fact that she did look like an older Cleo.

But he couldn't allow himself to believe it.

It was one thing to have grieved his daughter's death, and done his best to move forward, but thinking about what she could have endured if she was still alive was too much. The pressure on his shoulders grew, not only did he now have to get Raven out of here alive but the girl as well. Even if she wasn't Cleo, she looked enough like her that he couldn't allow anything else to happen to her.

"Our final offering tonight is a beautiful young thing, just thirteen years old, the voice of an angel, and a virgin," the announcer said as the Cleo girl was prodded to walk across the stage. The audience murmured at the revelation that she was a virgin and Max knew that the girl was going to bring in a fortune for Le Entregar.

He had rejected the idea when Raven first suggested that she believed Cleo was still alive. He had fought against it when they both saw the girl who looked so much like their lost daughter. But when the girl was given a microphone and began to sing, he knew.

Knew for certain.

The girl was Cleo.

As impossible as it seemed that Cleo could be standing before them, that the one time Raven was able to actually get close enough to Le Entregar to get to one of their auctions that their daughter would be there, it was true.

Even as a toddler, Cleo had had a voice like an angel and this girl had Cleo's voice.

Raven was shaking violently in his arms now. If anyone happened to notice her, they would know something was going on, but he knew that she couldn't contain her reaction even if she tried. She was weeping for their lost baby who was suddenly standing before them, and Max himself was fighting back tears.

The auction ended, the men chatted in small groups, bragging about who they had bought and what deal they had gotten, but Max grabbed Raven and dragged her straight to their room not caring what anyone thought or if anyone thought that their behavior was strange. He had to get her alone, they had to talk about what they'd just seen, and they had to get that information to Bear so he knew how much more important this mission had become.

In their room, he quickly went to his suitcase and pulled out a device that would jam the cameras in the room from transmitting data. They didn't have long, if he kept them jammed for too long then someone was bound to notice and would no doubt come to check and see what was going on.

"It was Cleo," Raven said as soon as he turned to face her.

"We can't know that for sure," he said because until they did a DNA test to confirm it, he couldn't allow himself to completely believe it.

"You saw her, you heard her," Raven said. Her entire body was shaking, and she was jittery and anxious.

"I did, but there's nothing we can do about it right now. When Alpha team come in and everything is settled down, we'll talk to her, run tests."

"I'm not waiting. I need to get to her now. Tonight. We need confirmation now. *I* need confirmation of it now." Desperation was rolling off her, and he was terrified that if they didn't come up with a plan, she would do something stupid.

"We don't know how to get to her. They'll be keeping them in the basement, we know that, it will be well guarded, we can't just go waltzing down there," he reminded her.

"Then we get them to take us there."

"How?"

Raven thought for a moment then her eyes lit up. "I bet that's where they train the women."

"Probably, at least in part," he agreed, not sure where she was headed.

"So, I bet they have plenty of ways to torture and punish the women down there. When they first come here they're going to fight, but you saw them today, they all did as they were told without argument. They didn't just agree to that, they had to be trained to behave that way. I'm your slave, tell them I did something wrong, that you want to teach me a lesson, that might get us down there."

"No," he said immediately. That was a slippery slope. If he did that there was no telling where it would stop.

"Yes," she said fiercely. "That's our baby down there. Our

baby. It will work, I know it will. Earlier at dinner, when you wanted to make sure they didn't think we were the ones sending the message you yelled in front of everyone that I'd come when you were touching me. Use that. No one will think twice about it. We'll go out there, find the office, I'll put the malware onto the computer, if we're caught you can pretend you were just looking for someone because you want a way to punish me. That will get us access to the basement, and then I might be able to get close enough to the women to find Cleo."

"I won't let anyone hurt you, Raven."

"I don't care, Max," she exploded. "Let them hurt me, let them hit me or beat me, I don't care if they rape me. There isn't anything I wouldn't do for my baby. They can do whatever they want to me, I would gladly suffer through anything to get to her. I don't care, Max, I don't care about anything but Cleo. Help me get to her. Please."

* * *

10:48 P.M.

She knew that Max wasn't pleased with this plan, but it was the only way to get into the basement.

Raven knew that was her daughter on that stage tonight, she would know Cleo anywhere, and ten years couldn't change that. No amount of time could. Max knew it too, although he was trying to pretend that he didn't. She understood that he was just trying to protect himself.

This wasn't going to be pleasant. She had no idea what her punishment would be or if Max would get a say in the matter, but she didn't care. She had to get to her daughter, and tell Cleo that she was here now and that everything would be okay.

"It's done," she told Max, and he turned from the doorway where he was keeping watch. After leaving their room, they'd come downstairs and found the office unattended. It seemed most people were still in the auction room, and Le Entregar probably didn't feel the need to make sure no one got in here, they likely thought no one would even try. In their minds, if you were here to break up the auction you would have done it during the auction, but that left too many chances for something to go wrong.

"Uploaded?"

"Yes, as of right now everything on this computer, on the system, is being transferred to Tex."

"How long will it take? Do we need to stay here?"

"No, the program allows him to get remote access. He'd already be in there, sifting through the information and making copies."

"Will someone be able to find the program?"

"Only if they are specifically looking for it, otherwise no. Tex and I made it so that it's undetectable. So, we can get out of here and know that Tex is downloading everything on here and putting it to good use."

"All right." He grabbed her hand as she crossed the office and tugged her into his arms, planting a quick kiss on her lips. "You sure you want to do this? If that is Cleo, she'll get out of here when Alpha team comes in."

"I want to do it. And you know it's Cleo. What if something goes wrong and they kill us all before Bear and the others can get to us? I don't want my baby to die alone and scared. I want her to know that her parents love her. That they never gave up on her, that they came for her. If we're going to die, I want it to be with my little girl in my arms."

"We're not going to die." Max's arms tightened around her, and she squeezed him back, so glad they'd gotten this chance to reconnect. "And I *did* give up on Cleo."

"You told yourself what you had to in order to survive," she corrected him, no longer angry that he had believed that Cleo was dead. "Now it's time to get our baby and bring her home where she belongs."

"All right, babe. I hate this but let's do it. You sure you're ready."

"Yes." She was, but she wasn't. She was scared about what was going to happen to her, but nothing mattered more than getting to Cleo. She would take whatever she had to to make it happen. After all, she'd survived being raped and cut up with a knife, and she had survived losing her daughter. There was nothing these men could do to her that would be worse than that.

Raven was already naked, they'd needed her to be when they left their room because their cover story was that Max was looking for one of the Le Entregar men to demand access to their basement to punish his wayward slave.

"I'm sorry in advance, midnight," Max said, regret and pain in his eyes as he looked down at her and tenderly stroked the skin of her cheek.

"I know you are. I haven't taken anything you've said or done to me personally, Max. I know this is just an act, it's not going to change how I see you when this is over. If anything, it's going to make me respect you more because I know how much you hate it but you're doing it anyway. For me."

"I love you, Raven."

"I love you back."

They shared a brief kiss and then Max grabbed her hair

and began dragging her through the corridors, striding so fast she had to run to keep up, not an easy thing to do when he had her basically up on her tiptoes.

"What are you doing down here, sir?" a man asked as he approached them.

"Looking for one of you," Max snapped, his tone haughty.

The man's gaze bounced between her and Max. "Is something wrong, sir?"

"Yes, as a matter of fact there is. Do you know how long I spent training this one?" He shoved her forward hard enough that she stumbled and hit the ground hard. "Hours, weeks, spent with her, training her just the way I liked them. But this one has a hard head. Or should I say a super sensitive body." He laughed like he'd just said something insanely funny. "She keeps coming when she hasn't been given permission. She needs to be taught a lesson."

The man's face turned smug and amused. "A lesson, sir?"

"Yes, and I was hoping that you might allow me access to your training rooms."

"Training rooms, sir?"

"Don't play dumb," Max snapped. "You think I don't know that you train these women before you sell them? That they just parade across the stage and stand there waiting to be bid on for fun? Please, you train them here, and I want access to that room. Now," he demanded.

"We don't allow our guests access to that floor, sir," the man said with exaggerated patience.

"I'm not just any guest though, am I?" Max shot back. "How many years did I work for Le Entregar? How many enemies did I take out so that you could remain untouched? How many auctions have I attended? I always make a purchase and you've never once had a problem with the money not going through. I demand to be taken to your training rooms immediately."

Raven stayed where she was, huddled on the floor, curled in on herself, trying to look like a terrified slave, the terror part not hard to fake. Mentally, she cheered that Bear and the others had been able to get as much information out of Joseph Calder as they had. She'd had quite a bit, but he'd provided so much more, and because of that they might actually make this work.

The man didn't look pleased, but he nodded. "You have been a valuable asset to Le Entregar. Fine. Grab your slave and bring her to the basement."

Relief almost made her smile, and she was grateful for the protective curtain of hair hanging loose around her face that hid her.

Max reached down and snapped a hand around one of her wrists, dragging her to her feet and roughly pulling her along behind him as he followed the man through a maze of corridors to a door. Another man with an automatic weapon in his hands stood guard beside the door, but he nodded and stepped aside when they approached.

The man punched in a code, opened the metal door, and then led them down a steep staircase to a dark, dingy room. The room had ropes and chains hanging from the ceiling and embedded in the floor and walls. There were an array of paddles and whips lined up in a cabinet up against one wall, and a variety of chairs, tables, and benches that she was sure had purposes a lot more nefarious than they looked.

"What is your pleasure?" the man asked Max, indicating the room.

Dragging her with him, he walked around the room, surveying everything as though he was trying to make up his mind. Eventually, he stopped by a set of metal cuffs hanging from chains from the ceiling. "This one."

"Very good choice, sir."

The man nodded, and another man appeared out of nowhere, he grabbed Raven and snapped the cuffs around her wrists. Adjusting something, her arms were pulled up until she had no choice but to balance precariously on her tiptoes. He then knelt in front of her, and grabbed one of her legs, which would have sent her wobbling wildly if he hadn't held onto her. He snapped another cuff around her ankle, then pulled her other leg out to the side and snapped it into a cuff as well, leaving her spread-eagled, balanced on her tiptoes, with her arms stretched painfully above her head. It wouldn't take long for her calves to burn with pain, and there was no wall behind her for her to lean against which meant that once she started to hurt there would be no reprieve from the pain.

"Which do you wish to use on her, sir?" the man asked, indicating the whips and paddles. He had a wicked gleam in his eyes like he couldn't wait to feed off her pain.

"None. Yet," Max added. "I wanted her body burning and trembling with pain, rather than with pleasure when I whip her."

With that, he turned and headed back up the stairs, both men followed, and the light was switched off, leaving Raven alone in the darkness to face her pain. She prayed that her daughter was down here and that she'd get a chance to make contact with her, otherwise she was in for a whole lot of suffering and no reward.

11:37 P.M.

. . .

He hated this.

It was the one thing Max hadn't wanted to have happen while they were here. For him and Raven to be separated.

Walking away, leaving her behind in the basement, naked and very quickly to be in excruciating pain, went against everything he was as a man, as her husband—well ex-husband but soon to be husband again—as the father of her child, and as a PJ. He should be with her, protecting her, watching over her, keeping her safe, instead he had left her alone to suffer.

When he reached his room, Max slammed the door behind him, and prayed that anyone who might hear it would just assume that he was angry with his slave who had misbehaved.

He stormed across his room and snatched up his phone, he didn't want to have to make the call in here, but he also didn't want to go looking for one of the common areas to make it in there. Even though it was almost midnight, he knew that a lot of the men were still hanging around, laughing, drinking, and congratulating one another on their purchases.

They'd picked three as the time for Alpha team to breach the compound unless he or Raven indicated otherwise. They would know by now that everything in here was progressing as they'd hoped because Tex already had access to the computers, and they knew that there were more guards here than they had initially believed and hopefully made appropriate arrangements, but there was no way they could know about his and Raven's discovery.

A door slammed just down the hall and Max had an idea. If he made his call here, Le Entregar would know that he was up to something. With Raven no longer under his protection, they could decide to take it out on her, use her to get him to talk, give up what he was really doing here.

That he could not allow to happen.

Changing out of the suit he'd worn for the auction, Max threw on jeans and a black long sleeve t-shirt, simple clothes but ones he could move freely in should he need to take anyone down. He also snagged one of his knives and the gun and felt infinitely better now that he was armed.

Max slipped out of his room, walked purposefully down the corridor, and stopped outside the room where he could see light spilling out under the door. He pressed an ear to the door, listened but couldn't hear voices inside. Perfect. Whoever's room that was he was in there alone. The last thing Max wanted was for one of the slaves who worked here to get caught up in this.

Picking the lock was child's play, and he was slipping into the room, the door closed behind him, already approaching the man who was undressing before he even realized that anyone else was in the room.

The man's eyes widened in shock, but Max was on him before he could make a sound. He wrapped an arm around the other man's neck, pulling him up tight against his body so he couldn't fight back—not that he was all that worried about that, the man was clearly drunk and out of shape—he applied pressure until the man dropped. Max tossed the man's body onto the bed, then put his cell phone beside him.

Max would make his call and be out of the room, leaving the man to look like he'd passed out drunk after making a phone call should anyone come looking for him.

Keeping his eyes fixed on the man so he'd notice if he started coming round, Max dialed Bear's number.

"Problems?" Bear's gruff voice came down the line.

"Yes."

"Explain."

"Raven and I are split up."

"Someone onto you?"

"No. Not exactly anyway. We found something at the auction. Some*one*."

"Who?" Bear demanded.

"Cleo."

The silence stretched out for so long that he actually had to remove the phone from his ear to check that they were still connected. "Bear?"

"What do you mean Cleo? You found information on who bought her?"

"No. We saw a kid at the auction who looks just like what Cleo would have looked like if she was still alive."

"Max ..."

"I know," he cut off the other man. "I know, man. But you weren't here, and you didn't see her. The girl sang. She sounded like an angel. Cleo used to sing like an angel. I know it's crazy. I know it's unlikely. Raven is the only one who believed that Cleo was still alive."

"*Is?*"

Max sighed. "Okay. Was. Raven *was* the only one who believed that Cleo was still alive."

"You believe the kid is yours?"

"Ninety plus percent certain. When we get out of here, we'll do tests to confirm it, but yeah, I think it's Cleo."

"How did you and Raven get split up?"

"She wants access to the girl so we came up with a plan to get her into the basement so she'd get a chance to see the women who were sold tonight."

"Do I want to know what plan?"

"Don't think you do, brother. Point is, we're not together anymore and I don't have eyes on her."

"Whatever they're using to jam signals means we can't access the camera and microphone in her earrings," Bear warned.

He didn't like it but that was what he'd expected to hear. "You guys have to be careful when you come in. There are guards everywhere." Max sighed again. "Look, man, that's why Raven wanted to get close to Cleo. She's worried the guards are going to shoot everyone as soon as they know you're here. She doesn't want Cleo to die alone."

"No one is dying today, Max. No one on our side anyway," Bear said firmly. "We brought in back up, we'll get you both out, the girl too, and all the other women there. Le Entregar are going down."

"I'm going to go and get Raven before you guys come in, I want her up here in our room where I can protect her, but just in case things go sideways I wanted you guys to know that we're not together."

"Noted. Hang in there, brother, we'll have you and your girls out of there in a couple of hours."

"Hopefully," Max whispered to himself as he lowered the phone and looked to the door. No one had come barging in to see who was on the phone and why, but he'd been here longer than he should, he needed to get back to his room.

As he slipped out the door the man on the bed was just beginning to stir. Max hurried down the hall to his room, and he had no sooner gone inside when he heard footsteps pounding down the hallway.

Someone was coming running.

Guards he would guess. Come to check on the unlucky man a few doors down.

Max couldn't help but grin, he didn't feel even a little bad that the man whose room he had borrowed was about to find himself in a hell of a lot of trouble. The man more than deserved it for how he spent his cash.

"I told you it wasn't me," a voice yelled a moment later, and he could hear the commotion.

Deciding it wouldn't be unreasonable for him to stick his head out into the hall to see what was going on, Max did just that. The man from down the hall had an armed guard on either side of them, each holding onto one of his arms and dragging him along between them. There was also an armed guard in front of him and one behind him. Le Entregar certainly didn't do anything by halves.

"It was him," the man spat when he caught sight of him. "He broke into my room, knocked me out. I didn't make any phone calls. I can't. I thought you guys did some sort of ... I don't know ... thing, to make it so we couldn't call or send messages to anyone."

Obviously, the guards didn't believe him because they barely even spared a glance in his direction as they walked their prisoner down the hall.

"I didn't do anything. You got the wrong man. It's him, he's right there, go get him, ask him your questions," the man hollered as he was taken away.

"What was that about?" asked another guest as his head popped out of the room across the hall.

Max shrugged as though he were barely interested. "Guess that guy got caught trying to make a phone call."

"He said you did it," the man pointed out.

"Phone call obviously came from his room or they would have been dragging me away to be questioned," he said. "Think the guy's drunk. Probably missed out on buying the woman he wanted tonight. I, on the other hand, did not." He gave a smarmy wink, and the guy immediately relaxed and smiled back.

"I got the angel-voiced virgin," he confessed.

It took every single ounce of self-control that Max had learned in his years in the military to stop himself from reacting how he wanted to. What he wanted to do was launch himself at the man, cut off the body part the man used to abuse women and girls and feed it to him, before strangling him slowly, squeezing the life out of him with his bare hands.

Instead, he shot the man a wide smile. "Dude, good purchase. Every man here wanted a piece of that sweet young thing." Unfortunately, that was true. He'd seen how every man in that room had salivated over Cleo.

Boiling fury made it hard to keep his smile in place.

"You make a bid on her?" the man asked.

"Yeah, but I had to pull out when the price got too high."

"Too bad," the man said smugly. "Can't wait to get her home tomorrow, try her out. Nothing like breaking in a virgin."

"Right," he said, his hands curling into fists.

Before he could do something stupid like use one of those fists to show this man exactly what he thought of him, the man said goodnight and disappeared inside his room.

Max, too, went back into his room, locking the door, not because he thought it could keep anyone out but because he wanted to shut out the dirtiness of this place.

"Hold on, Raven," he whispered. "I'm coming for you, honey." Max dragged in a breath, then dropped his head into his hands. "And hold on, baby girl, Daddy is coming for you. Coming for both of my girls, and once I get you both back, I'm never letting either of you go ever again."

CHAPTER 8

November 1st

12:38 A.M.

Her body was trembling with pain and exhaustion.

Raven had no idea how long she'd been here, but it had to have been a couple of hours. So far, she hadn't seen anyone, and she was starting to lose hope.

Was all this suffering for nothing?

It wouldn't be long before Max came back down to get her. She knew he'd want to have her with him before Alpha team came in, which meant he'd come for her before three. When he did come, she wasn't sure she'd be able to stand, let alone walk on her own back to their room, but she was going to have to find a way. Max couldn't just scoop her up and carry her back. If he was really her master, he would relish her pain not try to abate it.

The thought of things going badly and her daughter being killed without knowing that she was loved, that she had people who cared about her, that she wasn't alone, was more than Raven could cope with. Even if they were all going to die, she needed to tell her daughter she loved her one more time.

Her shoulders ached, her wrists were torn bloody, she could feel the warm liquid dribbling down her arms. Her calves burned with a pain she hadn't felt in a long time. She was simultaneously boiling hot and icy cold, and thirsty. She'd been so busy playing at being a slave, and then coming up with this plan that she had forgotten to drink anything after they'd left Joseph Calder's house this morning.

"Here, I thought you might need some water," a soft voice whispered beside her.

Raven startled, for a second thinking she was hallucinating, she'd just been craving water, and then all of a sudden, someone was there offering her a drink. She had to be dreaming.

But when she opened her eyes, she saw a woman standing beside her. The woman had auburn hair and greeny-gray eyes. She was one of those who had been auctioned off earlier and was still dressed in the same white gown she'd been wearing as she'd been walked across the stage. She held a bottle of water in her hand, and she lifted it and raised an eyebrow, silently asking if Raven needed a drink.

"Thank you," Raven croaked, her throat dry as dust.

"You're welcome," the woman said quietly.

Since she was completely incapacitated, the woman held the bottle to her lips and tipped some water into her mouth. Raven swallowed greedily, immediately feeling a little burst of energy as the cool water flowed down her throat.

Too soon, the woman moved the bottle away. "You can

have more in a moment, if you drink too much too quickly it'll make you sick." She said it like she had firsthand knowledge of this and Raven was sure that she did.

"I'm Raven."

After a brief hesitation, the woman said, "Hope."

"I'd say nice to meet you, but …" Raven looked around the basement and left her sentence unfinished. She wasn't sure how much she should tell Hope. If she told her too much, there was a chance that Hope would let onto the guards that something was about to go down and that would ruin everything. But she also didn't want the woman suffering anymore, plus she needed her help to get Cleo in here. If she didn't explain herself then there was no way the woman would grab the girl and bring her here.

"Right, nothing nice about this," Hope agreed. "But you already know that. Nothing nice about this life at all. And it's only going to get worse." The woman's voice wobbled, and her eyes filled with tears.

Raven chewed on her lip, she had to do it, but she also had to make sure Hope knew the stakes. "I'm not a slave, Hope," she said quietly, looking around to make sure no one else was within earshot.

The woman's brow crinkled. "I saw the man bring you down here. He's your master, yes?"

"No, he's not. He's my husband, well, my ex-husband."

Hope's eyes widened almost impossibly. "Your husband did this to you?"

"No, I …" Raven wasn't sure how much to say and how to explain, and it was hard to think through the pain spearing through her body.

"He brought you here, he ordered you restrained, said he'd be back to hit you, wanted you to be in pain," Hope said, her voice getting louder.

"Shh," she hissed. The last thing they needed was for something to go wrong now, when they were so close to ending this. "I need you to be quiet, okay? Can you do that for me, Hope?"

Slowly Hope nodded.

"What I'm going to tell you, you can't tell anyone else, not even the others, I need you to promise me that."

"I promise."

"Good. I'm really not a slave, and the man you saw me with is really my ex-husband, and he would never hurt me. He brought me down here because I needed to get close to all of you. We're here undercover," she admitted.

Hope gasped.

"Don't say anything," Raven said quickly. "You can't react, you can't let on to anyone that you know. We have a team who will be coming in in just a couple of hours. Le Entregar is going down, and all of you are going home. But if you let on and one of the guards gets suspicious it could ruin everything. The reason they have so many guards in here is so that if anything happens, they can kill everyone, slaves and the men here to buy them." Hope needed to know just how much was riding on her keeping this secret. "So, you see why it's so important you don't let anyone know. I'm counting on you, Hope, please."

The woman visibly steeled herself, dragging in a deep breath and straightening her spine. "Here, drink some more water."

Raven drank a little more, feeling more refreshed but in just as much pain. "The team coming in is a good one, they work for me, well for the security company my siblings and I run. I promise you, Hope, Le Entregar will be destroyed."

Hope nodded. "It's personal to you," she noted.

"It is," Raven agreed.

"Why?"

"Because they took my daughter. Almost ten years ago, when she was only three years old. I find information on computers, it's what I do, I tracked her to Le Entregar, but I haven't been able to get this close to them. Until now. I came here to bring them down and find who bought my daughter, but ..." she broke off as a sob rumbled through her chest.

Hope rested a gentle hand on her shoulder. "But what?"

"She's here," Raven whispered.

"Who's here?"

"My baby girl. I didn't know she would be, but I saw her. Please can you go and get her, her name is Cleo, she's the young girl, the one who sang. Please can you get her and bring her to me?" she begged.

"She's really your daughter?"

"Yes, and that's how you can know that everything I've told you is the truth, and that me and my team will do anything to get you all out alive. I need to see her though, please."

Hope looked shell-shocked, but she nodded. "I'll go and get her."

Relief would have dropped her to her knees if she wasn't chained in place. The pain in her body receded, but the pain in her heart increased as she prepared herself to come face to face with the daughter she hadn't seen in a decade.

What was she going to say to Cleo?

How did she explain what had happened and how she'd never given up on her?

What had Cleo been through the last ten years? At least she could be comforted by the fact that her daughter was still a virgin, but that didn't mean Cleo hadn't been hurt.

The only thing she wanted to do was drag her child into her arms, but she couldn't because she was trussed up.

Frustrated, she yanked on the chains on her wrists, and then the ones on her ankles, but they didn't budge.

Raven gasped as Hope returned with Cleo.

Her daughter was standing before her.

Just a handful of feet separated them.

Cleo both looked completely different from the last time she'd seen her, and exactly the same. Her big brown eyes hadn't changed, only now they weren't full of light and joy they were dark and empty. Her hair was longer, she was of course taller, and just beginning to fill out, but she would recognize her daughter anywhere.

"My baby," she murmured.

Cleo looked at her confused, took a lock of hair, and twirled it around her finger. She used to do that as a child, and Raven choked on a sob.

"It's Mommy, Cleo."

Her daughter gasped. "My name is ... I'm not ... I can't ... he said I couldn't use that name. How did you know? I didn't tell anyone that my name used to be Cleo."

For a moment Raven couldn't speak. Her daughter's voice was beautiful, it sounded just like she remembered only a little deeper, a teen's voice now, not a little girl's. "I know you might not remember me, princess, but I'm your mom, and I'm here to bring you home."

1:01 A.M.

Home?

Cleo rebelled against the idea.

She didn't have a real home, and the place she'd lived

before being brought here was hardly the kind of place she wanted to go back to.

Wasn't the kind of place you called home either.

At least she didn't think it was.

But it was all she knew.

For as far back as she could remember, she'd lived in that place. That room. A simple bathroom—toilet, vanity, bath—beside the always locked door, the bunk beds against the walls, the TV mounted to the wall at the end, the tables and chairs in the middle of the room, the very few toys. That was where she lived. No windows, no way to access the outside world, just that room and the other kids like her who lived there.

The only time she got glimpses of the sky, the trees, other people, was when she was collected for a photoshoot and taken from the room she lived in to another room—a worse room—and she caught glimpses of life outside her prison through the windows.

She didn't have parents.

None of them did.

No Mom.

No Dad.

No brothers or sisters.

No grandparents, aunts or uncles.

And yet ...

Memories flashed through her mind. Giggling as she was tickled, sitting high above the world on a tall man's shoulders, eating ice cream, and someone reaching over to wipe her chin. Being scared and creeping down the hall and into a bedroom where she shook a body in the bed and called out, "I'm scared, Mama."

Mama.

The woman she'd called mother had looked a lot like this

woman, only she didn't have tattoos of flowers all over her skin.

No.

This had to be a trick.

One designed to cause her more pain.

More suffering.

She might be only thirteen years old, but Cleo already knew that the world was a dark place filled with monsters whose only goal was to hurt you.

"Baby?" the woman said. There was pain in her voice, and the blue eyes that stared back at her were filled with tears.

Those eyes.

Cleo was sure she had seen them before, but she wished she was positive.

She wasn't stupid, she knew why she was here. It wasn't like the man they all called The Boss hadn't told her all about it. She was too old now to do his photoshoots, his customers wanted little kids and she was a teenager now. But she could still make him money. He sold her to the people in this big house, and tonight she had been sold to another.

Because she was a virgin, she had made them all a lot of money, but a lot of good that did her. She knew what being a virgin meant, it meant she hadn't had sex, she also knew that was first on the agenda for whoever had bought her today.

It wasn't the way it was supposed to be.

Sex was for grownups, and it was supposed to be something you wanted to do with someone you wanted to do it with.

Not for her though.

What she wanted never mattered.

It wasn't how things were meant to be. On the few TV shows she'd seen, she knew kids were supposed to go to school, laugh and play and get up to mischief, learn to ride a bike, go swimming, and play at the park.

The park.

Her last memory of before was of being at the park. She was supposed to be playing on the slide but there had been a man with a puppy, he said he had more puppies and if she went with him she could play with them. She hadn't realized it was a trick until it was too late.

"Cleo, princess, I know you're scared, but your daddy and I will get you out of here," the woman—maybe her mother— said earnestly. "I just need you to be brave for a little bit longer." There was admiration and pride in the blue eyes that studied her. "You are a brave girl, Cleo, I know you are because you're standing here before me. You're a survivor, so I know you can do this."

The woman's confidence in her bolstered her own.

Could it be true?

Were they really getting out of here?

Was she really going to have a proper home?

Her voice was rusty because they weren't encouraged to be loud. If they got too boisterous, they were punished, so mostly they watched TV or whispered quietly amongst themselves. This woman made her feel safe, so she said, "He said my name isn't Cleo."

"What did he say it was, baby girl?"

"C. Just C. But ..." But she'd known that wasn't true. She knew her name was Cleo, she was sure of it, and she'd clung to that knowledge over the years. They could call her C, and she could pretend that it was her name, but every night before she went to sleep, she repeated it to herself. Reminded herself that she was Cleo. She wasn't sure why she'd done it, but it seemed important.

"But what, sweetheart?"

"But I always knew I wasn't C. I was Cleo. I *am* Cleo."

"Yes, my sweet little princess, you are Cleo. My Cleo. I know you don't remember me or your daddy, but we love you so much, and I never, *ever*, gave up on you. I've been looking for you ever since they took you from us. I thought about you every day, I loved you every day, and I looked for you every day. That's why I'm here, sweetheart. For you. To destroy the people who took you. I love you, Cleo, always and forever."

Memories tickled her mind.

Always and forever.

To the end of the milky way and back.

Around the moon and up to the stars.

And brighter than the sun.

She was snuggled in a big bed. A bright pink quilt was tucked around her. The walls of her room were pink, too, as were the curtains hanging at the window and the carpet on the floor. There were so many stuffed animals in the bed with her that there was hardly room for her. A man and a woman perched on the edge of the bed, one on either side of her, and the woman closed a book and set it on the nightstand. Then they both kissed her cheeks, and the three of them said those words together.

"To the end of the milky way and back," Cleo murmured aloud.

The woman's eyes brightened. "Around the moon and up to the stars."

"And brighter than the sun," they finished together.

"Mommy?" Cleo took a step toward the woman hanging from the ceiling. Instead of trying to fight it, instead of letting the fear and distrust that had been instilled in her hold her back, she allowed her mind to open and the memories she'd banished to flow freely into her conscious.

"Yes, my sweet little princess, it's me." Her mom beamed at her, happiness radiating off her despite Cleo knowing she had to be in agony strung up like that. She knew that because she'd been photographed in that position before.

"You came," Cleo murmured. Had she prayed her mom and dad would come for her? Yes. Maybe anyway, she thought she might have in the early days, thought she might actually have believed they would for sure come to get her, but that hope had quickly faded. She'd thought this was her life, was old enough to know that she would likely never make it to becoming an adult. But now her mother was here, before her, and she took another step closer.

"Nothing would have kept me from coming for you," her mom said fiercely.

"And daddy is here?"

"Yes, he'll be down to get us soon. We're going to have to leave you here just for a very short time, baby, people are coming in to get us all out, but to keep our cover your daddy will have to take me back to our room. But we are not leaving you behind. Any of you," mom said, throwing a quick glance at Hope who was standing quietly beside them, watching their reunion with misty eyes. "So that's why I need you to be brave just a little longer, Cleo, and then this will all be over, and you can go home. We've all missed you so much, me and your daddy, and your aunts and uncles. Everyone is going to be so happy to have you back."

Right now, she didn't care about her aunts and uncles, or even her dad or going home, right now there was only one thing she wanted to do. "Can I give you a hug, Mom?" she asked shyly.

Tears began to stream down her mother's cheeks. "You better get over here and hug your mom."

Cleo wrapped her arms around her mom's waist and

rested her cheek against her chest, a sigh of relief echoed from deep down inside her. This was what she'd been dreaming about for as long as she could remember.

To be held by her mother.

"I love you, Mommy," she whispered as her own tears began to fall.

Her mother sucked in a breath. "You have no idea how much I've missed hearing you say that. I love you too, sweetheart, so, so much."

* * *

2:25 A.M.

He was about to lose his mind.

Max had always been someone who was patient and calm under pressure. As a kid, his parents' constant screaming matches had forced him to perfect the skill. If he had done anything to draw attention to himself his parents viewed that as an invitation to drag him into their arguments. That always included him either being insulted by both of them as they blamed one another for all his perceived shortcomings, or they tried to force him to choose sides. Problem with that was he didn't want to choose either side. He'd gotten out of that house as soon as was possible. It was why he had joined the military in the first place, he'd wanted to get as far away from the both of them as possible.

So, learning to sit quietly, play dead, do nothing to draw any attention to himself had been part of his life for as long as he could remember. It had served him well in the military when you often had to spend hours waiting for the perfect moment to strike.

Today, though, the ability had fled.

He'd paced so many times up and down the small bedroom that he had probably hit close to the same number of steps as if he'd been in PT.

Everything felt wrong. Knowing his daughter was downstairs in the basement, having been bought, and leaving her there, even knowing that she might be being hurt or abused. Leaving Raven behind, strung up, in pain and suffering, without him there to watch her back.

It was wrong.

He wanted his girls here, with him, where they belonged.

His girls.

A smile tugged at the corners of his mouth despite the anxiety churning in his gut. He'd missed them both so much, and there wasn't anything he wouldn't do to get them out of here and safely home.

Even if it meant sacrificing himself.

Max prayed that all three of them got out of here, along with the other victims, but if it came down to it, he would give his own life in a moment to ensure his girls lived.

A glance at his watch told him it was time to go. There were only thirty minutes left before Alpha team would be coming in, enough time for him to collect Raven and get her back here, but not enough time that he would have to pretend to rape her once he got her back to his room. If he'd made his move too early, he would have had to go through with that, there was every chance given the way they'd staged the drama to get Raven access to the basement that someone would be watching the footage from his room to see what he did with her when he got her back here.

Striding confidently down the halls, Max made his way toward the basement door. He didn't bother asking anyone's permission, it wasn't like they thought he wouldn't be coming back for his slave at some point.

A different guard was standing by the door when he reached it, and since he didn't have the code, he had to defer to the man.

"Open up," he said with an impatient nod at the keypad.

"No visitors," the man said in heavily accented English.

Max sighed dramatically. "I'm not a visitor, I used to work for Le Entregar, made a fortune doing it too," he said proudly. From what they'd learned about Joseph Calder, the man was always bragging about his newly acquired wealth.

"No visitors," the man repeated.

Struggling to keep his cool, the last thing he needed to do was let out his pent-up anger and frustration on the guard, not when they were so close to finally bringing down the most dangerous trafficking ring in the world. Instead, Max frowned at the man. "My slave is down there. Being punished for bad behavior. I'm ready to collect her and take her to my room."

The man gave him a funny look but nodded and turned to the control panel. He punched in a code, opened the door, and then stepped aside to give him access. Max didn't bother offering any thanks just took off down the stairs, uncaring if he looked a little too eager, he'd just hope anyone watching thought he was anxious to punish his slave and not that he was near dizzy with desperation to get to Raven and make sure she was all right. He also couldn't wait to find out if she had made contact with Cleo and if their daughter remembered them.

It was wishful thinking, he knew that. Cleo had only been three when she was taken, she'd just turned thirteen, there was no way his little girl remembered him. Still …

He couldn't help but hope his daughter had at least one or two fuzzy memories of him.

At the bottom of the stairs, Max froze.

Raven was gone.

The chains hanging from the ceiling now hung empty, there was a discarded bottle of water lying on the ground nearby, but there was no sign of Raven.

Where was she?

Fury battled with fear inside him.

Fear that Raven was dead or had been taken and used by one of the men here. As far as anyone else was concerned she was a slave, which meant she was ripe for the taking. Fury that he had gone along with this plan even though he hadn't liked it. He'd known it was safer to keep Raven with him as a supposed slave she was vulnerable here, but he'd allowed his feelings for his daughter to convince him to do something he knew was wrong.

Now it was too late.

Storming through the basement, Max bellowed, "Where is she?"

No one came running out to answer his question, and as he walked through one room after another in the large space, he couldn't see anyone.

The place was quiet.

Too quiet.

Almost eerily quiet.

Where were the women from the auction? He knew they were being kept down here, but they seemed to have disappeared.

"Something the matter, Mr. Calder?" a man asked, approaching from another guarded door. From talking to the other men here, he'd managed to learn the names of two more of the six Le Entregar leaders in addition to the one who had been Joseph Calder's contact, they'd learned his name from him. This man was Mr. Ling Kim, the Asian representative.

"You know very well something's wrong. I brought my slave down here because she needed to be punished. I was ready to collect her, I can't go to sleep until I've gotten off, but she's gone. Where is she? What kind of operation are you running here? This is supposed to be a secure facility, and yet I leave my slave in an armed room and come back to find her gone. Unacceptable," he snarled.

Mr. Kim frowned, and the armed guard took a step toward him. "You are a guest here, do not forget that, Mr. Calder. Just because you have worked for us in the past, and benefited greatly from that job, never forget that we can rescinded your invitation to be here at any time."

Max wasn't going to be intimidated, and he doubted Joseph Calder would have been either. Instead, he took a step closer and flexed his large hands. "Where is she?" he demanded, over-enunciating each word.

"I will look into it. I assume she was gathered up with the other women when they were sent off to be prepared to leave with their owners later today. A mistake I'm sure," the man said, offering him a smile that was anything but warm and reassuring.

There was no mistake, he'd bet his life on it. Raven had been taken on purpose, but for what reason? Did they know something was going on? Did they suspect him, or he and Raven both? Did the man whose room he'd snuck into to make his call convince them that he was innocent and get them to focus on him?

Whatever was going on, he needed eyes on Raven immediately. He couldn't protect her if they were separated, and in just under thirty minutes this place was going to be filled with gunfire.

He offered a nasty smile of his own, baring his teeth and allowing every molecule of dangerous warrior that lived inside him to shine through. "A mistake, yes, well one I'm sure you'll be in a hurry to rectify. After all, I am a return customer, one with enormous amounts of knowledge about your little enterprise here. Information I am sure you wouldn't want me to accidentally get into the wrong hands. It would be just a mistake of course. I want my slave delivered to my room within the next ten minutes."

With that, he turned his back on the man and stalked back the way he'd come. Something was definitely going on, and he didn't like it. Everything he loved was in this house, his daughter and the woman he had always loved, he needed them both to get out of here alive. Max had spent enough of his life carrying a heavy burden of guilt but losing Raven and Cleo because he messed up would be more guilt than he could bear.

That guilt would kill him as surely as the bullets that would soon be flying through these halls.

* * *

2:30 A.M.

An Asian man came toward them.

Ling Kim.

One of the six men who ran Le Entregar.

Raven quickly made sure her gaze was locked on the floor. After her daughter had hugged her—something she was still struggling to process and believe was real—she'd told Hope to take Cleo back to the others, the last thing she needed was for her daughter to be punished for talking to another slave.

As soon as she'd left Cleo in the care of the other women, Hope had returned. Raven had argued with the woman, told her to go stay with the others, that she was risking punishment by hanging around, but Hope had a stubborn streak and had refused to leave.

Not that she'd tell the younger woman, but Raven appreciated her company. Hope had brought her more water, and the two of them had spoken in hushed whispers, conscious of the fact that someone could come up on them at any moment. She'd learned that Hope was a photojournalist who had been in Colombia reporting on the effects that the cartels and violence had on the people living in small remote villages. She'd been snatched from her bed in the small hut she'd been staying in one night and brought here. Hope said she'd tried to escape a few times but never made it, and only received beatings for her efforts, and had been trained in what was expected of her as a slave.

Hope had fight left in her, fire and defiance burned in her green-gray eyes, and Raven was glad, the pretty redhead was going to need it to survive and rebuild her life after this horrendous ordeal.

As Mr. Kim approached, Hope also dropped her gaze to the floor, and let go of the water bottle which fell with a quiet thud, spilling the last of the water.

Two men with guns flanked him. One immediately moved toward Hope, grabbing her wrist in a grip Raven knew was just shy of tight enough to snap the bones. While Hope flinched, she didn't utter a sound, not even a whimper, and didn't make any attempts to fight against the man holding her.

The other man came toward her, leaning his shoulder into her stomach as he bent and unlocked the metal cuffs around her ankles. Her legs were numb, her muscles screaming in pain from the hours spent balanced on her tiptoes and didn't possess the power to hold her up. She collapsed against the man, who stood, balancing her on his shoulder, while he unhooked her wrists.

Even though she tried not to cry out, when her dead arms dropped to hang down the man's back, and he stood, jostling her aching body, she couldn't help a half-sob falling from her lips.

"Slaves don't make sounds," Mr. Kim snapped.

For the next few moments, Raven couldn't even think of whether she should keep up the charade, break cover, or keep pretending to be a slave but ask for her master because the pain tearing through her body was too strong. It made the edges of her vision go black, her breathing accelerated as she attempted to breathe through it, and her heart rate was through the roof. It was beating so hard in her chest she was sure it was going to leave bruises on her ribs.

By the time she was able to get herself under control they'd crossed the room where she'd been kept and were walking through a door into a smaller room.

Despite her fuzzy head and the pain threatening to break through the barriers she hastily tried to erect, Raven knew this wasn't good.

Something had changed.

There was no reason for them to have come and got her, that wasn't something you did with another man's slave, and she had no idea where they were taking her.

Did they know that Max wasn't Joseph Calder?

Did they know that she wasn't his slave?

As much as she wanted to demand they tell her what was

going on, where they were taking her, and why her master wasn't here, she kept quiet. Perhaps there was a logical explanation.

Only she couldn't come up with one.

Things weren't right, Raven knew it, felt it. She might not have ever served in the military like four of her five siblings, like Max and most of the men who worked at Prey, but that didn't mean she didn't know about trusting her gut. Right now, her gut was screaming at her that things were about to get really bad.

"Where is she?" a voice bellowed somewhere close by.

Max.

Relief swept through her leaving her shaky and dizzy. Max was here, he wouldn't let anything bad happen to her or Cleo. She wished so badly that she could see her daughter right now, know that Cleo was okay, offer whatever comfort her presence could.

"Take her to the office," Mr. Kim ordered. "Drop the redhead, but get the girl, the one who sings, take her too."

No.

Raven's body protested violently against the notion of her daughter in trouble, and she retched, throwing up down the back of the man carrying her. He muttered a curse in Spanish and tightened his grip on her until his fingertips bit painfully into her burning thighs.

A door guarded by a man with a gun opened and she was carried through, a moment later, a terrified-looking Cleo joined her. She longed to reach out to her daughter and console her somehow, but there was no way these people could know that Cleo was her child, so she kept her mouth shut.

The door slammed shut behind them with a finality she felt down to her bones.

It felt very much like she and Cleo both were living on borrowed time. And what was going to happen to Max? He was looking for her so he knew something was wrong, but what could he do to stop it from happening, and how much longer was it until Alpha team came bursting in to save them all?

Stall.

She had to find a way to stall.

If Max had come to collect her then it was probably only thirty minutes or so until Alpha team came in. She could buy them that much time. She had to, it wasn't like it was an option. She wasn't going to allow her daughter to be hurt ever again.

They were taken into the same office where she had infected the computer earlier. The man carrying her threw her down onto the floor, hard enough that more pain slammed into her already struggling body. Her limbs were still dead and heavy, and as blood flow began to return, they were screaming with fiery agony, and she knew with the vicious cramps in her legs she wasn't going to be able to make a run for it.

Talking was her only way out of this, but that meant breaking cover.

Cleo was tossed down beside her, and the girl immediately curled into her side. Having her daughter rely on her strengthened her resolve, allowed her to push the pain to the back of her mind and focus.

No longer bothering to keep her gaze fixed on the floor, she took in the six men in the room. These powerful, rich men ran Le Entregar. Each of them came from a different continent and ran operations there. It was the perfect way to dominate the human-trafficking market, they had home ground advantage all around the world.

The six men were lounging around the room. A man with skin as dark as night sat at the desk—she knew he was a Nigerian man named Emmanuel Aliyu and had been Joseph Calder's contact in Le Entregar. A Hispanic man—she didn't know his name—and a man with olive skin—Greek Alejandro Cirillo—were sitting on a couch. Ling Kim stood by the door, and the other two men, one with golden-brown eyes that seemed to glow, and the other with a lazy smile that reminded her of a lion watching its prey, were pouring themselves drinks. She didn't know their names but knew they had to be the North American and Australian representatives.

The one with the lazy smile was the first to speak. "It's a pleasure to finally meet your acquaintance, Raven Oswald."

She sucked in a shocked breath.

They knew who she was. That meant they knew why she was here. Which meant that Max was in danger.

How could she warn him?

She couldn't.

It also meant they were likely prepared for an assault on the complex, which meant that Bear and his team would be in for the fight of their lives.

And how was she going to get Cleo out of here alive?

Doing the only thing she could, Raven straightened her spine, summoned the courage that had enabled her to enter the house where two men were murdering her parents, the courage that had helped her get up each morning after her daughter was stolen, and met the men's gazes squarely.

"The day you took my child I vowed that I would destroy you," she said, surprised by how calm her voice sounded when she was quaking inside. "Now that day has finally arrived."

* * *

2:56 A.M.

Max decided he'd given them enough time to produce Raven. That they hadn't meant only one thing as far as he was concerned.

Their cover was blown.

He didn't know how. Either they'd decided to listen to the man from the room down the hall and believed Max was really the one to make that call, or they'd noticed that the cameras and microphones in his room had been temporarily jammed, or some other reason, but it seemed likely that Le Entregar knew they had traitors in their midst.

Leaving his room, he headed for the office. If he wanted to make waves he would start there. Any minute now Alpha team would be coming in, the best he could hope for if this mission was compromised was that he could stir up some trouble inside to bring as many of the guards in here as possible so that Alpha team had an easier ride.

If he hadn't already decided that they knew who he and Raven were, walking through the halls would have convinced him. The place looked like a ghost town. There were no guards in the hallways, and when he passed the bar and the common areas, that a couple of hours ago had been full of drunk men and the women kept as slaves here, he found them empty.

Le Entregar was expecting an attack and had mobilized their army to take on whoever was coming.

When he approached the hall that led to the main office, he slowed down. He wasn't playing this smart, he was letting his emotions get in the way, cloud what he knew was sound judgment and the training he'd been given.

Emotion had no place in his head right now.

Of course the thought of Raven and Cleo in danger left him breathless, borderline panicked, and terrified beyond imagining, but if he didn't get himself under control he would get all three of them killed.

That was unacceptable.

Getting low to the floor, he took a peek around the corner and found two armed men standing outside the office.

Distraction.

He needed a distraction, something to lure the men away. If he could get them here, kill them, get control of their weapons then maybe he stood a chance at getting inside that room.

Raven was in there, he knew it as clearly as he knew his own name. Not only did he feel it, but it was the only thing that made logical sense, they'd taken Raven for a reason. There was no way they didn't know about her, likely her status as co-owner of one of the world's best security firms meant they'd been hesitant to go after her, but now she was here, and no way would they waste that opportunity.

Gripping his knife, it was small but still deadly, Max knocked down a painting hanging on the wall. The thud it made was quiet but loud enough that the guards would hear it and come to investigate.

Sure enough, a moment later one came cautiously around the corner.

Max didn't hesitate.

Wrapping an arm around the man's neck, he plunged the knife into his chest, sliding it between his ribs with expert precision and piercing the heart.

He lowered the man to the ground and snagged his weapon, feeling a lot better with a fully loaded M16 in his hands.

Now he had to decide how to take out the second guard. He didn't have long to make up his mind, it was after three so Alpha team and whoever they'd brought with them were already on their way in. If he shot him, he gave away the element of surprise, but there was no way the second guard would be as easy to take. If he came looking, he would know something had happened to his partner.

Deciding with Alpha already breaching the perimeter he had nothing to lose, he darted around the corner and fired off a single shot, taking down his target.

Now he had a clear run at the office. He took it because he didn't know how many were inside or what condition Raven would be in when he got to her.

The room was dark when he edged open the door, and immediately Raven screamed his name.

"Max, look out!"

He heard her grunt of pain, felt a moment of fury that someone had struck her before a bullet slammed into his chest.

The pain was enough to have him blacking out and his final conscious thought was that once again he had failed the people he loved.

Pain.

That was the first thing that registered.

Fear.

That was the second.

Where was Raven? Was she still alive? How badly was she hurt?

"Easy, man," someone said when he tried to struggle to his feet. "You got hit in the chest."

"Not the first time," he wheezed. "Probably not the last either."

Bear huffed a chuckle. "You were lucky, if you hadn't been wearing the vest, you'd be dead."

Packing the Kevlar vest was the best decision he'd made. He'd known it was a risk, but it was a calculated one, he'd thought it was more likely they'd run all the suitcases through an x-ray machine to check for weapons, rather than hand search each one. Obviously, that risk had paid off because the vest had been left in his suitcase ready and waiting to be put to use.

"Raven?" he asked, allowing Bear to help him up. He'd have a massive bruise, but it definitely beat a bullet flying through his heart.

"Gone."

"Damn," he muttered. That wasn't what he wanted to hear but what he was expecting to hear. "Do you have eyes on Cleo?"

"No. She's gone too," Bear said. "Charlie team cleared the basement, they found the women but Cleo wasn't amongst them."

Max cursed again. "That means they have both of them."

"They have to know who she is," Bear agreed.

"They're taking them both hostage. They know this place is breached, maybe know about the computer being hacked too, they're either going to use them to get us to back off or they're going to exhort money from Prey." Neither option boded well for Raven and Cleo.

"We have this place secure," Bear said. "The guards were well trained, but they were expecting an attack from the outside, we parachuted in, took them by surprise from behind. Bravo team is securing the guests, the medics are checking over the women, and the rest of my team is searching for any other guards hiding about."

"What about the leaders, you got them?" he asked. If they didn't bring down the six men who ran Le Entregar then there was nothing stopping them from just setting up somewhere new and starting over. Raven wouldn't allow that to happen, and neither would he, his family would never be able to completely move on so long as those men were out there.

"Tex wants to talk," Bear announced, handing him a comms set.

As soon as he put it on, Tex started talking. "I've been going through the information from the computers, and I've identified the other three men. The North American is Dusty Evans, South American is Jorje Hernandez, and the Australian is Aston Greene."

"So we know all six of them." That was a relief. It meant that even if one of them slipped through the cracks they'd be able to track them down.

"Yes and no," Tex replied.

"What does that mean?"

"It means I'm seeing signs that there is actually a seventh member of the ring. One who is actually the leader. The other six men work under him but I'm not seeing a name, not anywhere. There's still a lot of data to get through, but I don't know if we're going to find a name in there," Tex explained.

Another member of Le Entregar, that wasn't what he wanted to hear. Joseph Calder hadn't mentioned anything about him. None of the men he'd spoken to here knew anything about it, and when he'd done a little digging into the six owners the only names he'd gotten were the three they'd known before Tex told them the others.

No one knew anything about this mysterious man.

"We'll find him, Max," Tex assured him.

Maybe.

But unless they took one of the Le Entregar alive, it was unlikely they'd ever get the name.

"There's movement on the roof," Tex announced.

"Helos. We have to get up there." That was where Raven and Cleo were, he knew it.

"I've got access to all the cameras in the house, I don't have eyes on Raven, Cleo, or Le Entregar," Tex told them.

"There must be a secret escape route from in here," he said already moving to search the room. That was why they'd congregated in here, they knew they had an escape route as the estate was overrun. They didn't care about the men who worked for them, they would happily sacrifice the guards for their own lives, and they cared nothing for the men who paid for the privilege of coming here to purchase women. As for the women, there would always be more to abduct, train, and sell.

"Bringing up plans for the house," Tex spoke in his ear. "Right corner of the room, beside the fireplace. There's a space, I'd bet anything that behind the fireplace is a set of stairs that lead up to the roof."

Max moved to that corner of the room, and he and Bear began to look for a switch, or a button, or lever, something to reveal the secret passageway.

He was about to give up when part of the wall finally moved.

"You stay here," Bear said, nudging him out of the way.

"No way."

"You were out cold when I found you."

"And now I'm conscious and ready to go." It was true, his chest ached, but fear for his family was dulling the pain. "We don't have time to argue, nor do we have time to waste. I'm the only other one here, and I'm not letting you go alone."

Bear glowered in his usual gruff manner but relented with a nod, and the two of them started to creep through the narrow tunnel. A steep set of stairs did indeed lead up behind the fireplace, then a short corridor.

"You got the drone, Bear?" Tex asked.

"Yeah."

"Set it up, it's small and quiet and can give you a visual of what you're walking into," Tex said.

Bear removed the small drone from his pack and turned it on. "You controlling it, Tex?"

"Yes, you two just concentrate on not getting shot," Tex said.

While the drone moved on ahead of them, he and Bear moved slower, more cautiously. They went up a second flight of stairs, meaning they were now on the third floor, but there was still another short corridor, and more stairs up ahead.

"I see them," Tex announced.

"Raven and Cleo?" he asked tightly.

"Got eyes on them," Tex confirmed.

Relief hit him hard, and he staggered briefly before refocusing himself. "They alive?"

"Yes. Both conscious and on their feet."

"How many others?" Bear asked.

Tex paused before answering. "I see five of the Le Entregar, five men I'm assuming are the pilots, and five armed guards, gonna guess they're each man's personal bodyguard."

"What about the sixth Le Entregar?" Max asked.

"Helo is taking off, the sixth man must be in it," Tex replied.

"Which one?" Bear asked.

Another pause. "I don't see Jorje Hernandez, he must be the one in the helo," Tex answered. "I count four people on that helo, one looks like a woman. Could be a slave."

"Are the pilots armed?" Bear asked.

"Negative."

"Le Entregar?" Bear asked.

"No, looks like only the bodyguards are armed," Tex informed them.

"Five threats to neutralize, we can do that," Max said confidently.

"Better hurry, they're preparing the next helicopter," Tex said.

"You go in high, I go in low," Bear said.

Max nodded, and the two of them moved stealthily toward the final set of stairs that would bring them up to the roof.

They had the element of surprise on their side. They'd already taken out a man each before the others reacted and returned fire.

Instead of spraying bullets like the guards were doing, he and Bear both took careful aim, using the walls for cover, and hit what they were aiming at.

The pilots obviously weren't armed because they dropped to their knees, hands on their heads when Bear ordered them to.

He didn't stop to see what the Le Entregar men were doing because one of the helicopters was lifting off.

Raven and Cleo were nowhere to be seen.

Then he looked at the helo and saw Raven's pale face staring down at him.

* * *

3:21 A.M.

She stared down at him.

He stared up at her.

They both knew it might be the last time they ever saw one another alive.

Raven knew that she would do whatever it took to get herself and Cleo out of this mess, or she would die trying, just as she knew that Max would spend the rest of his life searching the globe to find them.

But sometimes you didn't get what you wanted no matter how hard you fought for it.

She knew that.

If fighting hard and wanting something meant you got it, her parents would never have been murdered, and she wouldn't have been raped and sliced up. She would never have lost her daughter either, and even if she had, she would have found her well before now.

"Where are you taking us?" she demanded, angling her body as best as she could to make sure Cleo was tucked behind her. It wasn't like that would protect the girl, but it was better than nothing. As long as she was standing, she would always put herself between her daughter and danger.

"Somewhere where you won't be able to cause us any more trouble," the Greek Alejandro Cirillo replied.

"You know who I am. You know that Prey will use every resource at its disposal to find me. There's nowhere you can put us where they won't find us," she said. Prey had brought them all a whole lot of money on top of the huge inheritance they'd received upon their parents' deaths. They also had contacts all over the globe, she knew, she'd used them both in her personal search for Cleo and when working jobs.

"And yet we had your girl for almost a decade," Alejandro mocked.

She didn't rise to the bait. She had minutes at most to do something if she didn't want herself and Cleo to disappear. Despite what she'd said and her belief that Max and her siblings would never give up on her, plenty of corners of the globe were hidden by the darkness brought by money, power, and fear.

"There is someone waiting to see you, someone who has been waiting a very long time to finally meet you," Alejandro goaded, but again she wasn't going to rise to the bait. She had to come up with a plan.

They hadn't bothered to restrain her in any way, they probably thought her body was too weak and cramped from being strung up for hours for her to be considered a viable threat. Plus there was Alejandro's armed bodyguard who sat beside his boss looking bored. In their minds she was just a stupid, helpless woman, injured with a gun pointed at her, there was nothing she could do.

They would be wrong.

There was something they had done to give her an edge.

They'd put a headset on her. That gave her the ability to communicate with them, they'd probably done it because it was clear Alejandro had information he was excited to taunt her with, but she was going to use it to her advantage.

All she needed was one second to cause a distraction and then she could strike.

"You're not curious to know who wants to meet you?" Alejandro asked.

"As a cat," she quipped. Really, she couldn't care less. It was obviously another man involved in the running of Le Entregar that they hadn't known about. Tex had access to their computers now, so he'd find that man, she didn't have to meet him to find out who he was.

"He's the man who ordered the hit on your parents," Alejandro dropped his bombshell right as she prepared to make her move.

If she'd known what he was going to say she would have waited, gathered more intel. Intel that they would need if they were going to take down someone who'd been involved in their parents' deaths.

But she was already moving.

Opening her mouth, she screamed as loud as she could.

Her siblings had always teased her about how high-pitched her squeals were. Since they'd grown up very unconventionally on a remote property with no access to the outside world, completely self-sufficient and without technology, they'd spent a lot of time playing outside. One of their favorite games was to hide then jump out and scare each other. Her family had always said she had a scream that could scare the pants off a ghost.

Now she put every ounce of that power into her scream.

Wearing the headphones as they were, everyone in the helicopter bar Cleo who hadn't been given a headset and had her hands pressed to her ears, immediately winced and automatically went to remove the source of the sudden pain, the headphones.

Raven lunged forward, going for the weapon. If she could get to it, she could take control of the helo, order the pilot to take them back to the mansion, and take Alejandro into custody to be interrogated.

Just as her fingers curled around the gun the guard reacted, slamming it up and into the side of her head. The blow was hard enough that she saw stars, but she didn't back off. Backing off meant dying, more than that it meant her daughter dying.

So instead, she reached blindly for the trigger and pulled it.

For once she wasn't worried about the blood that would flow or the life that could end once again at her hand.

This was survival.

Her daughter's survival.

No amount of fear about blood or violence was going to stop her from doing what needed to be done.

No one was more surprised than her when she actually managed to hit her target, and the bodyguard slumped in his seat, his grip on the weapon loosening enough that she could tug it free.

Before she could aim at Alejandro, he kicked at her. He got her in the shin and pain screamed through her leg, and he followed up with a blow to her stomach. That blow made her gag, and she lost her grip on the weapon which clattered uselessly to the helicopter's floor.

Not willing to be beaten when the stakes were so high, Raven went down after it.

Alejandro moved as well, delivering another kick, this one to her chest. Already damaged in the car accident a few days ago she felt her ribs crack under the pressure.

He drew his leg back to kick again, and she lifted an arm to try to block the next blow, but it got her anyway. Pain spiraled up her arm, but she didn't think he'd broken her arm and this time she decided she better find a way to be active instead of reactive or he was going to kill her.

When his leg started to move, Raven reached out and grabbed his foot pulling as hard as her battered and broken body could manage and somehow was able to unbalance him enough that he stumbled backward.

Since she was still holding onto him, she moved with him toward the open helicopter doorway.

They'd taken off in a hurry under a hail of bullet she knew had come from Max and Prey, so no one had bothered to close the door or do up their seatbelts. The seatbelt thing she had used to her advantage but now the open door was about to spell her death.

Alejandro's eyes widened as he realized what was happening. He tried to reach out, grab hold of something, anything, to stop his fall but there was nothing there.

He screamed as he tumbled out of the helicopter taking her with him.

This was it.

She was going to die.

And her daughter was still on that helicopter, still being taken toward someone who had ordered her parents—and no doubt her and her siblings as well—murdered.

The sensation of falling made her stomach churn but at she was yanked back at the last second.

The gun.

Raven hadn't even realized she was holding it, but it caught in something and halted what would have been a plummet to her death.

Not that she was out of the woods.

The gun had stopped her plummeting down to earth, but she was still hanging out of a helicopter.

She had to pull herself back up, but she wasn't sure her body had the strength. She probably had a concussion, broken ribs, if her arm wasn't broken it was at least bruised, plus she was dehydrated, and her muscles were still weak and sore from being chained up in the basement for hours.

She couldn't do it.

She wanted to, but her body wasn't cooperating.

Then she caught sight of her daughter's face.

Cleo's eyes were wide with fear, her body shaking violently, tears streamed down her cheeks, and she was moving, her hands reaching out trying to help.

No.

That couldn't happen.

She couldn't risk falling and taking her daughter down with her.

Somehow, she found strength she didn't think she had and managed to pull herself back up and into the helicopter where she collapsed against the floor, the gun still in her hand.

"Mom!"

Raven read the word on her daughter's lips rather than hearing Cleo's voice above the noise of the rotors.

She reached out to Cleo, shaky herself now that they were both alive and Alejandro and his bodyguard were gone. But behind her daughter she saw the pilot move, producing a weapon of his own.

Again she didn't think, didn't worry about her phobia of blood, or how much she hated violence, she just swung the gun that had already saved her life once and fired, hitting the pilot between the eyes.

Cleo screamed.

The helicopter began to drop now that no one was flying it.

And Raven knew that once again her daughter's life was in jeopardy.

* * *

3:32 A.M.

. . .

Her mom was alive, but the pilot was dead.

No one was flying.

The helicopter was going to crash.

The hope flowing through Cleo's veins just moments ago when her mom somehow managed to pull herself back into the helicopter now evaporated.

Raven reached out, picked up one of the headsets and set it over her ears, then grabbed the one she'd been wearing earlier before moving across the seats and shoving the now dead pilot onto the floor so she could sit in the pilot's seat.

"It's okay, sweetie, just sit down, buckle yourself in, it's been a while since I've done this," Mom said.

For a long moment Cleo couldn't move.

Too much was happening too quickly.

Just a couple of weeks ago she'd been living in the house with the other kids, being photographed regularly, just like she had been all her life. Then all of a sudden, she was at that mansion, being kept in the basement with other girls and women, being taught how to serve someone as their sex slave. Then her mom was there, and she'd thought maybe everything was going to be okay, but then they were both dragged away and into this helicopter. She'd been so sure her mom would be killed, but somehow she'd survived and now she was flying the helicopter back toward the mansion.

It was too much.

"It's going to be okay, Cleo, I promise. Sit down and buckle up," Mom said softly.

"But … you're going back to that place," she whispered, bracing for backlash. Talking back wasn't allowed where she'd been living—either the house or the mansion they'd just left—and while she didn't think her mom would punish her for speaking up, she wasn't certain.

"It's okay, sweetie. Your dad was on the roof as we were

flying away. That means he and my friends have taken out all the bad guys."

"Are … are you sure?" She wanted to believe that so badly, but she didn't have much experience with good things.

"Positive."

Still a little tentative, Cleo climbed over the seat to sit beside her mother. She kept her feet up on the seat so she didn't touch the dead pilot, and pressed her knees to her chest, curling her arms around her legs and holding tight.

Was it really over?

Was she really going to go home?

That scared her as much as it excited her. She didn't really remember what home was like, and even though she knew certain things from TV shows she'd seen, she didn't really know what it was like to live a normal life.

Cleo knew she wasn't a normal girl.

She also knew she would *never* be a normal girl.

She'd just been through too much.

The ride back was bumpier than the ride out had been. While it was clear her mother knew how to fly a helicopter—they hadn't crashed yet—it was also clear that her skills were rusty. Still, as long as they made it back in one piece that was all that mattered.

Wearing the headphones made it much more pleasant. The rotors had been so loud, and no one had given her a headset. She'd known that the others were all talking about something, but she had no idea what.

Not that it mattered she supposed.

The mansion came back into view, and as they got closer, she could see people moving around on the roof where they'd taken off from.

The helicopter dipped precariously and for a second Cleo

was sure they weren't going to make it, that they were going to plunge to their deaths this close to safety.

But they didn't.

One second the roof was coming up to meet them at an alarming pace, and then they were touching down, and the rotors were turned off.

The sudden silence seemed deafening.

A man came running toward them, and Cleo shrunk away from the door. It was one thing to know that she was safe, it was another to see a huge man rushing at her.

No.

Not just one huge man.

There was at least half a dozen of them, all rushing the helicopter.

"Raven!" the one at the front of the pack yelled.

Raven?

Birds.

For as long as Cleo could remember, she'd had a fascination with birds but if she'd ever known why she'd long since forgotten.

Was it because her mother was named after a bird?

A flock of birds.

In her mind, there was more than one bird, but she had no idea why. All she knew was that she'd always felt safe when she thought of the flock.

The door was wrenched open, and the first man reached for Mom. Cleo's instinct was to grab her mother, pull her back, keep her close, make sure neither of them was hurt, but her mother sagged in the man's hold.

"You scared me to death, midnight," the man said, unbuckling Mom's seatbelt and pulling her into his arms. "When I saw you hanging out of the helo my heart stopped beating."

"You got us all pretty good with that one, Raven," said a huge man with a beard who reminded her of a grizzly bear.

"Sorry," Mom said.

"Are you okay?" The man held Mom with one arm, and his other hand reached out and touched the blood streaking the side of her face.

"I am now," Mom said, suddenly sounding exhausted. Then she turned and looked at Cleo, a reassuring smile on her face. "Cleo, sweetie, it's your daddy."

The man looked at her, and there were tears in his eyes.

She remembered those eyes. Remembered them smiling down at her, remembered the crinkles around them as he looked up at her, held her above his head and spun her around, and remembered them warm and kind as he tucked her into bed.

She saw those same eyes in the mirror when she took in her reflection.

They were her eyes.

His eyes.

"It's okay, sweetie," Mom encouraged.

Slowly she reached up and removed the headset, letting it slip from her fingers and join the dead pilot on the floor of the helicopter, but she didn't move.

Oh, she wanted to.

Wanted desperately to believe that it was all over, that she was going to get to go home, have a mom and dad again, a family, maybe siblings one day. She could go to school, have friends, maybe even get married, and have children of her own. And yet she was so scared to believe it could be true because if this was all one big trick, she'd be devastated.

Broken.

Unable to fix herself.

Her dad didn't say anything, just stared at her like he was

as scared to believe that she was real as she was to believe he was real.

It was that very same war so evident in his gaze that was raging inside her that encouraged Cleo to edge along the seat toward her parents.

When she was close to the edge her dad held out a hand. He hadn't said anything, and he didn't rush her, didn't get annoyed that she had to move slowly, cautiously, just watched her and kept his hand there.

It was an offering of peace, happiness, love, of a future.

All she had to do was reach out and take it.

Cleo lifted her hand, it was trembling, but her dad's was too. It seemed he was every bit as scared of her as she was of him. Scared but not *scared*, Cleo knew this man would never hurt her, she felt it.

It was that feeling that had her place her hand in his much larger one.

As soon as she did, his fingers curled around hers, and she was pulled forward and into his arms.

He buried his face in her hair as he clutched her and Mom tightly. "My girl, my girl, my girl," he murmured over and over again.

He was crying.

She didn't think she'd ever seen a man cry before.

Not a grown-up one anyway, lots of the boys at the house cried often.

But this was a grown-up, and he was crying openly as he held her and her mother. Her mom was crying too, and when she pressed her face against her mom's neck Cleo realized she was too.

Other than in the very early years when she was a very small girl, she hadn't believed that she was ever leaving that house, that she would ever see her parents again. Cleo assumed that her parents had thought the same about her, that she was gone, lost to them forever.

Now here they were, the three of them clinging to one another and crying a lifetime of tears, and finally everything felt okay.

No, not okay.

Good.

It felt good.

Everything was going to be okay.

At least that was what she thought.

Until her dad's urgent voice said, "Raven?"

He pulled back slightly, and when Cleo lifted her head, she saw that her mother's eyes were closed and she was hanging limply in Dad's grip.

Was she gone already?

Had she just found her mom only to lose her so quickly?

Cleo reached for her, not willing to let her go. She needed her, didn't her mom know that? "Mommy, don't leave me!"

* * *

3:49 A.M.

His daughter's terrified voice mirrored his own terror as she cried out for her mother not to leave her.

Max felt the same way.

Raven couldn't leave him—them—now. Not when they'd finally reconnected, when he'd told her about the crushing guilt he felt, when they'd successfully taken down Le Entregar—five of the six men were now dead, four here at the mansion, and the one who'd fallen from the helicopter, leaving only one remaining.

Not when they had their daughter back.

Their daughter who he had believed to be dead for almost ten years who was now crying in his arms.

"Raven?" he barked her name in an order, but she didn't respond.

Just hung limply in his hold, her eyes closed, blood streaking her beautiful face, red marks already turning into bruises on her gorgeous body.

"Here, man, give me Raven and you take care of your kid," Bear said, holding out his arms to take Raven.

Max hesitated. He didn't want to let go of his wife—well, ex-wife but he'd be rectifying that mistake as soon as they got home—but he didn't want to let go of his daughter either.

Since he knew what choice Raven would want him to make, he reluctantly allowed Bear to gather up Raven's still unconscious form while he used both arms to lift Cleo and cradle her against his chest.

"You hurt, princess?" he asked as he followed Bear who bypassed the dead bodies on the roof and headed for the narrow staircase that would eventually lead them back down to the office.

"N-no," Cleo replied, her gaze fixed on Bear and Raven.

"You can tell me if you're injured," he said, not at all convinced that she was all right.

"I'm not hurt, but Mom …"

"What did they do to your mom, honey?" Arrow asked, following quickly behind them. Max prayed whatever was wrong with Raven was something the medic could fix because it would take them at least a couple of hours to get her to a hospital.

"The man with the gun hit her head when she tried to grab it," Cleo replied. "She shot him. Then the other man kicked her lots of times before she tripped him and he fell.

She fell too. I thought she was going to die." Cleo started crying again and his own eyes misted. When he'd seen Raven dangling from the helo he'd about had a heart attack.

"Do you know where he kicked her, sweetie?" Arrow asked as he dropped to his knees beside Raven and picked up her wrist as soon as Bear laid her down on the couch.

"Her stomach, her chest, and her arm," Cleo answered without missing a beat. "They were talking about something, but I didn't hear, I didn't have the headphones on. But Mom screamed, and it distracted them and then she just attacked them." Cleo's eyes—so like his own—were wide with surprise and awe.

Arrow, on the other hand, huffed a chuckle as he started listening to Raven's heart. "I bet it did."

"Raven's screams are legendary," Bear added. Although the gruff man didn't smile, one corner of his mouth did lift in what could barely be classified as a smirk.

"Arrow? Is she okay?" Max asked, his attention focused on the woman he loved lying so still.

"Dehydrated, probable concussion, likely broken or at least cracked ribs, possible internal bleeding," Arrow rattled off as he opened his med kit. "I'll get some fluids and painkillers into her, but we'll have to get her to a hospital for x-rays and scans."

"Is she going to die?" Cleo asked, brown eyes wide with fear.

Turning to face her, the expression on his face fierce, Arrow said, "No way we're going to let your mom die."

Cleo's eyes—eyes which had seen way too much for her barely thirteen years—assessed the medic as though needing to ascertain whether or not he was pacifying her. Obviously, she liked what she saw because she gave a single nod then began to squirm in his arms.

Even though Max didn't want to put her down, maybe if he held her for long enough he might believe he'd gotten his miracle and gotten her back, he could feel his daughter's desperation to be closer to her mother. He set her on her feet, made sure she was steady, and then watched as she quickly crossed the few feet between her and the couch and knelt beside Arrow so she could take Raven's hand.

"I'm going to put in an IV," Arrow explained as he grabbed a bag of fluids from his pack and nodded to Bear to hold it up while Arrow inserted a needle into the inside of Raven's elbow. "Since your mom hasn't drunk enough water in the last few days her body has become dehydrated, so giving her fluids will help her a lot. I'm also going to give her something to help her with pain."

"Will she wake up when you give it to her?" Cleo asked.

"I hope so," Arrow replied. "But she might not. It depends what made her go to sleep."

That was what was worrying Max.

Raven's head injury could be worse than they thought, or she could be bleeding internally. There was always the chance that she was hurt badly enough that she wouldn't wake up.

Ever.

"We're going to get your mom on a plane, and if she's stable, that means if her pulse and her blood pressure and oxygen levels all stay within acceptable ranges, then we'll fly her back to New York and get her to the hospital. If she's unstable we'll go to Miami, take her to a hospital there, so she can get the help she needs," Arrow explained to Cleo. His obvious attempts to keep Cleo calm with information appeared to be working. From the looks Arrow kept throwing his way, Max knew that the walking through of everything the medic was doing was for his benefit too.

"One thing you need to know about your mom, Cleo, is that she's strong. She flew that helicopter even though she was injured, no one is tougher than her," Max told his daughter. If there was one thing he wanted Cleo to hold onto it was that Raven would fight with everything she had to come back to her.

To him.

To them.

He knew he needed to hold onto that as well.

"That's true, sweetie," Arrow agreed as he covered Raven in a blanket. Even though she was naked, all the guys on Alpha team had been studiously avoiding looking at her, and Max appreciated their professionalism and desire to not make Raven uncomfortable when she woke up.

"Mom said that she was looking for me all this time," Cleo said, almost as though she were afraid to hear it wasn't true.

"She did, Cleo. Your mom *never* gave up on you. Ever. She'd been looking for you every day since you were taken from us," he told his daughter.

Cleo cocked her head and studied him. "Only mom?"

"I'm sorry, princess. I thought that they had killed you," he admitted. If they were going to help Cleo work through everything she had lived through—the details of which he didn't know and wanted to ask about but now wasn't the time—they would have to be honest. Brutally honest. And that started with admitting all the ways he'd failed her. "Your mom though, she never gave up on you. She believed in her heart that you were out there, and nothing was going to stop her from finding you."

His daughter nodded. She didn't offer him absolution from his failings but neither did she tell him that she hated him or couldn't forgive him for giving up on her. Max knew he deserved it, but hoped the fact that she didn't immediately tell him to get away from her meant their relationship wasn't beyond repair.

"I'm going to organize our transport," Arrow announced, standing and moving to a corner of the room to give them some space and time together.

Max moved closer to the couch where Raven lay. Bear had made a makeshift IV pole to hang the fluids from so he too moved away leaving Max alone with his girls.

Carefully, he lifted Raven's shoulders so he could sit with her head resting in his lap. Cleo watched him, and when he held out a hand to her, she didn't hesitate this time to take it and allow him to guide her to her feet. Max lifted Raven's shoulders again to make room for Cleo on his lap, and then he let Raven's head rest in their daughter's lap.

His girls.

Back where they belonged in his arms.

With both of them holding onto her, Raven's eyelashes fluttered on her cheeks before her eyes blinked slowly open.

There was a moment of panic in the blue depths before her gaze registered their presence. Then he saw her relief.

He felt it too.

Soul deep relief.

Their daughter was finally back where she belonged, here with them, and as horrible as whatever had happened to her had been, they would find a way to move forward.

"Love you both," Raven whispered as tears began to trail down her face.

"I love you too, midnight, and my princess." Max wrapped his arm around Cleo's shoulders, and she leaned into him immediately. "Our family is finally back together, and I'm not ever letting either of you go again."

CHAPTER 9

November 2nd

8:44 A.M.

"You should be sleeping," Max rebuked gently as his large hand stroked her hair.

They were lying on the bed in one of Prey's private planes. Arrow was in and out checking on her, taking her vitals, but despite that she was relaxed and happy. Her head was pillowed on Max's shoulder, her casted arm resting on his stomach, Cleo was asleep, snuggled against her other side, and she finally felt at peace for the first time in a decade.

"I've slept most of the last twenty-four hours," Raven reminded him. After Arrow had checked her out at the mansion, he'd loaded all of them onto a plane, and they'd flown to Miami for a hospital stopover. As predicted, she had a concussion, three broken ribs, thankfully no internal bleeding just a whole lot of bruising, and her arm did indeed have a hairline fracture. She'd slept off and on, comforted by knowing that not only were Max and Cleo by her side, but Alpha team was keeping watch over them. She had also taken several showers to scrub off the temporary tattoos which were mostly faded away now.

"But you should still be in the hospital," Max countered.

"Cleo needs to go home. She needs to start settling into her new life. We need to find her a therapist, a tutor at first until she's ready to start school, and I want her to have her family around her." Right now, everything was about her daughter and what Cleo needed, her own pain and discomfort could be easily pushed to the background.

"Cleo also needs her mother," Max reminded her, "and right now her mother is hurting and needs to be resting so she can recover."

"I am recovering," she said, tilting her face so she could breathe in his scent. "You, me, our daughter, everything is perfect. Almost," she added because she hadn't achieved everything that she wanted. They had Cleo back, which was the most important thing, and Le Entregar was disbanded, but only five of the six men who ran it were dead—they'd all committed suicide by drawing weapons on Max and Alpha team while she was in the helicopter—the other was still out there. And there was another man they had known nothing about—someone who had something to do with her parents' deaths.

Her siblings were going to lose it when she told them.

They'd thought it was a crime of opportunity. Two men, escaped from prison, on the run, stumble on a remote farmhouse, take advantage of the opportunity to rape and murder the couple who lived there. That was what Raven had believed, but now she knew differently.

Plus, there was the fact that the pretty redhead Hope who had helped her hadn't been found with the other women. She'd been spotted on the helicopter with Jorje Hernandez and was still out there somewhere, still a prisoner. Raven couldn't accept that, they had to find and rescue the woman.

She was thinking of asking Falcon to take a team and go after her. Her little brother was a little lost at the moment. After losing his team when they were betrayed, then staying away from the family for almost two years in an effort to keep them safe, things had blown up earlier in the year when the people responsible had targeted Olivia. Her soon-to-be sister-in-law had barely survived with her life, and Falcon had been badly injured when he's traded himself for her. It had taken him months to recover and now that he was back to his old self, he needed something to focus on, something to help pull him out of the black hole he was slowly succumbing to. Searching for Hope could be that something.

"It's not over yet," she murmured.

"Not yet, but it will be. We'll find Hope, and we'll figure out this thing about your parents, right now let's just focus on Cleo," Max said, touching his lips to her temple.

"Hey, sleepyheads, we're about to start our descent so you guys need to get into seats and buckle up," Arrow announced as he breezed into the room. "Raven, I don't want you walking on your own, you're still weak, should still be in the hospital," he added with an arched brow. Arrow had not been happy when she'd insisted on flying back to New York today. "I'll check your vitals then Max can carry you to your seat."

"Let me wake Cleo first," she said as she stroked her daughter's hair. "Wake up, honey, we're almost home," she whispered.

Cleo woke slowly, blearily, but there was no fear in her eyes which Raven took to be a good sign. Her daughter had felt safe enough with her and Max and Alpha team to sleep soundly, and she seemed comfortable enough around the big men who could be intimidating even when they weren't trying to be.

Arrow checked her out, then Max carried her into the main cabin, and they all took their seats and put their seatbelts on. It didn't take long for Brick to put the plane down and before she'd even had a chance to unbuckle, the plane door was open, and her family was clambering inside. Well, most of them anyway, Sparrow and Hawk were still serving overseas, but her older brother Eagle and his fiancée Olivia were there, and her younger brother Falcon as well as baby of the family Dove.

She felt rather than saw Cleo stiffen beside her and Raven reached over with her good hand and curled her fingers around her daughter's. "It's okay, sweetie, this is my family. Your family. Two of my siblings can't be here, your Aunt Sparrow is a pilot in the Air Force, and your Uncle Hawk is a Green Beret in the Army. But this is your Aunt Dove, and your Uncles Falcon and Eagle, and this is Uncle Eagle's fiancée Olivia. I know you probably don't remember them, but they love you very much and they've all helped me to look for you."

Cleo was studying everyone with her head tilted to the side and her brow furrowed, she didn't look afraid, but she did look thoughtful. "A flock of birds," she murmured.

"What was that, sweetie?"

"I always liked birds. In my head there was a flock of birds that watched over me. When I heard your name was Raven, I thought it was just that, but it's more than that, it's all of you. You've all been watching over me." Her face lit up at the thought as though she'd found out her guardian angels were in fact real flesh and blood people. People who would be here with her through everything that would come over the next few weeks and months, and for the rest of her life.

Eagle was the first to approach Cleo. "You know your mom didn't give up on you. Not once."

Cleo turned to give her the first smile she'd seen on her daughter's face since she found her again. "Thank you."

"You don't ever have to thank me for loving you," Raven told Cleo.

"I don't want to freak you out, kiddo, but I really want to give you a hug," Eagle said. Leave it to her big brother to be straightforward and not bother to beat around the bush. Despite his alpha tendencies, sometimes controlling behavior, and need to always be in control, her brother had a big heart. If he loved you, you were his, and he would do anything for you.

To Raven's surprise, Cleo didn't even hesitate, she practically leaped off her seat and into Eagle's outstretched arms. The sight of her daughter embracing her family had tears brimming in her eyes, and Max reached out to wrap an arm around her shoulders.

"Let me look at you," Dove said when Eagle set Cleo on her feet. Sassy, spunky, full of spirit Dove was crying as she reached out to run a hand through Cleo's long brown locks, which were hanging loose down her back. "You're so big, so grown up, so pretty. And tough. Tougher than any of us, except maybe your mom."

Cleo beamed at the compliment. "I kind of remember you all, but kind of don't."

"It doesn't matter if you remember us or not, sweet pea, we're your family and we love you to pieces," Dove said fiercely before hugging the teen.

Raven was crying openly now, and when tough as nails, remote and emotionally closed off Falcon pulled his niece into his arms and hugged her hard, she began to sob noisily. Each sob was agony on her broken ribs, like breathing through broken glass, but the tears were happy tears, and she didn't try to hold them back.

"Mom?" Cleo asked, sounding concerned.

"Just happy, sweetie," she said through the tears, vaguely aware that Max had scooped her up and set her on his lap. "I finally have you back, and your dad is here, and Eagle, Falcon, and Dove, and Olivia. If Sparrow and Hawk were here too, I'd have my whole family around me. Everything is perfect."

"Don't think tears are going to get you off the hook, little sister," Eagle said, crossing the plane to pick her up and hug her gently. "Putting yourself in danger like that was crazy."

"Worked didn't it?" she said with a smile, knowing her brother was just worried.

"If you call worked beating beaten and almost falling out of a helicopter," Dove huffed.

"I think you did amazing," Falcon said, taking her from Eagle and hugging her. "You did what you had to do for your family, you didn't let your fears stop you from killing those men and saving yourself and your daughter. I'm proud of you."

His words made her start crying all over again. "Thank you, Falcon."

"Better dry those tears, there's one more person who flew all the way out here to see you and meet your girl," Eagle said when Falcon set her back down on Max's lap.

"Tex!" she exclaimed when she saw the handsome former SEAL enter the plane. Her friend was more comfortable in front of his computer, and even though she'd known him for years they'd only met in person a handful of times. "Cleo, this is my friend Tex. I met him a few years after you were taken, and he's helped me run down leads ever since. I never could have found you without him."

"Our entire family will always be in your debt," Eagle told Tex.

Tex waved off their thanks. "Seeing this beautiful young lady home with her family where she belongs is thanks enough. You ever need anything, Cleo, you call and ask."

Cleo looked overwhelmed by the number of people there to support her but pleased too if the smile on her face was anything to go by. Raven, too, was grateful for all the support. Her family—both blood and by choice—had been by her side as she searched for her daughter, and they would be by her side as Cleo adjusted to her new reality. She'd never felt so surrounded by love as she did in this moment.

* * *

11:52 A.M.

"Whoa," Cleo murmured as she stepped off the elevator into the enormous penthouse. Was this really where she was going to live? There were huge floor-to-ceiling windows that gave an amazing view of Manhattan, and the living room alone was larger than the cramped room where she and the other kids had lived together.

Now she'd have her own room. A whole room just for her. And toys and clothes, probably anything she wanted.

She felt almost giddy with her new reality.

"Is this where you live?" she asked, awestruck as she spun in a slow circle in the middle of the living room and then crossed to press her nose to the window and look down at the world below her.

The world.

She was actually part of the real world again.

Cleo thought she should probably feel more afraid, more affected by what had happened to her, and she was sure she would, but right now she was riding a high. She was alive, she was free, she had a mom and a dad, plus a whole family of warrior aunts and uncles who made her feel safe.

"This is my place," Mom replied from the couch where Dad had set her when he'd carried her into the room.

She turned and looked between her parents. "But not yours?" she asked Dad.

"No, princess, your mom and I are divorced," Dad replied.

"Oh." She'd thought that she was getting a mom and a dad, but maybe her parents had just come together to rescue her. Cleo had thought that they loved each other. From the way they looked at each other and were always touching each other it looked like they did, but what did she know? She'd spent pretty much her entire life being locked in a room, deprived of almost all human love and affection, being forced to take photos for bad men to look at. Maybe they didn't love each other, maybe her dad would be leaving now.

"Hey." Her dad waited until she looked at him before continuing, "That's something I plan to rectify. Real soon," he added as he picked up Mom's hand and touched his lips to it.

"You're going to get married again?" Cleo brightened at the idea. She wanted a real family, she wanted everything normal people had. Maybe if she surrounded herself with enough normal it would rub off on her and she'd become normal too.

"Oh, yeah. We're doing a big wedding this time, everything we didn't have when we got married before. We're going to have flowers, candles, dancing, and a big white dress. I want the whole family there, aunts, uncles ..."

"And cousins," Uncle Eagle announced, placing his hand on his fiancée's stomach.

"You're pregnant?" Aunt Dove squealed, clapping her hands and throwing her arms around both Eagle and Olivia.

"We just found out last night," Olivia replied, smiling up at Eagle. "We wanted to tell you all at the same time."

"Another baby in the family, I can't wait." Aunt Dove was beaming and everyone else looked just as excited, but all of a sudden, Cleo wasn't feeling as happy to be back home.

A new baby in the family meant that she was ...

What?

Was she still needed?

Still wanted?

The baby would be normal, not like her. She was thirteen, and she had no friends, she didn't know how to read or write, she didn't know the first thing about how to live a normal life. Who wouldn't be excited about a new baby when the alternative was dealing with her?

"I don't like the look on your face. Come here, sweetie," Mom said, patting the sofa beside her.

"How did you know?" Cleo asked as she crossed the room and curled up beside her mom.

"Because I'm your mother." Mom smiled before growing serious. "You want to tell us what made you look so sad?"

Dad looked around at the others. "If you want, everyone else can go and you can just talk to your mom and me. Or just your mom if that's what you want."

Cleo looked around the room. No one was looking at her like she was crazy, and no one was looking at her like she was a burden, it seemed like everyone here cared about her. "You can stay, them too."

The smile on her dad's face made her relax a little, maybe she was reading too much into it. It seemed like her mom had been through something pretty awful, and from what she could figure out it looked like her family owned some sort of bodyguard company or something. They had probably seen and heard everything, they weren't going to be surprised by anything she said.

"We have an appointment set up for you to speak with a therapist tomorrow morning," Mom said. "She works for Prey, that's our family's security company, and she's very good. It's your choice whether you feel more comfortable talking to her or to us, but we are all here to hear anything you have to say."

"No one touched me, you know badly," Cleo blurted out. She knew a lot more about the evil in the world than she should, and she knew that her parents would be worried about what had happened to her. Especially her mom who had spent all these years searching for her.

"Are you sure, baby? They were selling you as a virgin, but that doesn't mean someone didn't touch you in ways they shouldn't." Her mom looked pained to say the words but didn't shy away from them, and that made Cleo feel better. Maybe she really could talk to them about anything.

"I'm sure. They took photos of me and other kids." She hesitated for a moment then decided she had nothing to lose by telling them everything. "Sometimes they made us touch ourselves or one of the other kids, but none of the grownups ever touched us. What's going to happen to the other kids? I'm home now, safe, but they're not. They're still there. They need help."

It was her Uncle Eagle who knelt in front of her and rested his hands on her knees. She looked at them, worried that his touch would freak her out but it didn't, it just made her feel a teeny bit more connected to the world. "Cleo, I'm going to make you a promise here and now. We will find those other kids. I already have people at Prey working on locating them, so later I'm going to ask you to sit down and tell me everything you can remember about that place, and what you saw when you were leaving, but not today. Today is for you to start getting used to being home again, being around all of us."

"You really think you can find them?" she asked.

"One thing you should know about me, princess, I don't make promises I can't keep. No matter how long it takes, we'll find the men who were keeping you and save those other kids," Eagle said, his blue gaze steady as it held hers.

"Hope too," Mom said firmly. The nice woman had been the one to reunite her with her mom, and now she was still out there somewhere. Hope wasn't safe, and she was glad that they were looking for her too.

"Hope too," Eagle agreed, turning his gaze to his sister.

"I know we don't know each other because I only met Eagle this year," Olivia said, stepping up to perch on the arm of the chair beside her. "But I don't want you to feel like our baby is stealing the attention you need. Nothing could replace you, and you have people around you who would—and did—move heaven and earth to get to you. Trust me, it means a lot to have people who have your back, and you have that. I know what it's like to be alone, I know you do too, but you're not alone anymore. You have your mom and dad, you have uncles and aunts who adore you to pieces, you have me too, and you'll have this baby. Don't push your family away. You look like a smart girl, and you're obviously a survivor, so you need to make sure you utilize the resources available to you. That's us," Olivia said with a nudge and a grin.

Cleo found herself grinning back. She liked Olivia, she liked all of these people, even though she might not really remember them, but she remembered that they loved her.

They were her very own flock of protective birds and she knew that they weren't going anywhere. It was a comforting thought. For so long she'd been alone and scared. She'd thought that she was never going to be free and now she was.

Her cage had been opened, and now she was free to fly. She could soar through the air, be anything she wanted, go anywhere she wanted, and while she knew it wasn't always going to be easy, she also knew that here, in the arms of her family, she had a safe place to fall.

What more could she ask for?

* * *

7:37 P.M.

It felt good to be back.

Max had always gotten along well with Raven's siblings. He'd never met them back when they were kids, and he and Raven would meet up at midnight when he was staying on his grandparents' farm. The first time he'd met some of them was actually when he and Raven were married. Raven was almost twenty when he'd tracked her down to the city, Eagle was already in the military, and Falcon had already left for boot camp, so he'd met Sparrow, Hawk, and Dove then. When he got Raven pregnant, he'd immediately proposed, he'd figured he would have married her at some point anyway and he wanted them to be officially together before the baby was born, so they'd been married at the courthouse in front of a justice of the peace with all five of her siblings there.

This time though, he was giving her the wedding she deserved.

He was giving her *everything* she deserved.

He watched her as she talked to Falcon. Both of them looked serious, and he assumed that the two of them were talking about Hope, the woman who had risked her own safety to take care of Raven and reunite her with Cleo. Max knew that no one in the Oswald family would allow the woman to remain captive. They'd find her, throwing every resource they could into it.

Raven looked tired, he'd been trying to make sure she ate and drank enough water, and he was giving her painkillers as often as he could. With the injuries she'd received care of Alejandro Cirillo's beating, he had no idea how she'd managed to pull herself back into that helo and then fly herself and Cleo to safety. And that she had set aside her aversion to violence and blood to do what had to be done made him so very proud of her. Even now, despite the fact he knew she had to be in pain and exhausted, her expression was clear as she talked to her brother.

Max shifted his gaze to Cleo who was giggling with Dove and playing with makeup. The two of them had already made a date for tomorrow to do some online shopping, buy Cleo all the clothes she needed. He was glad and grateful that Cleo had a whole family to rally around her, but he also knew he needed to apologize to her.

It was because of him she'd spent the last decade in hellish conditions being forced to pose for photos that would be sold and used as child pornography.

"Hey, princess, mind if I borrow you for a moment?" he asked as he crossed to the table filled with dozens of makeup products, most of which he couldn't name if his life depended on it.

Cleo looked up at him. "I guess so."

"I'll go check in with Raven, see how she's doing, if she

needs anything," Dove said. She gave his shoulder a squeeze before she headed off toward the sofa where Raven and Falcon were deep in discussion.

There was no easy way to say this, and he was prepared for Cleo to withdraw once she knew, but he had to tell her how sorry he was for failing her. Whatever she needed him to do to earn her trust back he'd do in a heartbeat. Taking the chair Dove had vacated, Max met his daughter's gaze squarely. "I'm the one who was with you at the park the day you were taken. You were playing, and so many other kids and parents were around that I was lulled into a false sense of security. I took my eyes off you for a moment to answer a text, and when I looked back up, you were gone. *I'm* the reason you were taken, princess. I'm so very, very sorry."

Cleo cast a glance at Raven. "Is that why you and mom broke up?"

"Yes, but not in the way you're thinking. I love your mom very much, she's the only woman who's ever held my heart, I hated leaving but I thought I was doing her a favor. My guilt was the only thing I could see for a while, but now I know leaving her was a mistake. One I will always regret. You and your mom are the best things that have ever happened to me, and I hate that I was the cause of both of your suffering. I understand if you'd like me to stay away for a while, but whatever you need me to do to try to earn your trust and your love back I will do. Anything."

His daughter studied him with eyes much too old for a barely thirteen-year-old. "It sounds like you've suffered enough. All the kids there, we all had the same story, a man with a puppy, a man with candy, a man with balloons, they knew how to lure us away. I don't want you to go, I want you to stay with mom and me. If you left, mom would be sad, and

I don't want her to be sad anymore. And I want you here too. You make me feel safe."

Overwhelming relief at his daughter's ability to forgive the unforgivable, Max felt his heart crack open and a million emotions poured out. "Can I hug you, princess?"

Cleo smiled this time and wrapped her arms around his neck so tightly he was surprised he didn't pass out. Max hugged her back almost as hard. He had a second chance with his family, and he was determined not to waste it.

When he finally looked up, he found everyone watching them. Raven, Dove, and Olivia were crying, Eagle was grinning, even Falcon had a small smile on his face. If Raven had given up on Cleo, even just once, then they wouldn't all be here today, finally reunited, a family put back together.

His soon-to-be wife was something special.

Something amazing actually, he was in awe of her strength and determination.

But right now, she was fading, Cleo too. It had been a big day on the back of a very emotional few days, and both his girls needed rest now.

"Not to kick you all out or anything, but Raven and Cleo need some sleep," he announced, his arms still around his daughter.

The others gathered up their things, hugged Raven and Cleo goodbye, and fifteen minutes later he was alone with his family. Just the three of them in what would now be all of their home.

"When I moved in, I set up all the things from your room at our old place in a room here, even painted the walls the same color," Raven said as the three of them walked hand in hand down the hall to what would be Cleo's room.

"Pink," Cleo said with a grin as she stepped inside the room.

For Max it was like stepping back in time, all of Cleo's stuffed animals, toys, and books were there, her bed, and dresser, the giant doll's house her uncles had made for her for her third birthday, the enormous teddy bear her aunts had given her for her first birthday.

"I know you're not a toddler anymore and we can replace everything with things you want now," Raven said.

Cleo hesitated and looked up at them. "Can we leave it like this for now? I know it makes me a baby, but I guess in some ways I *am* still a baby. I don't know how to read or write or anything else girls my age know."

His heart broke with how upset she looked about that. More than that, she looked at them like she was afraid they would be disappointed in her. Grabbing her shoulders, he leaned down so they were eye to eye. "You can learn all of that stuff, Cleo. And you already know all the important parts of life, you know how to be strong, how to survive, and how to forgive. You're already a better person than most adults, the rest will come in time."

"Okay," she agreed, then kissed his cheek.

"Aunt Dove picked you up a few clothes, so you can change into some PJs. Our room is just next door, so if you need anything at all, you come and get us or call out," Raven instructed.

A few minutes later, Cleo was in her PJs, teeth brushed, and under the covers. Raven perched on the side of the bed, and Max stood behind her. His girls' eyes met and they both grinned before they both started saying, "Always and forever. To the end of the milky way and back. Around the moon and up to the stars. And brighter than the sun."

There hadn't been a night that had passed since Cleo disappeared that he hadn't said those same words, the words Raven's parents had said with her and her siblings every night when she was tucked in as a child. The words that they had said to Cleo every night when they tucked her in. No matter where in the world he'd been, what he'd been doing, what mission he was on, he'd always said them to himself before going to sleep. It felt so much better hearing them said aloud by his daughter and Raven.

"Sweet dreams, sweetheart," Raven said, kissing Cleo's forehead.

"Get us if you need us," he reiterated as he also gave her a goodnight kiss before scooping Raven into his arms.

He carried her out of the room, switched off the light, and left the door open, then he headed for Raven's room. *Their* room now.

"Were you serious?" she asked, resting her head on his shoulder.

"About what?"

"Us getting married?"

Max set her on the bed and switched on the lamp on the nightstand. Then he sat beside her and took her hands in his. "Never been more serious about anything in my life. But I want to propose properly. I want to do everything properly this time. I don't want you to ever doubt that I'm with you because I love you. Never again are you going to worry I'm only with you because we share a child." He gave her a rueful smile. "At least one good thing came from me believing Cleo was already dead, now you know I wanted to be with you anyway."

"I'm sorry I ever doubted your love for me. Maybe if I hadn't, I wouldn't have let you walk away, wouldn't have let your guilt drive a wedge between us."

Tucking a lock of hair behind her ear, he asked her the question that had been burning a hole in his gut for the last decade. "Why didn't you ever blame me for Cleo's abduction?"

* * *

8:28 P.M.

Raven had wondered when he was going to ask her that question.

She'd actually thought he would have long before now.

"Because I know how easy it is to lose track of a small child. I almost lost Cleo once, worst ten minutes of my life," she admitted. "I got distracted with a phone call. Cleo and I were playing, but it was a message from Eagle, and I didn't get to hear from him much because he was still in the SEALs back then. When I looked back up, she was gone. She was two and she'd just gotten good at opening and closing doors. I spent ten minutes running through the house searching for her. My stomach was in knots, my heart was pounding, my head was spinning, I was in a panic. She was nowhere to be found, I looked everywhere. Then I got a call from the front desk to say that the penthouse lift had been used and Cleo had wandered out into the foyer as happy as can be. By the time I got to her I was sobbing, she couldn't understand why I was so upset, but I felt like the worst mother in the world. It could easily have been me at the park with her that day. It only takes one second for something to go wrong, I could hardly be angry with you for something that I'd done too."

"I remember that terror. When I looked up and found Cleo gone, I thought I was going to have a stroke," Max said, leaning down to rest his forehead against hers. "I wish I could take it all back. Making you think I only loved you because of Cleo, taking my eye off her, leaving you, letting my guilt consume me, giving up on Cleo when she needed me. I wish I could go back in time and change it all."

Raven lifted her hands to frame Max's handsome face, the thumb of her good hand caressing his cheek. "You know the thing about wishes? They're for the future not the past. You can't change what has been by wishing, but you can change what's to come. I love you, Max Hathaway. Always and forever. And I love our beautiful, brave, strong girl. Together we can help her get through this, and one day, I hope she's able to live a normal life."

"She will, midnight. I know that without a shadow of a doubt because she is her mother's daughter. You survived something horrific that would break most people, survived and thrived. You fought for your daughter, and watching you do what had to be done to bring down Le Entregar was awe-inspiring. And what you did the other day, babe, I almost had a heart attack when you fell out of the helicopter. How you managed to pull yourself back in with the extent of your injuries I'll never know." Max turned his head to touch a kiss to her cast. "You amaze me."

Right now she was feeling too battered and overwhelmed to feel amazing.

In fact she felt the opposite.

Her body pulsed with pain. It had been easier to ignore while she had to be strong for Cleo and Max, while she had to talk to her siblings about what Jorje Hernandez had told her about their parents' murders. While she had to make sure Prey was looking for Hope, but now ... now everything was starting to catch up with her.

She needed to feel something good, even just for a moment. She needed to turn her mind off, stop feeling worried and overwhelmed, stop thinking of all the things she had to do and how quickly she needed to get back to Prey, stop thinking about the long road Cleo had ahead of her.

"Make love to me, Max," she whispered, allowing the need she felt to seep into her voice.

"We can't make love, baby," he said, giving her a quick kiss. "You have broken ribs, a broken arm, concussion, bruises everywhere, you're in no condition to be doing anything but closing your eyes and going to sleep."

"I'll sleep after, but right now I need you."

"You've pushed yourself further than you should have already today. You should still be in the hospital, instead you entertained your brothers and sister all day."

If Max was going to try to insist on being all protective and sensible, then she was going to have to play dirty. Raven knew she needed this, needed to feel her connection to Max, needed to start their new lives together by joining their bodies.

Raven reached out and placed her good hand on his crotch, squeezing lightly and then smiling up at Max when she felt his body responding.

"You're not playing fair, midnight," he growled, catching her hand and lifting it to his mouth, taking one of her fingers between her lips and sucking on it.

"Wasn't trying to," she said, shivering delightfully.

"I don't want to hurt you," he said as he moved her hand so he could press a kiss to the inside of her wrist.

"I don't care about that right now, and we'll be careful, I'll just lie here and let you do all the work," she promised.

"Raven," he started.

"Please, Max. I want you. I *need* you."

"Ah, baby," he murmured, and she knew she'd won. "You let me do all the work, okay, and if it gets too much you tell me, and we stop. And you rest all day tomorrow, no more overtaxing yourself. I don't want you going in to Prey for at least two weeks. No working from home either."

"But Hope is still out there, she needs help, and I need to find out what Jorje Hernandez meant about someone else being involved in my parents' murders, not to mention all the other kids kept with Cleo," she protested.

"That's the deal, take it or leave it." As he said the words, he put a hand between her legs and stroked her through her sweatpants.

She shifted uncomfortably, his touch not nearly enough. "You're not playing fair."

"Wasn't trying to," he parroted her own words back at her, then winked and laughed. "It's not an unreasonable request. Olivia will make looking for Hope, the other kids, and looking into your parents' murders a priority, you know that. Right now, you need to take care of yourself and our daughter, and I'll be taking care of you."

"I want you to be taking care of me right now," she huffed, shifting her hips to try to increase the friction of his feather-light touches.

Max grabbed her hips and held her still. "Uh, uh, uh. You're supposed to be just lying there and letting me do the work."

"Then hurry up," she ordered, making him laugh again.

Instead of hurrying, Max took his time easing her sweatpants down her legs. She wasn't wearing panties because as sore as she was it had been easier just to have one garment to pull down when she had to visit the restroom. Although he didn't remove her sweatshirt, he did push it up enough to bare her breasts, then he stretched out above her, slipped a finger inside her and took one of her nipples into his mouth.

Raven moaned as his tongue flicked her nipple, making it

pebble. One finger wasn't enough though, she needed more, needed him to move faster, harder. "More," she murmured huskily.

"Trying not to hurt you here, babe," he reminded her with a grin.

"Another finger isn't going to hurt me."

"There you go, babe," he said, adding another finger, stretching her, but it still wasn't enough.

"Still need more," she said, shifting restlessly.

"I got you, midnight. Just lie back and enjoy the ride."

Max curled his fingers so he could hit that hidden spot inside her, and his thumb found its way to her needly little bundle of nerves. His lips covered her other nipple, and he suckled it. The triple hit had her body tingling as pleasure began to pulse through it. It started slow like small ripples, but it quickly grew, touching every part of her, tossing her toward the inevitable crescendo.

"Inside me. Now. Gonna come," she said breathlessly as she pushed on Max's shoulders.

He complied, burying himself inside her in one smooth thrust.

While she knew it would come later, there was no pain right now. Her injuries forgotten, all her body felt at the moment was the magical carpet ride Max was taking her on.

His lips captured hers, his thumb continued to work her little bud, and seconds later she was flying into a whole new world as pleasure crashed down upon her, blurring her surroundings and replacing them with feelings so strong they couldn't be described.

"I love you, my sweet midnight," Max's voice cut through the haze, and she blinked to see his warm gaze on her.

"I love you back," she whispered.

"I'll never leave you again, Raven, that's a promise. From

here until eternity, I will be here by your side to protect you and take care of you, and our daughter." He slid out of her and gathered her into his arms.

"And I'll be by your side to protect you and take care of you, and our daughter," she returned. "We're a team."

"The best team ever."

"Can't argue with that. You make me stronger, smarter, better than I'd be on my own. You make my world a better place. A happier place, and for that I'll always be grateful."

Max touched his lips to her forehead. Held them there for a long moment. "You got that all wrong, sweetheart. I'm the grateful one. You're more than I deserve, and I will make sure nothing ever hurts you again."

Raven kissed the only man she'd ever loved. With her daughter asleep down the hall, and Max holding her, her world was perfect.

Falcon Oswald honors his promise to his sister to find Hope but gets more than he bargained for in the fiery redhead in the third book in the action packed and emotionally charged Prey Security series!

Protecting Falcon coming July 12th 2022

ALSO BY JANE BLYTHE

Prey Security Series

PROTECTING EAGLE

PROTECTING RAVEN

Saving SEALs Series

SAVING RYDER

SAVING ERIC

SAVING OWEN

SAVING LOGAN

SAVING GRAYSON

SAVING CHARLIE

Candella Sisters' Heroes Series

LITTLE DOLLS

LITTLE HEARTS

Broken Gems Series

CRACKED SAPPHIRE

CRUSHED RUBY

FRACTURED DIAMOND

SHATTERED AMETHYST

SPLINTERED EMERALD

SALVAGING MARIGOLD

River's End Rescues Series

COCKY SAVIOR

SOME REGRETS ARE FOREVER

PROTECT

SOME LIES WILL HAUNT YOU

SOME QUESTIONS HAVE NO ANSWERS

SOME TRUTH CAN BE DISTORTED

SOME TRUST CAN BE REBUILT

SOME MISTAKES ARE UNFORGIVABLE

Detective Parker Bell Series

A SECRET TO THE GRAVE

WINTER WONDERLAND

DEAD OR ALIVE

LITTLE GIRL LOST

FORGOTTEN

Count to Ten Series

ONE

TWO

THREE

FOUR

FIVE

SIX

BURNING SECRETS

SEVEN

EIGHT

NINE

TEN

Christmas Romantic Suspense Series

CHRISTMAS HOSTAGE

CHRISTMAS CAPTIVE

CHRISTMAS VICTIM

YULETIDE PROTECTOR

Conquering Fear Series

(Co-written with Amanda Siegrist)

DROWNING IN YOU

OUT OF THE DARKNESS

There are many more books in this fan fiction world than listed here, for an up-to-date list go to www.AcesPress.com

You can also visit our Amazon page at:
http://www.amazon.com/author/operationalpha

Special Forces: Operation Alpha World
Christie Adams: Charity's Heart
Linzi Baxter: Unlocking Dreams
Misha Blake: Flash
Anna Blakely: Rescuing Gracelynn
Julia Bright: Saving Lorelei
Cara Carnes: Protecting Mari
Kendra Mei Chailyn: Beast
Melissa Kay Clarke: Rescuing Annabeth
Samantha A. Cole: Handling Haven
Lorelei Confer: Protecting Sara
KaLyn Cooper: Spring Unveiled
Janie Crouch: Storm
Jordan Dane: Redemption for Avery
Tarina Deaton: Found in the Lost
Riley Edwards: Protecting Olivia
Dorothy Ewels: Knight's Queen
Lila Ferrari: Protecting Joy
Nicole Flockton: Protecting Maria
Hope Ford: Rescuing Karina
Alexa Gregory: Backdraft
Michele Gwynn: Rescuing Emma
Casey Hagen: Shielding Nebraska
Desiree Holt: Protecting Maddie
Kris Jacen, Be With Me
Jesse Jacobson: Protecting Honor

Rayne Lewis: Justice for Mary
Callie Love & Ann Omasta: Hawaii Hottie
A.M. Mahler: Griffin
Ellie Masters: Sybil's Protector
Trish McCallan: Hero Under Fire
Rachel McNeely: The SEAL's Surprise Baby
KD Michaels: Saving Laura
Olivia Michaels: Protecting Harper
Annie Miller: Securing Willow
Keira Montclair: Wolf and the Wild Scots
MJ Nightingale: Protecting Beauty
Victoria Paige: Reclaiming Izabel
Debra Parmley: Protecting Pippa
Danielle Pays: Defending Sarina
Lainey Reese: Protecting New York
KeKe Renée: Protecting Bria
TL Reeve and Michele Ryan: Extracting Mateo
Deanna L. Rowley: Saving Veronica
Angela Rush: Charlotte
Rose Smith: Saving Satin
Lynne St. James: SEAL's Spitfire
Sarah Stone: Shielding Grace
Jen Talty: Burning Desire
Reina Torres, Rescuing Hi'ilani
Savvi V: Loving Lex
LJ Vickery: Circus Comes to Town
Rachel Young: Because of Marissa
R. C. Wynne: Shadows Renewed

Delta Team Three Series
Lori Ryan: Nori's Delta
Becca Jameson: Destiny's Delta
Lynne St James, Gwen's Delta

Elle James: Ivy's Delta
Riley Edwards: Hope's Delta

Police and Fire: Operation Alpha World
Freya Barker: Burning for Autumn
B.P. Beth: Scott
Jane Blythe: Salvaging Marigold
Julia Bright, Justice for Amber
Hadley Finn: Exton
Emily Gray: Shelter for Allegra
Alexa Gregory: Backdraft
Deanndra Hall: Shelter for Sharla
India Kells: Shadow Killer
CM Steele: Guarding Hope
Reina Torres: Justice for Sloane
Aubree Valentine, Justice for Danielle
Maddie Wade: Finding English
Laine Vess: Justice for Lauren

Tarpley VFD Series
Silver James, Fighting for Elena
Deanndra Hall, Fighting for Carly
Haven Rose, Fighting for Calliope
MJ Nightingale, Fighting for Jemma
TL Reeve, Fighting for Brittney
Nicole Flockton, Fighting for Nadia

As you know, this book included at least one character from Susan Stoker's books. To check out more, see below.

SEAL Team Hawaii Series

Finding Elodie
Finding Lexie
Finding Kenna
Finding Monica
Finding Carly (Oct 2022)
Finding Ashlyn (Feb 2023)
Finding Jodelle (July 2023)

Eagle Point Search & Rescue

Searching for Lilly
Searching for Elsie (Jun 2022)
Searching for Bristol (Nov 2022)
Searching for Caryn (April 2023)
Searching for Finley (TBA)
Searching for Heather (TBA)
Searching for Khloe (TBA)

The Refuge Series

Deserving Alaska (Aug 2022)
Deserving Henley (Jan 2023)
Deserving Reese (TBA)
Deserving Cora (TBA)
Deserving Lara (TBA)
Deserving Maisy (TBA)
Deserving Ryleigh (TBA)

Delta Team Two Series

Shielding Gillian

Shielding Kinley
Shielding Aspen
Shielding Jayme (novella)
Shielding Riley
Shielding Devyn
Shielding Ember
Shielding Sierra

SEAL of Protection: Legacy Series

Securing Caite (FREE!)
Securing Brenae (novella)
Securing Sidney
Securing Piper
Securing Zoey
Securing Avery
Securing Kalee
Securing Jane

Delta Force Heroes Series

Rescuing Rayne (FREE!)
Rescuing Aimee (novella)
Rescuing Emily
Rescuing Harley
Marrying Emily (novella)
Rescuing Kassie
Rescuing Bryn
Rescuing Casey
Rescuing Sadie (novella)
Rescuing Wendy
Rescuing Mary
Rescuing Macie (novella)
Rescuing Annie

Badge of Honor: Texas Heroes Series

Justice for Mackenzie (FREE!)

Justice for Mickie

Justice for Corrie

Justice for Laine (novella)

Shelter for Elizabeth

Justice for Boone

Shelter for Adeline

Shelter for Sophie

Justice for Erin

Justice for Milena

Shelter for Blythe

Justice for Hope

Shelter for Quinn

Shelter for Koren

Shelter for Penelope

SEAL of Protection Series

Protecting Caroline (FREE!)

Protecting Alabama

Protecting Fiona

Marrying Caroline (novella)

Protecting Summer

Protecting Cheyenne

Protecting Jessyka

Protecting Julie (novella)

Protecting Melody

Protecting the Future

Protecting Kiera (novella)

Protecting Alabama's Kids (novella)

Protecting Dakota

New York Times, USA Today and *Wall Street Journal* Bestselling

Author Susan Stoker has a heart as big as the state of Tennessee where she lives, but this all American girl has also spent the last fourteen years living in Missouri, California, Colorado, Indiana, and Texas. She's married to a retired Army man who now gets to follow *her* around the country.

www.stokeraces.com
www.AcesPress.com
susan@stokeraces.com

Made in the USA
Coppell, TX
01 June 2022

78371657R00157